ONE TO GO

ONE TO GO

MIKE PACE

Oceanview Publishing
Longboat Key, Florida

ISBN: 978-1-60809-135-5

Published in the United States of America by Oceanview Publishing
Longboat Key, Florida

www.oceanviewpub.com
10 9 8 7 6 5 4 3 2 1

PRINTED IN THE UNITED STATES OF AMERICA

To Anne, my rock

CHAPTER 1

Tom Booker watched the numbers descend, his confidence growing with each passing floor that no one else would board before he reached the garage. 8—7—He tugged the collar of his green polo under his blazer, and smoothed down his unruly hair. He wanted to look good for Janie. 6—5—*Ding.*

The elevator stopped, the doors opened, and Robert "Bat" Masterson entered. Tom's heart leapt to his throat. Masterson was the third named partner in Smith, Hale and Masterson, one of the most prestigious law firms in the nation's capital and, at over 500 lawyers, one of the largest.

Approaching sixty, Masterson—tall, tan, with patrician features—looked at least ten years younger. Except for silver tinges over each temple, his hair remained as thick and black as it appeared on campaign billboards lining the roads of Fort Worth twenty years earlier. Masterson's nickname derived from the renowned Dodge City gunfighter who at one point served as Wyatt Earp's deputy, and was popularized by a '50s TV show. Masterson, who claimed Bat was his ancestor, loved the image of the tough lawman, and didn't discourage the press from referring to him as a gunslinger when defending his white-collar clients.

Since Smith had died decades earlier and Hale recently retired, Masterson was the most senior of senior partners.

"Good morning," said Masterson. "Mr. Hooker, is it not?"

"It's Booker, sir." He'd only spoken to the man once before, during the reception for new associates held shortly after he'd joined the firm.

He saw Masterson was wearing the official SHM Saturday casual uniform: tan slacks, loafers, polo shirt, and navy-blue blazer. When Tom dressed that morning, he'd briefly considered foregoing the uniform for more comfortable jeans, but thankfully hadn't succumbed.

"Yes, of course," said Masterson. "And in which department do you now find yourself, Mr. Booker?"

"Corporate, sir." The firm's policy required new associates to rotate through four or five legal specialties during the first two years, the theory being the rotation would allow both the new lawyer and the firm to find the best fit. The newbies also had to do a pro bono stint so the firm could meet its bar obligations to the poor and downtrodden without pulling time away from attorneys billing at much higher rates.

"Maybe we'll see you in WC soon."

WC was shorthand for white-collar litigation. Most in Washington considered Masterson, a former US attorney general and Texas governor, the best white-collar defense counsel in town, if not the whole country. The voters had booted Bat's former boss out of the Oval Office two years earlier, and Bat's name was on the shortlist of potential challengers for his party's presidential nomination to take on the new incumbent two years hence.

"Heading for the library?" asked Masterson. He was about to touch the button for the second floor.

Tom could easily lie—the chances of Masterson missing a lowly associate over the next several hours were virtually nil. But the key word was "virtually." "No, sir. Got to pick up my daughter for a short field trip." He added quickly, "But I'll be back in a couple of hours to make up the time."

"Family's important, of course." His expression left no doubt that Masterson believed time spent by an associate on a Saturday morning doing anything other than cranking out billable hours cost the most senior partner money, and therefore was by definition not important.

The elevator reached the lobby, and Masterson exited. "See you this afternoon, Mr. Booker."

"Of course, sir."

The doors closed. Tom took a deep breath, then punched the already-lit *G* button, willing the elevator to drop the last two floors before anyone else came aboard.

Once in the garage, he jogged to the silver Lexus GS 430. Almost five years old, it had been his one extravagant purchase when he'd been hired by SHM out of Georgetown Law.

He started the engine and drove quickly up the ramp and out of the garage, almost hitting two young men in suits and ties. Both gave him the finger. Lobbyists, thought Tom. They still wore ties on Saturdays.

The annoying warning chime began as soon as he turned onto M Street, and he buckled his seat belt with one hand as he turned south onto New Hampshire. He glanced at the dashboard clock. *Shit.* Gayle was going to kill him.

After catching the fourth red light, he reluctantly pulled out his phone. Talking on a cell while driving was technically against the law in the District, but everyone knew if the law were strictly enforced, the federal government and the businesses of all those who made a living off it would screech to a halt. Besides, he was stopped at a light so he wasn't technically driving.

When he heard the connection, he grimaced, knowing what was coming next.

"Where the hell are you? Janie, Angie, and two other seven-year-olds are standing here in my kitchen, waiting for you."

"Sorry, I—"

"Just how do you expect to drive here, pick them up, and get them back to the Air and Space Museum in less than forty-five minutes?"

"O'Neal needed the buy-sell agreement before—"

"*I don't care!* It's always something. Always putting your work and yourself before family."

The response shot from his mouth before he could stop it. "One might consider sleeping with our daughter's pediatrician putting yourself before family." *Damn. Remember, pause, then speak. Pause, then speak.*

"You son of a bitch."

Tom took a deep breath. Excellent chance Janie was within earshot, and the last thing she needed now after seven months of dealing with her parents' break-up was another fight. He lowered his voice. "Look, I'm almost to the Roosevelt Bridge. Can you take her? I can meet you at the museum entrance and take the handoff."

"My daughter's not a football. Besides, David and I have plans. If you're not here in fifteen minutes, maybe I can persuade Rosie to take them." She ended the call.

My daughter. The change from *our* daughter to *my* daughter several months earlier had not gone unnoticed. Gayle, Janie, and Dr. Dave—he insisted his patients and their moms call him Dr. Dave—lived in Tom's former house in Arlington, while Tom now called a cramped, one-bedroom apartment in the Adams Morgan area of the city home. Adams Morgan was known for its eclectic charm, a string of the best Latino restaurants in the city, and the violent drug culture along its borders.

Rosie was Rosie Battaglia, Gayle's sister. She, her husband, Gino, and their young daughter, Angie, lived east of Connecticut Avenue in upper Northwest DC near the Maryland line, the fancy-schmantzy part of the city.

The previous evening, Janie had invited Angie for a sleepover. Tom wished the sleepover had occurred at Angie's; it would've made his trip from downtown much shorter.

The last light before the bridge. One car in front of him, an ancient beige Buick with Ohio plates. The light turned yellow.

"Go, go!" But instead of speeding up, the sedan slowed down, then stopped at the intersection. Tom pounded the steering wheel with his fist. He checked the dashboard clock again. No way was he going to make it in time.

He could feel his face flush as his frustration escalated. He glanced at the glove compartment. *Just a sip to take the edge off?*

The light changed. He hit the gas, tailgating the Buick, barely avoiding knocking up against its bumper.

When he rounded the curve, he saw flashing lights on the bridge, an accident backing up traffic to a standstill. *Shit.* His deadline only a few minutes off, he considered abandoning the drive to Arlington, calling back, and begging Rosie to take the girls. He could intercept them at the museum.

Or, he could try the Memorial. What the hell? Maybe Gayle would give him a grace period.

He pulled around the Buick and drove south along the river, then made the turn onto the bridge and headed west across the Potomac, quickly sliding into the passing lane where a single yellow line separated him from oncoming eastbound traffic.

In the far distance, he saw a green Dodge minivan heading toward him from the western entrance to the bridge. Rosie had a green minivan. Could Gayle have sent the kids off with Rosie early? Why didn't she call him?

He dug out his cell, glanced down, and scrolled to her number. He'd developed a system where he held the phone up at eye level with his right hand so he could still keep his eyes on the road.

He punched in the text: *on Mem bridge. Did they leave?* He hit "Send."

The minivan was getting closer. He remembered Rosie had tied an orange ribbon on her antenna so she could spot her car in a parking lot. A red Ford pickup truck in front of the minivan wove back and forth in its lane, making it difficult for Tom to see the Dodge's aerial.

He heard the *chime,* and glanced down to read Gayle's message. *Yes. Couldn't wait. R not happy. Meet at A & S.*

Great. Why couldn't she—?

His thoughts were interrupted by screeching tires and and blaring horns.

He looked up and saw he'd drifted into the oncoming lane, heading straight for the green minivan.

He jammed his foot on the brakes and cut hard right.

Instead of responding, the Lexus spun like a Frisbee across the pavement, first crashing head-on into the front of the minivan, then ricocheting into the rear of the red truck. The truck hit the curb hard at an odd angle. It flipped up into the air, appeared to hover for a long moment before landing upside down in the middle of the road. The impact of the collision knocked the minivan up onto the sidewalk where it glanced off a light pole, then rolled up onto its two right tires. Teetering next to the bridge rail, it was about to flip into the Potomac.

A split-second image of a dirty orange ribbon filled his brain.

In a flash, he saw Janie's face pressed up against the van window.

Then he saw nothing.

CHAPTER 2

Full consciousness arrived a split-second ahead of the searing pain and the smell of smoke. Looking past the deflated airbag, he saw that the windshield, though shattered, remained mostly intact. Thank God for safety glass. Through the windshield's cracked mosaic, he was able to make out the crumpled hood of the Lexus mashed into a light post.

He conducted a visual check of his limbs—all were accounted for and appeared to be attached and functioning. The crash had twisted his bucket seat so he was now facing the passenger side where the car's impact with the light post had collapsed the roof to knee height.

The flipped-over red truck was the source of the smoke. The truck's cab had been crushed to a level almost even with the truck bed. The smoke rose from the truck's undercarriage.

Except, it wasn't rising.

He smelled the smoke, saw it pluming from the truck, but it didn't move; the dark vapors appeared frozen, as if he were viewing a photo of the smoke rather than the smoke itself.

He shook the cobwebs from his head, but the smoke remained static, no doubt an optical illusion caused by the shattered safety glass.

His eyes returned to the passenger seat. My God, what if he'd been on time and picked up Janie? He would've packed three of the girls into the backseat, and strapped Janie into the front bucket. Janie would be dead, maybe the others as well.

He wrenched his head around, and saw the green minivan, teetering on two wheels, about to flip into the river.

Janie.

He struggled to get out of the car, but the driver's side door was jammed shut. Not surprisingly, the electric window wouldn't move.

The seat belt buckle had slipped around so he was half sitting on it. He pushed the release button. Jammed.

Wiggling his hips against the belt, he gasped as stabbing pain shot across his lower back and down his left leg. The belt loosened. The bolts that fastened the belt bracket to the floor had been partially dislodged. He grabbed the belt at the point nearest the bracket and, with a quick glance across the road at the teetering minivan, pulled, using not only his arms and shoulders, but his whole body. His cry of pain mixed with triumph as the bracket popped loose. The smell of smoke strengthened. He twisted under and out of the seat belt.

He kicked out the windshield, and immediately pain fired from his hip and shot down his left leg, grabbing the breath from his lungs.

Ignoring the cuts to his arms from the broken glass, he dragged his body through the opening, then slid headfirst down the side of the car to the pavement and crawled to his feet.

Focusing only on the teetering minivan, he staggered to the center line. In the back of his mind, he wondered why he wasn't hearing the sound of approaching sirens. Then he realized he wasn't hearing anything. Had the impact from the collision caused hearing loss? Would it be permanent?

No time for that, he had to get to his daughter. The smell of smoke and burning rubber was nearly suffocating. He saw for the first time that smoke and flames rose from the minivan's engine. He had to pull her out before the gas tank caught on fire.

But, again, the flames weren't moving.

He turned back to the pickup. The smoke appeared to be frozen in the air.

He spun completely around. None of the other cars on the bridge moved. A few tourists who'd been strolling along the sidewalk seemed frozen in time. One woman walking a black poodle was suspended just as she was about to take a step. She should be falling over as her center of gravity hovered out and away from the single foot on the ground.

Tom made his way across the road to the minivan. Shouldn't it be tipping over? He saw Janie's face snug up against the rear window. Her mouth gaped open wide, her palms pressed against the glass. Her body leaned toward the pavement, but didn't fall. She wasn't moving, not a twitch.

She didn't frigging move!

He saw Angie and two other girls flipped and turned inside—all of them suspended in midair.

For a moment he stared into Janie's eyes. An unusual color of blue ice, he'd always been secretly proud when someone would tell her, "Oh, you've got your father's eyes." And while those eyes didn't move, he couldn't shake the feeling she could see him.

He tried to pry open the rear door. Didn't budge.

Maybe if he broke the glass of the rear window. He shuffled as fast as he could back to the overturned pickup to check for tools. His back spasmed as he crouched down, and he had to pause to catch his breath. The driver, a teenage boy, was upside down and had not been wearing his seat belt. The boy's unseeing eyes stared at Tom from his partially severed head. Blood soaked the bench seat and everything inside the cab. Tom struggled to force down the bile rising in his throat as he searched for a hammer or some other tool he could use to bash in the Dodge's rear window. Nothing.

He glanced back at the teetering van. There were other cars on the bridge. Somebody's got to have a hammer. He gasped from the pain in his back and leg as he rose to his feet. Looking east toward the Memorial, he spotted another truck, a white van with *Welch Plumbing* painted on the side, and hobbled toward it.

As he passed the red pickup's undercarriage, he reached out and moved his hand through the rising smoke—*except it wasn't rising.* He felt nothing.

Then, out of the corner of his eye, he saw movement from the far eastern end of the bridge.

Two people jogged toward him.

CHAPTER 3

As they got closer, he could make out that one was female. Ignoring the pain, he ran/shuffled toward the couple, waving his arms frantically in the air.

"Help! Help!"

The man and woman each smiled and waved back, continuing their easy pace. They must not have heard him.

"Help! Accident!"

Tom reached them near the center point of the bridge. They were young, tan, good looking in a clean, wholesome way. Both blond with ice-blue eyes. Not twins, but enough of a resemblance they easily could be brother and sister. With crisp white shorts and matching lime-green t-shirts, they resembled models from an Abercrombie & Fitch or J.Crew ad out for an easy jog on a warm, late September morning. And they appeared wholly oblivious to the scene surrounding them.

"Do you have a phone?" Tom shouted.

The male reached into his pocket, retrieved a cell phone, and showed it to him.

"Call 911! Hurry, my daughter—!"

"That's not really necessary, Tom," the man responded with a gleaming smile.

"You already called? Great. Look, my daughter and a bunch of other kids are in that green van. You got to help me get the door open." He shuffled toward the van. "We have to be careful, 'cause if the van tips over—wait, how did you know my name?" He stopped and turned back to the couple. It hit him—his surroundings frozen in a moment of time, two beautiful people greeting him.

Holy shit. He was dead.

"You're not dead, Tom," said the girl.

"How do you know what I'm thinking?"

They both responded with a wide grin.

"C'mon, we have to get the girls out of the van now." Doing his best to ignore the pain, he shuffled as fast as he could toward the minivan, expecting them to follow.

When he'd gone about thirty feet, he turned back. They hadn't moved.

Then in a sliver of a second, they were standing immediately in front of him.

"Who *are* you?"

"I'm Chad, and this is Britney. Pleasure to meet you, Tom." They each offered their hands.

Tom assumed there was a logical explanation for the bizarre behavior of these two preppy jerks, but he didn't have time to focus on it. He had to get Janie out of the Dodge. He ignored their extended hands, and ran the best he could to the minivan.

When he arrived, nothing had changed. The vehicle remained teetering on two wheels, and Janie's expression was still frozen. She hadn't moved a muscle.

He heard the girl—Britney?—directly behind him. "It's kind've weird, don't you think?"

He looked back. They both stood there, still with their hands extended. "I mean, the frozen-in-time thing. Spooky."

"I agree," said Chad, never losing his smile. "Way spooky."

Who the hell were these people? "I don't know what's going on, but if you can do anything, please help me get her out of there."

"As a matter of fact, Tom, we can help," said Chad.

"Absolutely," added Britney.

Chad wrapped a comforting arm around Tom's shoulder, and gently turned him so they were both facing the minivan. "I'm sure you'd agree that life's about making decisions. Trivial decisions—what am I going to wear today? What am I having for breakfast? And consequential decisions—the choice of a career, the selection of a spouse. Sometimes we're forced to make life or death decisions. Can you think of an example of a life or death decision, Tom?"

"Please, just help—"

"Try, Tom."

"I don't know, pulling the plug on a loved one."

"Excellent," said Britney. "You get an *A*-plus."

Chad waved his arm in front of the wreckage. "See, Tom, you have a life or death decision to make right now."

"Actually, it's a life or *deaths* decision," said Britney.

"You're right," said Chad, chuckling. "I stand corrected. A life or *deaths* decision."

"What the hell are you talking about?" He looked over at the Lexus, half expecting to see his own body still in the cab. Or, despite what they'd said, maybe he really *was* dead. But if he was dead, where was he? And why would stabbing pain be shooting from the small of his back down his leg?"

There can be two different outcomes here," said Chad, gesturing to the wreckage. "Here's choice *A*."

He heard a *whirring* sound, like an old-time tape recorder rewinding. Suddenly, everything moved. Backward. Rewinding to seconds before the collision.

Tom couldn't believe his eyes. He saw the green minivan with Rosie driving eastbound on the bridge, behind the red pickup. He could make out the driver now—good-looking kid, maybe seventeen or eighteen—talking on his cell phone. He saw his Lexus approaching the other two vehicles, and he was driving. But that was impossible, because he was standing on the sidewalk.

He looked closer. *He was driving*.

"Kind've cool," said Britney.

Tom couldn't pull his eyes away. He saw himself look down to check Gayle's text.

"You shouldn't text and drive," said Chad.

"Driving distractions kill," said Britney.

He heard the honking horns and screeching tires. He smelled the burnt rubber. He watched, transfixed, as the Lexus spun out of control toward the minivan and the red truck.

Except there was no collision.

Rosie braked hard, the minivan screeched to a stop, allowing Tom's Lexus to spin out in front of her. The Lexus careened up over the curb, missing the light post by a whisker, then returned to the road. The red truck continued on its way. Tom could see Rosie through the window giving the Lexus driver—him—the finger. Obviously, she didn't get a good look at him and didn't recognize the car. She slowly pulled out again and headed east toward DC.

As the minivan passed, Tom could see Janie and the other girls giggling at Rosie's obscene gesture.

He waved both of his arms frantically. *"Janie!"*

He knew she couldn't hear him, but he was so excited to see her alive and safe he didn't care. He turned back to Chad.

"If this is a dream, I want to wake up now."

Chad ignored him.

Again, he heard the whirring sound, and the scene returned to where it had been moments earlier—frozen in time with an overturned pickup, a Lexus wrapped around a light post, and his daughter caught in mid-scream inside a green minivan hovering over the edge of a bridge on two wheels.

"And this is option *B*," said Chad. He swept his arm over the wreckage. This time the scene rewound just a few seconds.

Immediately the now familiar jumble of sights, sounds, and smells confronted Tom: a piercing scream from the woman with the poodle; the screech of brakes and blaring horns from other cars as they swerved to avoid crashing into the pickup; the acrid smell of smoke and burnt rubber.

He whipped his head back to the minivan. The flames from

the engine were moving now. They'd caught on the gas dribbling from the fuel tank, singeing the green paint below the filler cap.

God, no!

The flames moved up the side of the van toward the filler pipe.

And the van slowly tipped toward the river.

CHAPTER 4

"Janie!"

As Tom ran toward the van, he saw her face and hands still pressed tight against the glass, a look of stark terror on her face. He got close enough to see her mouth, *"Daddy!"*

Then, as if in slow motion, the van flipped over the railing and dropped upside down, crashing into the Potomac.

The jarring slap of the van hitting the water lasted only a split second before being supplanted by the huge *boom* of the minivan exploding into flames. The blast shot back a fireball rising above the level of the bridge, causing Tom to involuntarily jump back.

"NOOO!"

Tom ignored the sparks and bits of debris raining down on the bridge, and rushed to the railing. Below, he saw the vehicle totally consumed by flames. He thought he heard a faint cry for help rising from the fire. *Janie's voice?* Did he imagine it? Was he imagining the whole nightmare scene?

He heard shrieks, shouts, and the faint wail of an approaching siren. He had to get down there. Now.

He turned to see Chad and Britney standing calmly in the middle of the road as the chaos swirled around them.

"Help me!"

In a split second, they both stood in front of him. "Sorry, Tom, she's gone," said Chad.

"Afraid she's burnt to a crisp," said Britney, an expression of deep sympathy on her face. "And, sadly, it was painful."

"Very painful," added Chad in a comforting tone.

Tom balled his fist and swung as hard as he could at Chad's jaw. His fist passed through Chad's smiling face as if it weren't there, and the force of his swing knocked him to the pavement.

When he looked up, he heard the *whirring* sound, and the scene snapped back a few seconds. The minivan was back on the bridge, teetering on two wheels, frozen in time.

Chad offered a hand. Tom ignored it and struggled to his feet. He couldn't keep his voice from quivering. "Who *are* you?"

"We're the folks who are going to give you a chance to save your daughter," Chad responded.

"We love Janie," said Britney. "Cute as a button."

"No one wants to see her turned to charcoal," said Chad.

Britney laughed. "Well, maybe someone would."

Chad said, "You need to make a choice. Option *A* or—"

"Option *A!*" Tom shouted. "Option *A!*"

"Excellent choice," said Britney. "But, as I'm sure you can appreciate, there will need to be compensation."

"We think of it more as a kindness," said Chad. "We extend to you the kindness of saving Janie from a fiery death brought on by your own self-absorbed negligence—rules are for others, not for Tom Booker. In return, you will need to extend us a reciprocal kindness."

"So, you're saying you're some kind of—what? Angels?" He knew the sarcasm in his voice sounded forced.

Both chuckled. "You might say, 'right field, wrong team,'" replied Chad.

Tom stared at Chad with a perplexed look on his face, his mind swirling. What the preppy jerk suggested was impossible. He'd long ago dismissed the concept of an afterlife as a fairy tale perpetuated by human beings since they emerged from the goo. From Thor to Zeus to Jesus, God, and Allah, belief in a higher being offered a glimmer of hope that no matter how miserable one's life, it would conclude with a happy ending.

Looking at their faces, Tom sensed the couple could read his thoughts.

Chad and Britney each giggled as they held their hands out in front of their chests, forming a cross with their index fingers like a pathetic victim trying to ward off Dracula.

Tom turned his eyes away. His mind flashed back to his youth. As a boy he'd been raised in the Methodist church by very religious parents. When he was in high school, his dad had been killed by a drunk driver, and after that he'd refused to attend church services depite his mother's pleas. He couldn't buy her explanation that his father's death had been "God's will."

And then four years later his mother had been diagnosed with breast cancer. When the chemo and radiation and herbs and potions failed, he'd resorted to prayer, begging God to spare her. But He didn't, confirming to Tom that even if God did exist, He was a sadistic sonofabitch.

Still, given what he'd just witnessed, either he was hallucinating from injuries caused by the crash or—

He turned back to them. "Am I in"—the word caught in his throat—"hell?"

"A lot of people would say Washington's a living hell," responded Britney.

Chad laughed. "Very good, Brit." To Tom, "No, you're standing right here in the middle of Memorial Bridge."

"So here's the deal," said Brit. "There are five innocents in the minivan."

"You're calling Rosie an innocent?" asked Chad. "What about the muff dives with her Pilates instructor?"

"But she always came home to Gino with a smile on her face," responded Brit.

"Good point," said Chad.

"Will somebody just tell me what the hell's going on?"

" 'What the hell,' very clever," said Brit.

"In return for Option *A,* once every two weeks, one of the occupants in the minivan will die," said Chad. "See, they were going to die anyway—you killed them, sorry to keep bringing that up. But you've got to pay attention to the road ahead. And watch the hooch, Tom. Drinking's bad juju."

"Definitely bad juju," said Brit. "And while all of them would be heading north so to speak—"

"Even Rosie," said Chad.

Brit continued. "The boss saw an opportunity for a win-win transaction. Your daughter and her friends will be allowed to live, but in exchange, you must provide him another life."

"By *provide,* you mean...?"

"Snuff, exterminate, bump off—you get the point."

"That's crazy! I'm not a murderer."

"Of course you are," said Chad. "You just murdered five innocent people."

"Wouldn't you do anything to save your own daughter?" asked Brit.

Tom dropped his head in his hands. *This can't be real, this can't be—*

"We've made it easy for you," said Chad. "The substitute can be a scumbag or as pure as the driven snow. But everyone you snuff goes south, whether they would otherwise deserve it or not."

"Life for a life," said Brit. "What could be more fair than that?"

Finally, Tom got it. He breathed a sigh of relief. Chad's words were so outlandish, he now knew he had to be dreaming. Wait till he tells his buddy, Zig. Preppies from hell; Zig'll get a big laugh out of that one.

"Oh, we're real," said Brit.

Tom smiled. The only way they could read his mind is if he were having a crazy nightmare. Feeling cocky, he decided to call their bluff. "Prove it."

Chad shook his head. "What, you want us to spin our heads and spew green vomit? Sorry, Tom, but you're just going to have to trust us. Or not."

The expression on Brit's face could best be described as apologetic. "So, by Saturday midnight at the end of every second week, either you deliver us a soul, or I'm afraid we'll be compelled to take one from the van."

"Remember, Tom," said Chad, "you're the one who put yourself in this pickle."

"Gotta dash," said Brit. They both waved, then continued jogging west along the bridge.

CHAPTER 5

In a split second, Tom was in the Lexus driving west on the bridge. No pain. Anywhere. Not even a scratch on his safety-glass windshield. He quickly checked his rearview mirror. He could see the minivan heading east, trailing the red pickup.

Everything looked perfectly normal. He reached the western bridge entrance, circled the turnabout and headed back east across the Memorial.

What the hell happened? He must've caught himself drifting into the opposite lane, slammed on the brakes, and momentarily bumped his head on the steering wheel. Crazy. He still had goosebumps running the length of both arms. Again, his eyes found the dashboard glove compartment.

"Watch the hooch, Tom. Drinking's bad juju."

He needed to calm down or he really *was* going to cause an accident. He opened the glove compartment.

***

Twenty minutes later he emerged from the Colonial Parking garage on C Street, and popped a few more mints into his mouth as he jogged north to the museum.

When he crossed Independence, he noticed at least a dozen school groups gathered at the entrance. He smiled briefly, remembering fondly his days as a schoolteacher. Life had been a lot less complicated then.

Janie and her classmates, wearing their green Fairfield Elementary

Frog shirts, stood at the end of the line. It looked like Janie had obtained a Frog shirt for her visiting cousin and made Angie an honorary Frog. A few mothers patrolled outside the herd to make sure there were no stragglers. Rosie, arms folded, fuming, gave Tom the evil eye as soon as he crossed the street.

He ignored his former sister-in-law and waved to his daughter. When he reached her, she jumped into his arms. Nothing short of heaven could match the feeling of his child's arms wrapped tightly around his neck.

Heaven.

His mind flashed back to his daydream—vision, hallucination, whatever the hell it was. While seemingly extending for fifteen or twenty minutes, the blackout must've only lasted a split second, since he hadn't lost control of the wheel.

"Mommy was mad at you 'cause you were late."

"I know, honey. Sorry. But I'm here now."

Rosie approached. She didn't look happy. Come to think of it, she never looked happy.

"Thanks," said Tom. "Know it was an inconvenience."

"You make a commitment, you keep it, Tom."

"You're right. Sorry."

She was in full scowl mode. "No smart-ass comeback? You sick or something? You should know by now that family commitment comes first."

Tom thought, *maybe you should tell that to your sister who made a commitment not to cheat on her husband.* And as far as the smart-ass comment reference, he probably deserved that. He forced himself to hold his tongue. *One Mississippi—*

"Right. Traffic. I should've left earlier." No use telling her his boss expected a complete buy-sell memo for the firm's second largest client by 9:30 a.m., and if he screwed up and lost his job, his family commitment to provide alimony and child support payments would be significantly jeopardized.

"Aunt Rosie gave a man the finger," said Janie.

Rosie scolded, "Janie—"

"What happened?" asked Tom.

"Some idiot in a silver car cut me off on the bridge. Almost made me run into the redneck driving a pickup truck in front of me. Might've caused me to spin off the bridge, the jerk. Didn't he see I had *children* on board?"

"What's a redneck?" asked Janie.

Rosie exchanged glances with Tom. "His truck was red, honey. So we call someone who drives a red truck a redneck."

"So you're a greenneck, Aunt Rosie?"

"Exactly," said Tom.

Angie called from the gathering of Frogs. "Hurry up, they're letting us in!"

"I got it from here, Rosie. And thanks again."

"I swear, Tom, I don't know how you can call yourself a responsible father."

The response jumped from his brain to his mouth before he could implement *One Mississippi*. "Thanks for that. By the way, how's your Pilates instructor?"

She froze, then turned back to him with a look of panic, no longer the tough broad who felt it necessary to convey how put-upon she felt as a result of his screwup. Her eyes pleaded with him, then teared up. She quickly disappeared into the crowd. Tom had never seen her that way.

The woman was scared shitless.

CHAPTER 6

Napoleon's was packed, but Argus, the bartender, had reserved their usual seats at the end of the bar, the prime location for scoping out single women entering the establishment. Argus tapped them each another Stella—Zig's second, Tom's third. A small voice in the back of his head whispered, *slow down.*

A very small voice.

"So, she might be having a lesbo affair with her Pilates instructor, so what?" asked Zig.

"That's not the point. How would I know that? The only way I could've known is if my bridge vision—"

"Impossible," responded Zig, with a certainty born of his lofty status as a fourth-year associate at SHM.

Brian Zigler, Virginia undergrad, Harvard Law, had been assigned to Tom as his mentor when Tom joined the firm. SHM had instituted a mentoring program for new associates several years earlier, and had received glowing reviews from top law schools for the firm's sensitivity to the stress experienced by newcomers. Numerous other firms had copied the program, a feather in the cap of senior partners in the continuing battle for status among the city's legal elites.

Zig was single, and also lived in Adams Morgan. After the mentoring period had ended, they continued to hang out together. Zig had been there for him when he'd had to deal with the breakup, and Tom had moved to the area on Zig's recommendation.

"Then how could I have known?" asked Tom.

"Who the hell knows? First, you could be reading her reaction wrong. Second, if it is true, maybe she said something about her instructor that at the time seemed innocuous, but your subconscious noticed the tone of her voice, or a tic in her expression. Then when you had your flash-vision, your subconscious mind shot that idea forward to your conscious mind."

"You have no idea what you're talking about, do you?"

"Absolutely none."

They laughed, then clinked their glasses and drained half the contents.

Zig turned back to front-door surveillance. "Bogie entering the grid."

Tom saw an attractive brunette come through the door and head toward two other girls sitting mid-bar. Zig caught her eye and waved. She waved back, then greeted her friends.

"Who's she?" asked Tom.

"No idea," responded Zig. "But before the night's over, my friend, that will change."

Tom shook his head. Zig was not what anyone would call classically handsome. At an even six feet, he was two inches shorter than Tom. Red hair, acne scars, and maybe fifteen pounds overweight. But for some reason, women were attracted to him. Zig explained it as projecting confidence. He was probably right.

After Gayle had left him for another man, Tom fought his sexual insecurity by chasing every skirt who walked across his path. Zig suggested his conquests were solely the result of young women desiring to date a lawyer. To prove him wrong, thereafter Tom had told prospects he was an elementary schoolteacher, which, up until a couple of years ago, had been true. While he admittedly noticed some drop-off, he'd discovered there were more than enough women who didn't care what he did for a living.

"So, what were their names again?" asked Zig.

"Chad and Britney. He called her Brit."

"Hot?"

"I don't know, I guess so. I wasn't checkin' out her body, I was trying to save my daughter's life."

"Who did she look like in real life? If you were visionating, chances are you were projecting someone you know for real."

"Nobody. She was blond, tan—" *Afraid she's burnt to a crisp.* "slim, friendly—" *Sadly, it was painful.* Tom shuddered. "Look, I don't want to talk about it anymore."

"Fine by me."

Tom watched Zig slide off his stool and approach the brunette. Within a minute, he had all three girls laughing. He waved Tom over.

Unable to stop thinking about the bridge vision, he decided the best way to clear his mind was to clear his pipes.

He grabbed his beer, switched on his most charming smile, and headed for relief.

CHAPTER 7

The next seven days passed quickly. Tom called Janie three times during the week, and picked her up Friday after school for the weekend. They'd gone to a movie Friday night. Saturday afternoon, after getting up at five a.m. and putting in six hours at SHM, he'd taken her to visit his cousin, Estin, who lived in a small waterfront town south of Annapolis. They'd gone fishing for rock in Estin's boat, and had eaten crabs out on a deck overlooking the Chesapeake Bay. He'd kept his promise to Gayle and had limited himself to three beers. Estin was the town's sheriff and had administered a complimentary Breathalyzer—.07, no problem. Janie had a ball, and Tom couldn't remember having such a pleasant weekend himself in a long time.

When he dropped off Janie Sunday evening in Arlington, Rosie, her husband, Gino, and Angie were at the house. Tom thought Rosie seemed different—quiet, as if she were trying to put on a brave face. Probably his imagination.

Rosie was five years older than Gayle. Tom had seen pictures from her high school yearbook that established her as one of the hottest girls in school. Short, trim, big rack, she was the cheerleader always posing in the front row. She had the same dark complexion as their Italian father, while Gayle—tall, blond, blue-eyed—drew from their mother's northern European genes.

Rosie was still short, but her waist had thickened and her boobs had drooped. Gino was more than ten years older than his wife. After the marriage, he'd gone to work for his new father-in-law's residential construction business, and six years later had taken over control of the company.

Despite their age difference, Tom had always gotten along pretty well with Gino. Short, weighing over 250 pounds with arms the size of Tom's thighs, Gino was built like the proverbial brick shithouse. Both sports fans, Gino sometimes got 'Skins tickets from one of his suppliers, and a couple times a year he'd take Tom to a game. When Gayle had dumped him for Dr. Dave, Rosie had naturally sided with her sister, suggesting not too subtly that if Tom had paid more attention to his wife and daughter, Gayle wouldn't have been compelled to seek comfort elsewhere. Gino's analysis, on the other hand, was less subtle. As Tom heard him express once to Rosie when Gayle was out of earshot, "She screwed her doctor, so it's her fault, period."

At Janie's insistence, they'd brought back a dozen crabs from Maryland for her mom to enjoy. Janie spread newspapers on the kitchen table and, armed with the small wooden mallet Estin had given her, demonstrated to Gino, Rosie, and Angie the most efficient way to extract the sweet crabmeat. He knew every father thought his daughter was the most beautiful girl in the world, but, of course, with Janie it was true.

Tom noticed Rosie seemed detached, only speaking when her opinion was specifically solicited. On his way out the door, Tom pulled Gayle aside.

"So what's the deal with your sister? She doesn't seem her normal bitchy self."

"Got me. For the last week she's been in a deep funk. I pressed her as much as I could, but she keeps denying anything's wrong."

"What about Gino? Everything okay between them?"

"As far as I know."

He said good-bye, received a big hug from his daughter, then walked out the door. As he reached his car, he felt someone close behind him. He froze, then turned, fearful he might see—it was Rosie.

"Sorry, you startled me."

She put her hand on his arm. "I don't know how you found out, but I'm begging you, for Gino and Angela's sake, for my sake, please don't say anything."

His initial response was to deny he knew what she was talking about. But he had to be certain. "How long has it been going on?"

She bit her lip to fight back the tears. "Couple of years, but it's over. A silly fling. I told myself it was harmless, a little bit of excitement every Wednesday afternoon. The woman thing, I don't know. I never cheated on Gino, with a man, I mean. Somehow, doing it with a woman didn't seem like it really counted. I swear it meant nothing. I love my husband and my daughter. I'm begging you—"

"Your secret's safe."

She embraced him and whispered, "Thanks, Tommy."

Over her shoulder, Tom saw Gino standing in the doorway staring at them. He didn't look happy.

***

For the first few days of the next week, Tom was swamped with work and had little trouble blocking from his mind any thoughts of an impending deadline. He only had a short time left in Corporate, and he wanted to do the best job he could finishing his assignments. While he hadn't made up his mind completely, he strongly leaned toward slotting Corporate first on the preference list he'd fill out at the completion of his rotation. Ultimately, it was up to the department chair to decide who would join their practice group, but the associate's preferences were taken into account.

Still, as the week progressed he found it increasingly difficult to concentrate. He couldn't wait for Sunday to arrive.

Zig asked if he wanted to go out Saturday night on a double date. Actually, more of a blind date—the girl was the roommate of Marcie, a Hill staffer he'd met the previous week at a fundraiser for Liz Guthrie, the junior senator from Oklahoma. Zig had introduced Marcie to Tom at Napoleon's. After just one appletini, she'd been all over Zig. Barely five feet tall, she had a boyish figure—no hips, no boobs. Later, Zig had been quick to mention she'd been on the Oklahoma State gymnastics team, information conveyed with a clear message: you should see what she can do in bed.

To entice Tom, Zig pitched Marcie's roommate, Jess, as a "party girl," winking when he said it. To Zig's mild surprise, Tom agreed immediately. He didn't care whether she was a nympho or a cold-fish spinster who wore ankle-length black dresses and her hair in a tight bun. He needed a distraction.

Her full name was Jessica Hawkins. Attractive—slim, straw-berry-blond hair—she wore a tight, green V-neck sweater that matched the color of her eyes, a mid-thigh black skirt and six-inch heels. Her vibe definitely skewed closer to the nympho than the spinster end of the scale.

They went to the Hawk 'n' Dove on Capitol Hill, one of the oldest Irish pubs in the city, an institution dating back over forty-five years. Jess kept his attention through three taps of Guinness and a couple of buffalo burgers. Tom was impressed that she'd gone the burger and fries route instead of a girlie salad as Marcie had ordered.

Like her roommate, Jess lost little time before conveying she was really into Tom, and took every opportunity to touch his arm or shoulder throughout the evening's conversation. But as the night wore on, he'd sneak a glance at his watch, then scold himself for giving any credence to what he'd come to call his "bridge vision."

Zig suggested a round of Metaxa, and insisted the Greek brandy include a coffee bean, since that's the way it had been served to him when he visited Santorini two summers earlier. The liqueur went down smoothly, and after the second round, Tom felt a hand rubbing his knee. Assuming it wasn't Zig, he figured sex would be the ultimate diversion, and squeezed Jess' knee under the table.

The moment Tom touched her skin, Jess scrunched forward so his hand moved up her skirt. He slowly withdrew his hand, intentionally teasing her. But his movements seemed mechanical rather than sensual. Normally, he would be feeling some level of arousal at this point—what Zig called a semi—but the image of the bridge vision, which he'd pressed into the farthest reaches of his mind, continued to leak out.

Afraid she's burnt to a crisp—Sadly, it was painful.

A little after midnight, they finally exited the bar. Despite exceeding his self-imposed drink limit, Tom felt stone-cold sober and was absolutely certain he could pass a Breathalyzer. He suggested it might be more convenient if he took Jess home, and was greeted with three matched expressions which loosely translated into, "duh."

During the trip to Foggy Bottom, where Jess rented a small townhouse with Marcie, she leaned heavily into him as he drove. She hummed along to the music from an oldies station on the radio playing doo-wop music from the '50s and '60s:

"—and that set included three of the top 100 doo-wop ballads in history. The Penguins' 'Earth Angel,' 'Pennies from Heaven' from the Skyliners, and the Platters with 'My Prayer.' Next up, The Shirelles..."

Tom couldn't stand it any longer. He gently freed his right hand. "Uh, need to check on my daughter, just to make sure she's okay."

"Isn't it a little late?"

Tom could think of no rational response, so he ignored her and hit the speed dial on his cell phone. After the fourth ring, Gayle answered.

"Hi, it's me," said Tom.

Her voice was groggy with sleep. "Tom?"

He heard a male voice in the background mumbling, "Who is it?" They weren't married yet, but recently Gayle had transitioned Janie to accepting that Dr. Dave might be "camping out" with mommy some nights.

Tom glanced at Jess as he spoke into the phone. "Sorry to call this late—"

"Christ, it's almost one o'clock."

This time he didn't look at Jess. "I didn't realize how late it was."

"What do you want?"

"Just checking to see if Janie's okay."

"Why wouldn't she be okay?"

"Just checking, that's all."

"Are you drunk? Again?"

"Look, I know it sounds crazy, but could you go check on her?"

"I'm not going to get out of my warm bed to check on my daughter. Besides, I was up just a little bit ago, looked in, and she was fine."

He tried without complete success to drain the anxiety from his voice. "How long ago, what time?"

"Fifteen, twenty minutes ago, what the hell difference does it make?"

Tom glanced at the clock on the dashboard: 12:48 a.m. Even assuming she was off by 100 percent, Janie would've been confirmed safe after midnight. He couldn't help but breathe a deep sigh of relief. "Thanks, sorry for calling so late. Give my best to Dave."

He ended the call before she could say another word.

**

Three hours later he was sound asleep, with Jess spooned up naked against him in her canopy bed. Living up to and beyond her reputation, she'd been a sexual crazy woman, even offering to introduce him to the contents of what she called her toy box—a drawer in a bedside table filled with various sex-play devices—for the second round. He'd politely demurred and fallen instantly into a dreamless sleep.

"Hail to the Redskins, Hail Victory—"

Tom's eyes flew open. The Redskins fight song was his phone ringer.

"Braves on the war path—"

He scrambled out of bed and dug the phone from his pants pocket. The screen alerted him that Gayle was calling. *Janie.*

He answered quickly. "Gayle?"

She was crying so hard she could barely speak. "Tom, you need to get over here."

Oh, my God. "Is Janie—?"

"Not Janie—Rosie. She and Gino and Angela...staying over, and—"

"What happened?"

Lost among her sobs, her words were incoherent.

He shouted into the phone. "Gayle, what happened?"

"Gino—he beat Rosie to death."

CHAPTER 8

During the drive to Arlington, Tom turned the radio volume up full blast, hoping the Shirelles, the Five Satins, and the Marcels would help block his mind from any thoughts about green minivans and missed midnight deadlines.

It didn't work.

As he pulled in front of Gayle's house, an Arlington police cruiser was just leaving. He could see Gino in the backseat, wedged tightly between two cops. For a moment, Gino's eyes met his. Expecting to see anger or fear, Gino's expression could only be described as bewildered.

There was no sign of an ambulance; Rosie's body must've already been taken away. A small crowd of neighbors appeared to be dispersing.

Tom made his way up the steps. The door opened as he reached the porch. Janie, wearing her favorite purple Elmo pj's, shot through the doorway into his arms.

Her body wracked with each sob. "Daddy—Uncle Gino—"

"Shhhh." He gently pushed her head down onto his shoulder. Gayle was sitting in the living room, responding to questions from a young guy with a crew cut wearing wire-rim glasses. Probably an Arlington County police detective.

On the other side of the room, Tom could see into the kitchen where Dave was comforting Angie. The girl was wrapped in a blanket. She sat at the table in front of a small plate of Oreos and a full glass of milk. Dave's head was bandaged.

Gayle spotted him and stood, her favorite blue terrycloth robe wrapped tightly around her body. Tom couldn't remember ever seeing his former wife look so forlorn.

"Didn't see you come in. This is Detective Berger."

Not wanting to release his grip on Janie, Tom just nodded.

"What the hell happened?" asked Tom.

Gayle nodded toward Janie. Tom understood. "Maybe you and David can put the girls to bed while I finish up with the detective," said Gayle. "I didn't mean to wake you, but she wouldn't go to bed without seeing you."

"Glad you did."

Gayle alerted Dave, and the two men carried the girls upstairs to Janie's room. There were two twin beds, but the girls insisted on sleeping together. As soon as their heads hit the pillows, they were out.

On the way down the stairs, Tom considered asking Dave about his head wound, but concluded it best to hear the whole story from start to finish. When they reached the living room, Berger was just leaving. He asked for Tom's card in case he needed to contact him later for additional background on Gino. As soon as Berger left, they sat around the kitchen table, and Gayle poured everyone a cup of coffee. "We were celebrating Rosie's birthday. She wouldn't turn thirty-five till Tuesday, but we thought we'd celebrate it on the weekend."

"Gino had been acting weird all night," said Dave. "He'd had a few beers before they arrived and more than a few after they got here. Nobody was concerned; in fact, Gino and Rosie had decided they'd spend the night so they could all have a few drinks and not have to worry about driving home."

Tom knew Gino could put away the booze, but he was a big man, and Tom could honestly say he'd never seen the man drunk. He wondered if that information in the hands of the authorities would help or hurt Gino.

"So we'd just sung happy birthday," said Gayle, "and right before Rosie blew out the candles, Gino pulls this folded piece of notepaper from his pocket. Rosie, she just kind've froze up. Tom, I've never seen her so scared."

Dave's face lit up as he relived the events of a few hours earlier. "Then all hell broke loose. Gino stands, turns over the table. Cake, drinks go flying everywhere. The girls are screaming. And Gino, he's waving this note back and forth."

"What was it?" asked Tom. He didn't want to believe he might know the subject matter.

Dave continued. "Apparently, Rosie was having an affair." He exchanged glances with Gayle, who looked away. "With a woman. The note was Rosie telling the woman she was ending it. Somehow, Gino discovered the note before Rosie delivered it."

"So he starts screaming these vile, vile things at her," said Gayle. "Rosie and I, we're covered in cake and ice cream. We try to protect Angie and Janie, you know, get them out of the room. Gino grabs Rosie's hair and yanks her back. David tries to intervene, but Gino's a big man and he hits David and—"

"I slipped on the ice cream," said Dave. Tom figured if Gino Battaglia hit anybody full force they'd go down, ice cream or no ice cream, but he kept his thoughts to himself.

Gayle continued through her sobs, pausing frequently to catch her breath. Her eyes glazed over, and Tom could see she was reliving the horror.

"And then he, he holds Rosie's head by her hair in one hand, and he punches her in the face with his other. Oh my God." She dropped her head into her hands.

"That's enough," said Dave.

Gayle continued as if she hadn't heard him. "I think she went unconscious with the first punch. But Gino, he kept hitting and hitting, and I was screaming at him to stop and screaming at the girls to go to their rooms. I jumped on his back, but he knocked me off and kept hitting her, and after a while, she didn't have a face anymore. And the blood, everywhere the blood, and her cheek, there was this skin flap, and you could see her cheekbone, and he kept smashing and—"

Dave wrapped his arms around her, pulling her close, cutting her off. She buried her face into his shirt, her shoulders heaving violently with each sob.

"The girls didn't see all of it, but they saw enough," said Dave.

Tom ignored his cell phone buzzing in his pocket. "My God. Gino, did he say anything else?" asked Tom.

"Don't think so," said Dave. "He just had this strange look on his face at the end."

Gayle pulled away from Dave and reached for a paper towel to blow her nose. "He stared at her, this bloody rag doll, as if seeing her for the first time. Then he broke down and cried like a baby. Sat right there on the floor, rocking her back and forth until the cops came. It was like he'd just snapped out of some kind of trance."

Tom felt his phone buzz again. Maybe it was Jess, wondering what happened. He pulled the phone from his pocket. The screen showed a video of a young couple waving.

Oh my God. Chad and—

A text message flashed over their picture: *"Scratch one."*

"Tom, what's wrong?" asked Gayle. "You look like you've just seen a ghost."

Tom hit the "return call" button. Nothing happened. The smiling couple continued to wave. He turned off the power, but the video remained.

Another text: *"Two weeks."*

Then the screen went black.

CHAPTER 9

Tom lay on his bed, fully clothed, staring at the ceiling. Physically and mentally exhausted, he knew he needed to sleep, but the churning in his brain wouldn't allow him. Besides, part of him was afraid to sleep. What would he dream? What would he see? *Who* would he see?

He had to talk to somebody. But who? And what could he say that would sound believable? That one was easy—nothing.

He immediately considered the option that the cell phone message had been another hallucination. But he hadn't suffered any head trauma, he'd been wide awake, and hadn't ingested any weird drugs other than a few Irish beers and some Greek liqueur. And what if there was just a tiny *possibility* he wasn't hallucinating, and his daughter might actually die in two weeks? Would that be enough to do something? To take the threat seriously? What if there was only a 1 percent chance the Chad & Brit show was real?

His back stiffened and he rolled over onto his side. Logic. He was an attorney, trained to examine a problem logically. Okay, for the sake of argument—*arguendo*—assume there was some chance he hadn't been hallucinating. After all, who could've predicted Rosie would've been driving that morning, and that Gino Battaglia, who'd never shown anything but love and respect for his wife, would mash her face to a pulp shortly after the passing of the deadline. What, then, would he be prepared to do to save his daughter? Could he kill someone about to murder Janie? Of course, any parent would do that without hesitation. Could he kill a stranger about to murder any innocent child? Absolutely. Again, not an issue.

The sound came from behind him. He rolled over and saw his alarm had gone off. Sunday morning was the one day he didn't set the alarm, but he'd never gotten around to turning it off the night before. Giving up on sleep, he shuffled into the shower, turned on the hot water to only a few clicks short of scalding, and remained under the spray until the hot water faded to cold.

Tom was as tech addicted as everyone else under forty, and satisfied his daily news fix by tapping into online publications from his phone, iPad, or—that dinosaur of technology—the computer. The only exception was Sunday, the one day he didn't have to get up before dawn. On those mornings, he enjoyed eating a huge, leisurely breakfast with the *Washington Post* spread out across the kitchen table.

But this morning was not one for guilty self-indulgence. He barely nibbled at a piece of dry toast, and only drank his coffee because he needed the caffeine jolt to concentrate. He completely ignored every story in the paper except the one about the Battaglia murder leading the front page of the Metro section under the headline: *"Construction Co. President Charged with Beating Wife to Death."*

The article was sketchy—not much lead time between the murder and the morning edition, but it did include Gino's mug shot. The photo was strange: rather than coming across as a TV Mafia enforcer, which he actually resembled in real life, the man appeared frightened and confused.

He broke his habit and tapped on his iPad to read the *Post's* latest edition. Gayle was quoted liberally, and there was a picture of her holding Angie, face away from the camera. A statement from Ralph Ziti, the company's lawyer, lauded Gino as a model husband, father, and citizen, and hinting this may have been a case of temporary insanity brought on by post-traumatic stress from Gino's heroic turn in Iraq, or poorly prescribed medication for his back pain. Nowhere could he find any reference to a pleasant preppy couple from hell who forced Gino to kill his wife simply because his scatterbrained brother-in-law had negligently forgotten to slaughter a complete stranger before midnight.

Tom's cell buzzed. He grabbed it, simultaneously fearing and hoping he'd see Chad's face on the screen. He needed to talk to him, discuss alternatives. *Negotiate.* Most importantly, he needed to confirm that Chad and his companion were real. Well, maybe "real" was the wrong word. The only thing worse than confirmation they were authentic would be uncertainty. Then what would he do? Go out and kill a complete stranger on the off chance that if he didn't, Satan's disciples would kill his daughter? Asking himself the question was beyond surreal. But what was the answer? *What would he do?*

The call wasn't from hell; it was from Arlington, Virginia.

"How is she?" asked Tom.

"Janie's hanging in there," replied Gayle. "But Angie keeps asking for her daddy. God, to have to witness that—"

"What can I do?"

"Dave and I need to go deal with the coroner and the funeral home. Can you come and get the girls? You'll need to take Angie home to get some clothes. She'll obviously be staying with us."

"Be there in forty-five minutes. Any word on Gino?"

"A bail hearing's scheduled for tomorrow. We're sure the judge will keep him locked up. You're a lawyer, what do you think?"

"I don't do criminal, but sure makes sense to me."

***

Tom picked up the girls in Virginia and the ride back to the District was quiet. He'd been unsure how to deal with Angie. Should he act cheerful to try keep her mind off the horror she'd witnessed? Or appear somberly sympathetic?

In the end, he decided to take his lead from her. She'd elected to remain silent for most of the forty-minute trip, although over the last few miles she'd been drawn to the video game Janie played on her Nintendo. When he and Gayle had been together, he'd imposed a strict rule against video games in the car, or, even more so, at a restaurant. But now, he was thankful for the diversion.

Scratch one. He couldn't get those words out of his mind.

"Janie, who were the two girls who rode with you guys when you went to the museum a couple of weeks ago?"

"Uh, Abby Jackson—" She turned to Angie. "Who else?"

"Emma 2," replied Angie.

"Two Emmas?"

"We have four Emmas in Ms. Allen's class. Emma Stein's Emma 1, and Emma Wong's Emma 2. Why do you want to know?"

Tom used his right hand to punch the names into his iPhone notes app while keeping his left hand on the wheel.

"You're not allowed to text while driving, Daddy," said Janie.

"You're right, honey." He quickly finished inputting Emma 2, then made a show of putting the phone back in his pocket.

When they arrived at Angie's house, Tom used Gayle's key to unlock the door, then entered the large, two-story colonial with Janie and Angie following close behind him. He'd been in the Battaglia home on Rittenhouse Street on numerous occasions when he'd been married, and was familiar with the layout. He stopped in the foyer.

"You girls go on up and get Angie's clothes. And don't forget her toothbrush and bathroom stuff."

Angela only made it up two stairs when she froze.

"Angie?"

"Maybe you should come with us," said Janie.

He was such an idiot. "Of course." He followed them up to Angie's room and made a big show of checking her closet and looking under the bed. He offered the most reassuring smile he could muster. "Everything's fine."

"How long will I be gone?" asked Angie.

Very good question. "I don't know, honey. I'd pack for three or four days. We can do a wash, or we can always come back if you need more stuff."

"I think my suitcase is in my mom and dad's room," said Angie.

"I'll get it, sweetie."

Tom walked down the narrow hallway and entered the master bedroom. In the closet, he saw several suitcases of varying sizes on an upper shelf. Among them was a small pink case covered with pictures of the Muppets.

When he reached for the suitcase, his elbow caught the corner of one of the larger suitcases, moving it aside, revealing a small, polished maple box.

He pulled the box down and opened it. A silver pistol rested snugly in a green felt cut-out.

Tom didn't move. The words, "Ruger GP100" were engraved on the barrel.

He heard the girls in the hallway.

"Daddy?"

Tom stuffed the gun into his pocket, grabbed the pink Muppet case, and exited the room.

CHAPTER 10

He'd been sitting at his kitchen table, staring at the draft due diligence agreement on his computer screen for hours. Katherine O'Neil wanted it first thing in the morning, and Tom needed to finish his redraft so she'd see it in her computer inbox when she arrived. But while his eyes faced the document, his mind focused on the Ruger lying next to the laptop. He knew next to nothing about guns.

Strike that. He knew *nothing* about guns.

He'd shot a 12-gauge once when his cousins had taken him duck hunting the previous December. He'd frozen his ass off in a rickety duck blind, blowing rain and sleet, conditions his enthusiastic cousins said were perfect for ducks. As Tom had explained in as clear a logic as he could muster: that's why they're ducks and we're not. It had been misty, so when Estin said, "There's one!" he'd shot at what he thought was a flying duck. His cousins had laughed so hard he thought they'd knock down the damn blind. Seems he was shooting at a passing airplane on its approach into BWI airport.

Tom had never held, much less fired, a handgun. He'd grown up in a suburb of Baltimore, a safe, middle-class community with wide streets, shady trees, and good schools. He supposed the Second Amendment gave people the right to have guns in their homes, and when he thought about it, believed the idea of everyone turning in their guns for some violence-free Utopia was naïve. But he rarely thought about it. Now, he had to think about it.

Scratch one. What if the *one* had been Janie? What if the next one's Janie?

Then again, what if the whole Chad & Brit show wasn't real, and Rosie's death had been a coincidence? Coincidences happened, hence the need for the word. And here he was contemplating how to shoot a Ruger GP100 so he could kill a perfect stranger.

He'd looked up the weapon online and learned it was a double-action model, meaning he wouldn't need to fan the hammer with his palm like the gunslingers in old TV westerns. Just point and shoot. Snuff out a life. Easy peasy.

He knew he needed to talk to someone, but who? Zig? Zig knew of his bridge vision, but any suggestion that the vision might be real would result in his friend informing him in no uncertain terms he was bonkers—stress from Rosie's death, pressure at work—and take away his shiny Ruger.

And then, what if two weeks from now he'd get a hysterical call in the wee hours telling him Janie or Angie or Emma 2 was dead? No, he decided he couldn't tell a soul. *He would actually have to contemplate killing another human being.* But, not knowing whether Janie or one of the other three girls was on deck, he'd also have to make sure he didn't get caught because he might have to kill again.

Tom Booker, serial killer.

Okay, okay. Think logically. As his Georgetown professors used to say, think like a lawyer. Could he take a chance with his daughter's life? No. He rubbed his fingers down the barrel of the Ruger. He now had the means, and he had the motive to kill, to save Janie. But did he have the balls?

He picked up the 5 x 7 framed photo on his desk. Halloween, two years earlier. Janie's face filled the frame. She wore a Hello Kitty costume. Eyebrow pencil-applied whiskers, a wide grin with a missing front tooth. Eyes sparkling with life.

He'd have to find the balls.

And a victim.

CHAPTER 11

Over the next ten days, Tom felt like he was wearing someone else's body. He attended Rosie's funeral, focused on his legal work, and had beers with Zig at Napoleon's where they gossiped about their coworkers.

On Saturday, he took Jess out to dinner where he was charming and appeared interested in her every word. She looked sexy in a low-cut blouse and a short, yellow miniskirt. He'd barely taken a sip of his beer before she began rubbing first his thigh, then his groin under the table. She appeared perplexed, even hurt, when he didn't respond.

"Sorry, just a little self-conscious."

"No problem," said Jess. "I can wait. A little while." She giggled.

It was after midnight when they left the restaurant. They'd barely gotten out of the parking lot before Jess was bent over his lap, tugging at his zipper. He gently lifted her up.

"Too distracting." His attempt at a laugh was pathetic. "You don't want to cause an accident, do you?" *Don't you know, driving distractions kill?* "Let's wait till we get to your place."

"Maybe I can't wait that long." She kissed him, plunging her tongue down his throat. His view completely blocked by her head, he heard a horn blaring.

Bright headlights lit up the car's interior. He was driving in the oncoming lane. Swerving hard right, he just missed a head-on with a huge sedan. Sweat beaded on his forehead.

"Sorry, but let's just cool our jets here. We'll be at your place soon, then we—"

He saw her slowly rubbing her hips back and forth on the car seat. Jesus, was she going to masturbate right here in the car? Was this the way girls acted in Oklahoma?

"I got a better idea," she said. "Let's go to the Lincoln Memorial. It's faster."

"Faster?"

"Just do it, silly, or—" She made a move to bend over his lap again.

"Okay, okay."

Given the hour, it took little time to reach the memorial and find a parking space on Ohio Drive.

Her skirt devoid of pockets, Jess carried her cell phone in her left hand, and took his hand in her right, then led him up the marble steps to the memorial.

"Expecting a call?" asked Tom.

She winked. "Photo op."

"Is the memorial open?"

"Twenty-four hours," responded Jess. "On-site rangers leave at 11:30. After that, it's just routine patrol."

"And you know this how?"

She responded with a grin.

When they reached the memorial, she gently tugged him toward the Lincoln statue.

"Stand there, in front." Tom complied, and while she fussed with her phone to take the picture, he looked up into the sixteenth president's face. From the sharp angle, it was as if God himself was staring down at him with an expression of weary disapproval. He whispered, "I have no choice."

"What did you say?" asked Jess.

"Nothing."

"Then smile."

She took the photo. "Come on. Don't know when the next patrol's going to swing by."

Tom looked around. No doors, just four walls, each bearing Lincoln's famous words. "Come where?"

She led him behind the statue. From the front, Tom had assumed the statue was positioned flush against the wall, directly beneath the words: *In this temple, as in the hearts of the people for whom he saved the Union, the memory of Abraham Lincoln is enshrined forever.* But there was a gap between the wall and the back of Lincoln's chair—more of a throne—consistent with the artist's view of the memorial as a temple. A draped robe fell from Lincoln's shoulders down the back of the chair.

Jess pulled him into the tight space. They were hidden from everyone except somebody who might happen to walk around to the back of the statue.

She reached up high and set her phone deep into the folds of Lincoln's draped robe, then braced herself against the wall and lifted her skirt. No underwear.

Like a woman possessed, she pulled at his belt and zipper. Tom was surprised his body responded to her ministrations. Pleasantly surprised, actually. She wrapped her legs around him, and for a short time he forgot about death and lost himself in the essence of life.

***

By Thursday, he'd made no progress in finding a target. He'd early on come to an obvious decision—he would only target someone who deserved to die. A bad guy. He banished from his mind the natural follow-up questions: What if he couldn't find a bad guy? Would he let Janie die? Would he roll the dice and pray one of the other girl's number would come up? Could he pray for the death of an innocent child? Hopefully, matters wouldn't get to that point.

His only plan so far was to drive through the drug-infested streets of Southeast DC and lure a street dealer to his car. He'd shoot him, then drive away before anyone could mount a chase.

When reviewing the plan, he purposely glossed over the "shoot him" part. When the time came, could he really do it? Would he really do it? He had no idea.

Tom was familiar with the area from his five years as a teacher at Ray Jabazz Elementary School. The school was named for a famous tenor sax jazz musician who'd grown up in the nearby public housing complex and attended the school.

Tom had started off as an architecture major at Maryland, but after his mother's death, decided to follow in her footsteps and spend his life teaching young children. He'd never get rich, but he'd enjoy more personal fulfillment working with live kids than dead buildings.

In his first few years at Jabazz, he'd been fearful walking from the school to the parking lot a block away, particularly in the winter months when it was dark. But over time, he'd come in contact with some of the kids' more notorious family members, including a young drug kingpin named Chewy Lewis. After meeting Chewy, the word must've gone out to leave the teacher alone, and he'd never been bothered.

After he'd married Gayle, she'd made it plain she expected a lifestyle more elevated than a teacher's salary could provide. At her urging, he'd taken the LSATs and scored amazingly well. To his astonishment, he'd been admitted to Georgetown's night school, which allowed him to continue teaching while attending classes in the evening.

So, he would visit the old neighborhood and do it—the thing, the act, the *cold-blooded murder*—on Friday. He prayed he wouldn't run into anyone he knew.

Tom had gone over his plan a thousand times. A smart guy, he should be able to figure out how not to get caught. He wouldn't use his own car in case it got picked up on traffic cameras. Instead, he'd rent a car, but not from one of the big agencies; he'd find some small outfit that took cash and make sure the license plates were covered with mud. He'd wear a disguise, but not so obvious as to be noticeable—a hat, sunglasses, and gloves.

Drug dealers were always killing each other, so, hopefully, the cops wouldn't spend too much time investigating.

Hopefully.

CHAPTER 12

Friday, Tom felt sick to his stomach. He couldn't think about work, much less concentrate on drafting the SEC quarterly report for a large pharmaceutical company client. Katherine told him he looked ill and encouraged him to go home early. When he entered his apartment, he barely made it to the bathroom before he hurled the complete contents of his stomach. *This is crazy this is crazy this is crazy.*

As he'd done every few minutes for the last week, he checked his phone again, hoping for another sign from Chad. Nothing. He cleaned himself off and took a quick shower.

Needing to dress in dark clothing, he put on black slacks. He didn't have a black shirt, but did possess a black jacket that would serve the purpose. The night before, he'd used cash to buy a pair of cheap rubber-soled black shoes at a discount store. The only black shoes he owned were dress wing tips, hardly appropriate foot attire for an aspiring serial killer about to launch his career. He stuffed a black Redskins baseball hat, black winter gloves, sunglasses, and the star of the show—his Ruger GP100—into a small, paper grocery bag. After downing a quick shot of Jack Daniel's to steady his nerves, he exited his apartment and walked ten blocks before hailing a cab.

"Drop me off near the intersection of Florida and Benning Road."

"Goin' to 3D?" asked the driver, an elderly black man.

"The movies? No." *Who knew there was a theater showing 3-D films in that rough section of town?*

"Not movies. 3D. Third District, police."

Wonderful. His carefully devised plan would begin with a visit to the cops. An image flashed in his mind of being a highlight on some late night host's "Stupid Criminals Files." *So, this guy, Tom Booker—you're not gonna believe this—he starts his murder spree by askin' to be dropped off at the police station! Yuk, yuk, yuk. Looks like Mr. Booker got booked! Yuk, yuk, yuk.*

"Just head up to that area, and I'll tell you where to let me off." The driver shrugged, giving the impression he'd seen it all before and couldn't care less.

Tom put on his glasses and hat, then told the cabbie to pull over at the intersection of Florida and Maryland avenues. He got out and walked north on Florida, looking for the used-car lot he'd scoped out the previous evening. The tattered sign had read: "Happy Cals, We Rent Cars To." Apparently, spelling was not Cal's strong suit.

After a few blocks, he spotted the string of lightbulbs drooping from bent poles demarcating Happy Cal's car lot from abandoned warehouses on each side of the business.

When he reached the lot, it looked like no one was there. He made his way to the dilapidated trailer in the back of the lot, took a deep breath, and entered.

A middle-aged black man sat behind a tiny desk watching a portable TV that might've been new in the Carter administration. A tarnished nameplate on the desk read: "Happy Cal Smith."

As soon as Cal saw him, he tensed up. Probably not too many young white guys popping by at night wearing sunglasses. The man's eyes were red, and he appeared to be high on something other than life.

"How's it goin'?" asked Tom. "I understand you rent cars."

Cal relaxed, revealed two gold teeth with a wide smile, and extended his hand. "You come to the right place. I'm Happy Cal."

Tom purposely didn't offer his name.

"So what you got to rent?" he asked.

"Pretty much anything on the lot," said Cal. "What you lookin' for?"

"I saw a black Lincoln Town Car out there. Looks to be about ten years old."

"Oh, she sweet, ain't she? Let's go take a look."

"Does it run?"

"Of course she run. As I said, she a sweet ride."

"Don't need to take a look. One day. How much?"

Cal made a show of looking through a stack of papers. "Well, as I said, that car there, she in great condition. Could maybe let her go on a twenty-four hour rental for 100 bucks." His voice raised at the end, signaling that the price quote was more of a question, as in, "Is that too much, because if so I can come down a little."

"How about $500 and we dispense with the paperwork."

Cal gulped. "Five hundred, yeah maybe I could work that out. But how do I know you'll bring it back?"

"Two things. First, if I don't, you report the car stolen from your lot, file an insurance claim, and end up better than when you started. Second, I'm giving you my word."

Cal thought for a moment, then nodded. "Cash?"

"Of course."

**

Happy Cal's view of what constituted a sweet ride didn't necessarily coincide with Tom's. The Lincoln swayed so much on a curve, he had to practically come to a complete stop prior to navigating even the most gradual of turns. The interior smelled of cigarettes, maybe weed, and there was a suspicious-looking dark stain on the gray leather passenger seat. On the positive side, it had heavily tinted windows, and on a straightaway, could move out quickly.

Tom drove into Southeast and pulled over onto a dark street under a broken streetlight, then stepped out and scooped some muck from the gutter. After smearing the wet grime over both license plates, he got back into the car and drove slowly past Jabazz Elementary. He had great memories of his years teaching there. The faculty was welcoming and the kids amazing. Though most came from Section 8 housing and, sadly, would struggle in the face of teen pregnancy, poverty, drugs, and violence, at the elementary ages they were still full of life and promise.

He turned left on E Street, past Marion Park, and approached Washington Terrace, a run-down group of dirty, red-brick garden apartments. He knew the dealers would be out—they were as much a part of the scene as the dying trees and broken streetlamps. Small potatoes, he suspected the cops mostly left them alone.

Three guys sat on a half wall next to steps leading up to a patch of dirt that at one time might've been a lawn in front of the first building. They were drinking some kind of booze from a crinkled paper bag and passing a roach back and forth. Hopefully, they would be high enough so their reflexes would be dulled.

Tom pulled over half a block away, and put on his gloves. Damn, the fingers were thick; he hoped his index—*trigger?*—finger would fit through the trigger guard. Why didn't he buy a new pair of gloves? Why didn't he try on the gloves first to see if he could fire the gun? *Shit.*

He removed the Ruger and tried the gloved finger. It fit, but only after he jammed it through. He tucked the gun halfway under his right thigh. *I need to turn around right now. This is insane.* He thought of Janie. *Scratch one.* The hairs on the back of his neck stood up. His whole body shook.

He took a deep breath, pulled his hat down tight, and slowly drove forward.

When he pulled over in front of the three men, none of them moved. A part of him hoped they'd just sit still. A large part of him. As soon as one approached, he'd open the window, shoot one bullet into the man's head, then take off down E Street before the others could react. He was hoping that the soon-to-be dead guy's friends would assume Tom was a contract killer enforcing revenge for a past insult. While this assumption was based on a long string of movies and TV shows rather than personal knowledge, he was reasonably confident the two companions wouldn't call the cops. At least not right away.

Protected by the tinted glass, he studied the faces of the three men. All wore hoodies, but Tom was close enough to see their features. Two appeared to be in their early thirties, the third, maybe late teens. Did any of them deserve to die? He'd convinced himself that if they dealt drugs, they'd probably either murdered somebody or were accessories to murder. Even if not, their drugs were ruining lives. Didn't they deserve to go to hell? Certainly, more so than an innocent child.

One of the men stood up and approached the car. It was the kid. *Shit.* Tom wedged his finger through the trigger guard. The boy stood next to the car and bent down, his face inches from Tom, separated only by the tinted window. God, the kid was really a kid. Maybe fifteen, sixteen max. Why couldn't one of the others have come over?

Tom steeled himself. Everybody knew kids younger than this guy killed for sport. He was probably in a gang. Tom slowly pulled the gun out from under his thigh, then pressed the automatic window button.

Nothing happened. He pounded the button as hard as he could. Nothing. *Sweet ride, my ass!* He saw the door handle jiggle. The kid was opening the door. Tom hadn't bothered to lock the doors. Okay, as soon as the door opened a crack, he'd fire into the kid's chest. Maybe shoot twice to make sure. Bang, bang, just like on TV.

The door pulled open a few inches. Tom raised the gun, but the kid couldn't see it. Good, let him go quickly, without a last moment of fear. Just a quick *pop, pop*—you're opening the door to a car, then you're walking through the gates of hell.

Without the filter of the window tint, Tom was able to look into the boy's eyes. Big, brown, long lashes. Soft, like a deer.

"You lost, mister? Lookin' for the Southeast Freeway?"

The kid's voice was friendly, and higher pitched than Tom expected. His expression so—*innocent?* No matter. This kid or Janie. He had no real choice. Even if the boy hadn't killed anybody yet, there was a strong likelihood, growing up here with the odds stacked against him, it was only a matter of time. Hell, by taking him out now, he was probably saving a life. More than probably.

He raised the Ruger, needing both hands to reduce the shake. For the first time, the boy saw the gun. His eyes widened in fear. For a split second, their eyes locked. Tom's finger tightened on the trigger—then stopped.

Shiiiit!

He tossed the gun on the passenger seat, yanked the door closed, and peeled off down E Street.

CHAPTER 13

Slouching against his trailer, smoking a joint, Happy Cal looked surprised to see Tom as he pulled in.

"Hey, you rented it for twenty-four hours, and there ain't no refunds."

Tom didn't bother to answer. He grabbed the paper bag off the seat and walked north toward New York Avenue. Along the route, he ditched his black jacket, gloves, and hat in a dumpster. He was unconcerned about the danger of the neighborhood; in fact, he hoped someone would try to mug him. His pal, Mr. Ruger, would take care of things, and his victim problem would be solved. As luck would have it, he reached New York Avenue unscathed, and flagged down a cab. Tom not only needed a drink, he felt a sudden urge to be among people. Normal people. *Normal.* On the drive to Adams Morgan, he was tempted to ask the cabbie to stop at one of the many seedy bars along the route, but held off until the taxi was heading down Columbia Road.

"Drop me at Napoleon's."

When he entered, the place was still jammed, normal for late on a Friday night. He spotted Zig sitting on his reserved stool in the back of the bar. Tom's seat was taken by Marcie, and when the crowd parted, he saw Jess standing with the two of them. She spotted him and waved him over.

"So, you don't answer my calls?" Zig asked.

Tom had forgotten he'd turned off his phone. He checked it and saw that Zig had called him twice and texted him once. "Sorry, been working at home and didn't realize the phone was off." He waved at Argus, who drew a Stella from the tap and set it in front of him. He drained almost all of it in one swig.

"Thirsty?" asked Jess.

He nodded, finished the rest, and waved for another.

"You sick or something?" asked Marcie. Tom looked at her quizzically. "You look a little pale."

"Wan," Jess observed.

"Definitely wan," added Zig.

Tom realized he should've gone straight home. Maybe he could play up the sick thing.

"Actually, think I may've caught a bug."

Immediately, the three of them dramatically stepped back from him.

He forced a laugh. "I'm sure it's not a big deal. Been feeling chills." He held up the bag. "I stopped at the drugstore for a few things, and thought I'd duck in for a beer to kill the germs."

"You need to take care of yourself," said Jess, showing genuine concern. "You're wearing yourself down, working so hard. Listen to your body."

"Good advice. Think I'll head back and kiss the sheets."

"If you want some company, I make a mean chicken soup," said Jess.

"Don't want to infect you. How about a rain check?"

"You got it." She gave him a tight hug. "Need to visit the little girls' room." She and Marcie worked their way through the crowd toward the restrooms.

"I'm out of here," said Tom.

As he turned, the paper bag bumped against the edge of the bar with a heavy *clunk*.

"Pretty heavy medicine," said Zig.

Before he could react, Zig snatched the bag from Tom's grasp and peeked inside. His eyes widened. He immediately closed the bag and lowered his voice.

"Okay, what gives?"

"Too many stories on the nightly news about drug violence in the area. Just being careful."

"I don't suppose it's registered."

"Better to be judged by twelve than carried by six."

"Cute. Where did you hear that?"

"*CSI.*"

"Go home and go to bed. You're beginning to worry me."

***

The next morning, Tom awoke late. He was surprised he'd slept at all, but his body had taken pity on him, and he'd been out a solid seven hours. No way could he concentrate at work, so he called in sick.

Never one for all-nighters before an exam, he did his best thinking in the morning. Refreshed by sleep, his mind spun at 100 mph while the hot stream of water pulsed from the showerhead. There was still a chance that Rosie's death was a coincidence. After all, there was no record of the text message on the phone, a fact that could be explained either by assuming the message had been a hallucination, or by assuming old Beelzebub had the power to project whatever he wanted onto a cell phone screen.

Could he take a chance? He still had the gun and about fifteen hours to do the deed. He considered putting the gun to his own temple. He would gladly give his life to save his daughter. But the identity of the girl who would be saved was unknown, so he could blow his brains out, Emma 2 would be saved, and Janie would die.

He thought extensively about going out hunting again after dark. Maybe, with no margin of error and the clock ticking down to midnight, he'd be able to summon the courage to pull the trigger.

Perhaps the key was not to get too close, don't look in the victim's eyes. A drive-by, so common now that the image had become a cliché on TV. He could rent another car from Happy Cal, drive to a different section of town, find a couple of dealers standing on a corner, and blast away. Having learned his lesson regarding appropriate hand attire when firing a Ruger, he'd purchase a box of transparent latex gloves at the Columbia Road Rite Aid.

Problem was, he'd only have a split second—no moment to reflect, no time for second thoughts—and he wasn't certain he could pull the trigger. Which left one option. He needed to be near Janie when midnight rolled around to protect her.

He stepped out of the shower and, without bothering to dry off, quickly found his phone.

***

"B-I-N-G-O, B-I-N-G-O, B-I-N-G-O, and Bingo was his name..."

Tom sang along with Janie and Angie who belted out the song from the backseat. He was proud of his daughter, who'd taken it upon herself to cheer up her cousin. They were heading back to his apartment after a trip to the movies and burgers at Chili's. During the ride to the theater, Angie barely spoke, but now she appeared a bit more animated.

Tom had concluded that the chances of him pointing a gun at a total stranger and pulling the trigger were slim, so the only real path open to him was to protect the girls from Chad and Brit. At first, he'd been surprised how readily Gayle had given up the girls for an overnight. Although, upon reflection, he could imagine the stress of having to deal with Angie on top of everyday motherhood responsibilities, so maybe the prospect of a day and night off would be welcome.

He still held out the slim hope that absolutely nothing would happen. However, if Chad were real—at least as real as a devil's disciple can be—Tom and his new buddy, Mr. Ruger, would be standing guard throughout the night. At one point he found himself hoping that maybe Chad would go for the low-hanging fruit and take one of the other girls, but he instantly became disgusted with himself for such a vile thought, and barred his mind from ever going there again.

It was a little after eight by the time they got back to his apartment. He'd already outfitted the couch with a pillow and blanket for himself so the girls could use the bed. Since it wasn't a school night, they gathered on the couch with a bag of Oreos and watched the Disney Channel.

His phone rang. He tensed, then realized four more hours had to pass before he might—*would?*—hear from Chad and Brit.

It was Gayle. Probably wanting to know if he could keep the girls a little longer.

"Tom, Gino made bail."

"What? On a murder charge?"

His tone of voice didn't go unnoticed. "Daddy, is that Mommy?" asked Janie.

He saw Angie's face blanch. The reference to murder left no doubt in her mind whom he was talking about. "Yes, sweetie, it's Mommy." He got up and walked into the bedroom. "What happened?"

"There was a bail-review hearing yesterday. He drew a soft-hearted judge. She found the death was the result of an alleged crime of passion. Gino had no priors and strong community ties. She ruled he wasn't a threat to the community and there was no risk of flight. He was just released this afternoon after posting his half of the company as bond."

"How'd you find out?"

"He just called me. Said he was house bound, wearing one of those ankle monitors. He wants to see Angie. She's not permitted in his presence without an adult, and my first instinct was not to let that child anywhere near the man, even with someone else present. I told him we'd check with child services in the morning and get back to him. Then he started crying, begging to just see her for a few minutes. He says he needs to tell her how sorry he is and how he didn't mean it."

"And—?"

"Look, I witnessed him beat my own sister to death, so no one has more reason to hate the man than me. I can't explain it, but a part of me believes he may have had some kind of seizure. You've seen them together. Never a hint of violence, and if he'd ever laid a finger on her, she'd have told me. I'm torn. What I saw in the kitchen was a monster. But that's just it. A monster, something that wasn't real. Not the big teddy bear I've known for years."

"So—"

"I told him you'd swing by for a few minutes."

"Are you nuts?"

"You should've heard him, Tom. There was something in his voice. I said the only way I'd authorize it would be if you were present at all times."

"Jeez—"

"You go to the door, he answers it, he says what he has to say, you leave. That's the deal, and he readily agreed. Angie will probably be nervous, so you can take Janie with you to keep her company."

"But if you're right and he went tilt—"

"He sounded normal. Upset, but normal. Not like he was going to take his own life or anything. As I said, hard to explain."

Take his own life. A horrible thought occurred to Tom. *No, no way.* He looked into the bedroom at the two innocent faces watching him, worried, wondering. Could he really take a chance? His voice rasped as he spoke.

"I'll gather up the girls."

CHAPTER 14

Tom considered leaving Janie in the car, but she wouldn't hear of it. Both girls huddled behind his legs as Gino came to the door. When Gino saw Angie, he couldn't hold back his tears. He bent down and opened his arms.

"Baby—"

For a moment, Angie hesitated, then she ran to her father and buried herself in his embrace. Gino swept up his daughter.

"Baby, I'm so sorry. I swear to you, I didn't mean to hurt Mommy."

"Aunt Gayle said you just got sick and germs went to your brain and made you do it, but you didn't really mean it."

"Maybe Aunt Gayle's right, honey." He looked at Tom. "Thank you. I know bringing her over wasn't an easy decision."

"No problem."

"Uncle Tom's going to take you home now," said Gino. "But tomorrow, we're going to talk to the court lady and see if you can stay longer next time." He hastily added, "With Uncle Tom or Aunt Gayle present, of course."

Tom glanced down at his daughter. His mouth felt full of cotton. "Uh, look, if you want us to come in for a few minutes, I don't see any harm."

Gino smiled from ear to ear, and without another word, carried his daughter into the house. Tom and Janie followed and closed the door. They moved to the family room, Gino and Angie refusing to let go of each other.

"Why don't Janie and I go into the kitchen and have a soda so you two can talk," said Tom.

Gino nodded. "Take off your jacket and make yourself comfortable."

"Thanks, I'll keep it on. Little chilly in here." He walked into the kitchen with Janie following close behind. She sat down at the kitchen table and he poured a couple of Cokes over ice. If ever he needed a little something to take the edge off, it was now. He opened Gino's liquor cabinet, retrieved a half-filled bottle of Jack, and poured two fingers into his Coke.

"Is Uncle Gino going to jail?" asked Janie.

"I don't know for sure, but he probably will. He did a very bad thing."

"I know, he killed Aunt Rosie. But you know what?"

"What?"

"I don't think he meant it. I think it was the brain germs."

How was he supposed to respond to that? Tell her she's right, and the only reason Uncle Gino smashed Aunt Rosie's brain to mush was because her father goofed up and decided not to murder anybody?

"I think it was the brain germs too, honey, but that will be for a judge and jury to decide."

"If he goes to jail, who's gonna take care of Angie?"

"We all will, sweetie." He looked through the door to the family room, where he saw Gino sitting inches from his daughter talking earnestly. Tom couldn't hear what he was saying, but he didn't need to. Gino would be explaining how he loved her mother and he doesn't know what got into him. And maybe he did get sick, and the sickness made him do it, and he loved her very much, and no matter what happened, she needed to be strong.

Tom glanced at the kitchen clock—almost eleven thirty already. His chest tightened. Could he do this? He drained his drink and reentered the family room.

"Sorry, but it's after eleven," said Tom. "Need to get these girls to bed."

"Catchin' a cold? Your voice sounds funny."

"Sore throat. Bug goin' around." *Forget about my throat, you should feel the battery acid sloshing around in my stomach.*

"You need to take care of yourself," said Gino.

"Yeah." This time his throat was so tight, the word was barely more than mouthed.

"Angie, you go on back to Janie's house with Uncle Tom," said Gino. "I'm going to talk to Aunt Gayle tomorrow, and we're going to work something out so maybe you can come home. Would you like that?" She nodded, wiped her eyes with her sleeve, and gave Gino a last hug.

"You girls go on out to the car and lock the door," said Tom. "I'll be out in a minute. I need to talk to Uncle Gino."

Janie took her cousin's hand and walked her out of the house. Tom watched to make sure they were safe, then closed the door. Gino turned to him.

"I want you to know I didn't mean to kill her."

"I know. Let's go into the kitchen to talk." Gino followed Tom into the kitchen and sat down while Tom pulled two beers from the fridge.

"Don't think I'm supposed to be drinkin'," said Gino.

"One beer." Tom set the can of Bud in front of Gino and wondered why his former brother-in-law didn't comment on his shaking hand. Gino popped the top and took a long sip.

"What the hell am I gonna do?" asked Gino, dropping his head into his hands.

Tom cleared his voice. He needed to sound as normal as possible. *Normal. What a joke.* "You killed her, even though you know you didn't mean it. I'm afraid you're going to be sent away for a long time. Maybe the rest of your life."

"If I go to jail, what'll happen to Angie?"

"I swear to you that Gayle, Dave, and I will take care of her as if she were our own daughter."

Okay, what he was about to say next would be the first step down the road to hell. *Road to hell. Funny.* But couldn't he simply bring the girls back inside, partner up with Mr. Ruger, and watch over them till after the clock struck midnight? And what were the chances absolutely nothing would happen?

The chances. That was the problem, wasn't it? Could he really take the chance his daughter would die within the next few minutes?" *No.* He took a deep breath.

"Gino, I think it would be helpful for you to write a note to Angie. You know, something she can keep with her always."

"Probably should. Maybe tomorrow—"

"You could do it tomorrow, but why not now? I'll give it to her tonight. Think it'll make her feel better."

"Guess you're right." He nodded at a cabinet drawer. "Rosie keeps a pad and pen in there."

Tom walked to the cabinet, which fortunately was behind Gino. He pulled a pair of transparent latex gloves from his coat pocket and tried to slip them on, but his hands were shaking so badly it took twice as long.

"I know my life's over, Tom. Rosie's gone. And I'm going away for a long time. Got a nice insurance policy. Was thinking—"

"Probably feel the same way in your shoes." *Jesus, did he really just say that?*

Tom retrieved the pad and paper, then pivoted and quickly set both items down on the table. Gino was so lost in thought that he never noticed Tom's hands.

The big man stared at the blank tablet. "Don't know what to say."

"It doesn't have to be long, just say what you feel. How sorry you are, ask for forgiveness, you know, that kind of stuff."

Gino picked up the pen and began to write. Tom watched over his shoulder.

Dear Angie, I'm so sorry for what I did. I loved your mommy very much. My heart breaks for you. Please forgive me.

"Guess I should say I'll see her tomorrow."

Tom pulled the Ruger from his jacket pocket.

Gino looked up, startled. "What's goin' on? That looks like my gun."

Tom had rehearsed in his mind what he would say, and the words rushed out. "You're right. You're going to spend the rest of your life in prison. You're going to die there. You want Angie to see you like that? Remember you like that?"

Tom looked at the clock. *Four minutes.*

"She's going to need money for college and a wedding. I know you want her to have a nice wedding someday. Gayle and I will do what we can, but college is so expensive. You said you have a life insurance policy."

Three minutes.

Gino stared at the gun. Tears poured from his eyes. He whispered, "You think I'll go to heaven?"

How was he supposed to answer that one? *Sorry, Charlie, but you're headin' south.* In the great scheme of things, lying seemed so inconsequential.

"God knows you didn't mean to kill Rosie. I'm sure He will forgive you and allow you to enter His kingdom." He could barely get the words out. The acid in his stomach had refluxed up into his esophagus, setting it on fire. He needed to stop this nonsense.

Another glance at the clock. *Two minutes.*

Tom turned off the safety and, using both hands to steady the gun, handed it to Gino.

Gino wrapped his large right hand, a tough construction worker's hand, around the grip. He stared at the gun, but his eyes appeared distant. He put his finger on the trigger and took a deep breath. "Don't know if I got the guts to do it."

One minute.

Tom kept telling himself the man sitting in front of him beat an innocent woman to death with his bare hands. A life for a life.

He gulped, his words just above a whisper. "You want me to help?"

"You'd do that for me?"

Of course, I'd be pleased as punch to assist you. No, no, don't mention it. Least I could do.

Thirty seconds.

Tom wrapped his hand around Gino's trembling wrist as the man lifted the gun, pointing the shaking barrel at his temple. Tom wedged his index finger inside the trigger guard on top of Gino's thick finger.

Twenty seconds.

Gino looked up to him, tears streaming freely down his cheeks. "Tom, I just want to say—"

Don't you understand? There's no time to hear what you JUST WANT TO SAY!

Ten seconds.

He felt Gino's finger tighten, but not fast enough. Tom closed his eyes and squeezed.

The sound of the gun, amplified by the kitchen tile, reverberated through every cell in Tom's body. Gino's head crashed to the table. Tom jerked his hand away, and the gun fell to the floor. Tom couldn't move. His entire body shook.

Gino Battaglia was dead, his brains splattered across the tile floor. His sightless eyes stared up at Tom.

He glanced up at the clock. Time of death: 11:59 p.m.

Tom couldn't stop screaming.

CHAPTER 15

Tom was beyond exhaustion. The DC forensic team was finishing up; Gino's body had been photographed in situ, then taken away. Tom had just finished telling the detective his story for the third time.

The cop's name was Percy Castro. Late fifties, overweight. If Tom had to describe the detective in one word, it would be "rumpled." His clothing was rumpled, his thinning hair rumpled, and even his face appeared rumpled. Broad shoulders, huge hands, he was several inches shorter than Tom. His blue eyes, shrouded by heavy lids, signaled intelligence: this wasn't Castro's first rodeo.

After calling 911, Tom had telephoned Gayle, and she'd come and taken the girls back to Arlington. Tom had made sure neither girl entered the house, but Angie sensed something was wrong. When she asked if her daddy was okay, Tom didn't have the strength to lie, so he said that her daddy had decided to go see her mommy in heaven. When she burst into tears, he'd held the child tightly, not letting go until Gayle arrived which, fortunately, was five minutes before the cops.

Tom knew there was no way he could eliminate microscopic traces of blood, so after pocketing his gloves, he actually smeared more blood on his clothes, and made a point of picking up the gun and setting it on the table. The gloves were not to cover fingerprints, but powder blowback—thank you, *CSI*.

Castro gestured Tom toward the couch in the living room. As soon as Tom sat, he sunk so deep into the plush cushion his knees were almost at chin level. The cop took the straight-back chair opposite him, creating a line of sight downward to Tom, and exaggerating Castro's role as top dog.

"So, tell me what happened," said Castro. The cop's deep, ragged voice suggested he was or had been a heavy smoker.

Tom had been smart enough to prepare and rehearse his story in his head on the drive over. He'd figured if he actually went through with the plan, he'd be too shaken up to concoct a cogent explanation on the spot.

"I took Angie over to see Gino. When I was about to leave, Gino called me back to the kitchen and offered me a beer. He had in front of him a pad of paper with writing on it."

"Didn't it look like a suicide note?" asked Castro.

"I was in a hurry to leave and get the girls home. I glanced at it and the writing appeared to be the beginning of a letter to his daughter. Gino hugged me, which was strange, and made me promise to take care of Angie when he was gone. I assumed he meant when he was in jail."

"Where were you when he pulled the trigger?"

"Just as I reached the door, I heard the shot and rushed back to the kitchen. Gino was slumped over the kitchen table. At first, I couldn't tell for sure whether he was dead, then I saw the wound. I retrieved the gun from the floor, put it on the table. I figured Gino must have either had the gun in his pocket or it had been in a drawer. I called 911 and Gayle, my ex-wife."

"Why did you disturb the gun on the floor?"

"Didn't see it at first, then accidentally kicked it when I checked on Gino. I picked it up to get it off the floor."

Tom had designed his story to explain why he had blood on him and why he may have had fingerprints on the gun—he didn't trust himself that he could've wiped his prints perfectly clean. The note was powerful evidence: Gino had a perfect motive to take his own life and obviously there was no reason for Tom, a member of one of the most respected firms in Washington, to tell anything but the truth. Best Tom could tell, Castro bought every word.

"It's been a long night. Mind if I go home now?" asked Tom, the weariness in his voice the only authentic element of his performance.

"Sorry to keep you," said Castro. "Thanks for your time."

They shook hands and Tom left. As soon as he was out the door, he gasped for breath. His heart pounded and he began to tremble. *Stop it.* He had to hold it together.

He saw the paramedics loading the black body bag into the back of the ambulance. *He did that. He was respon—*

Wait, the bag moved. That's impossible. The body sat up and the bag unzipped. Gino Battaglia, now with a hole through his head, smiled, except his white teeth were gone, supplanted by blackened stubs. A white worm slithered through the stubs and dropped into the grass. He winked, and when he spoke, it wasn't Gino's voice. Instead, the sound was more a high-pitched squeak: *Thanks, Tommy. Keep 'em comin'.*

Tom pressed his fist to his mouth to stifle the scream, then looked again; the body bag was as it had been, now fully loaded into the ambulance.

A hallucination.

The minute he got into his car, he checked his cell phone, hoping for a message from Chad releasing his daughter in exchange for the soul of Gino Battaglia.

Nothing.

***

He lay in bed, staring at the ceiling. Three stiff shots of Jack hadn't helped. He could equivocate about Gino, having bludgeoned an innocent woman to death, deciding to take his own life rather than face life behind bars. All Tom had done was hasten the man's suicide by a few seconds. But the truth was, Thomas Michael Booker, middle class, above-average intelligence, well educated, generally a nice guy, had murdered Gino Battaglia.

For the hundredth time, he checked his cell phone. *Where the hell were the demon twins?* He wanted badly to call Gayle to check on Janie, but both girls needed sleep right now. Besides, what explanation would he offer?

His mind rushed over the details of the past hours. What

was he missing? What clue did he leave? Would the next knock at the door be Castro with a pair of handcuffs? After leaving Gino's, he'd pulled over behind an abandoned strip mall and burned his bloody latex gloves. He knew he didn't think of everything, but—*damn!* The gloves had Gino's blood on them, and he'd put the gloves in his pockets, which meant his pockets had traces of Gino's blood. He had to get rid of the jacket; no, that would look suspicious. Castro had seen him in the jacket. Dry-clean. Would dry-cleaning remove the blood? Probably. He'd take it to the dry-cleaners in the morning.

But wait, even if traces of blood remained, he'd made no attempt to hide the blood on his body, and had, in fact, made sure there was blood on his hands, or Castro would've wondered why there was blood on other parts of his clothing, but not on his hands. And if it was okay for him to have the victim's blood on his hands, it would make sense there would be blood in his jacket pockets. So he would dry-clean the jacket, but do so along with his shirts and suits on his normal day. Normal, that was the key.

Satisfied, he finally drifted off to sleep.

He dreamed of Gino, sitting at the kitchen table, looking up at him with that plaintive expression: *"You killed me Tom, but that's not the worst of it. I'm in hell now, for all eternity. I didn't deserve that, Tom. You should be here instead of me. I took a life, but it was against my will. You willfully murdered me. You should burn—"*

No!

Thanks, Tommy. Keep 'em comin'.

Tom woke in a sweat. His phone buzzed. He grabbed it from the night table. On the screen he saw a video of a familiar freckle-faced, seven-year-old wearing a green Frog shirt, kicking a soccer ball in her backyard. A text appeared across the video.

Angie saved. Thanks for Gino.

Still owe three.

CHAPTER 16

Tom slept until one p.m., then spent the rest of the day in his under-shorts and t-shirt, staring blankly at the TV. Sunday meant football, and the 'Skins were playing the Eagles at home. Ignoring breakfast, he popped open a bag of Cheetos, found a six-pack of beer, and parked himself in his old, red leather recliner. Over the next six hours, the phone rang four times—two calls from Zig and two from Gayle. He ignored them.

By eight, he'd watched the 'Skins lose and the Ravens win. He'd finished two family-size bags of Cheetos. His fingers, face, hair, undershorts, and the arms of his chair were covered in orange gunk. The six-pack had barely lasted until a last-second Eagles field goal had doomed the 'Skins, and he'd required the assistance of his friend, Mr. Daniel's, to help him make it through the Ravens' thrashing of the Packers.

He was into the second quarter of the Sunday night game—he had no idea who was playing, but could make out that one team wore red and the other team white—when Jess called. Through the blur, he knew enough to avoid talking to any human being in his condition, and elected not to answer.

***

When the alarm went off the next morning, he found himself still in the red recliner, covered in orange crumbs and beer stains. He looked to his left—his eyes hurt to move—and saw the fifth of whis-key was half gone. Had it been a new bottle? When he attempted to climb out of the recliner, he stumbled to the floor. The movement triggered a gag reflex and he vomited orange puke onto his rug.

Okay, that was it. No more booze. He was stopping right then and there. He'd turned to the bottle as a way to dull the pain immediately after his mother's death. Since then, he knew he'd increased his consumption, and while he certainly wasn't an alchoholic, he was well aware that sometimes he overindulged.

No way could he go to work. He did his best to clean up the mess, then stumbled into the kitchen and poured Cheerios directly from the box into his mouth. Hopefully, the dry cereal would soak up the putrid brew in his stomach.

His eyes caught the flashing "notice" light in the corner of his laptop, signaling a reminder from the firm. Every morning, the light would flash to alert firm personnel of upcoming appointments and events scheduled for the day.

He clicked on the icon and read the message. *Damn.* Today was the deadline to give notice of his preference for the next rotation. He was about to click on Corporate, when he saw he also had the option of selecting this round for his pro bono obligation. There were several pro bono options, but the one that caught his eye was a single opening at the Public Defender Service. What better place to find bad guys than in the criminal justice system? And what better way to gain access to said bad guys than as a part of that system? He wanted that slot at PDS. Correction, he *needed* it; after all, it was a matter of life and deaths.

He dragged his ass to the shower to begin the slow process of regaining full consciousness and washing sticky Cheetos powder from his hair.

***

Edie Rudnick smiled at him from across her desk. In her fifties, Edie looked like everybody's favorite aunt—round but not fat, silver hair pulled in a bun, and eyes in a constant state of twinkle. She was the most unflappable person Tom had ever met, which came in handy administering a staff of over 500 attorneys, ranging from mildly self-centered to egotistical pricks, plus paralegals, secretaries, mail room personnel, four IT guys, three accountants, and a full-time chef. Unmarried, she'd been with the firm for fifteen years, and she was rumored to have been Bat Masterson's mistress in the early days.

"You don't look so good, Tom. Are you ill?"

"Maybe a touch of flu. No big deal."

"The Irish flu, perhaps?"

He was screwed. Must be his breath. He'd gargled for ten minutes, but Gayle had always taken perverse pleasure in pointing out that when he drank, alcohol seemed to seep from every pore in his body.

Edie opened her desk drawer, removed a tin of Altoids mints, and slid them across the desk.

"When I have that strain of flu, I find these are helpful."

He decided right then and there that Edie Rudnick qualified for sainthood. The fact she happened to be Jewish was only a minor impediment. He popped three of the mints into his mouth.

"Thanks."

"So, I'm curious why you want to do your pro bono obligation now. Most associates do everything they can to put it off."

Left unsaid was the reason most associates wanted to put it off—they viewed nonbillable obligations as a distraction, an interruption that had the potential to throw them off their singular upward journey to the promised land—partner.

"I want to go to WC for my next firm rotation, and I figured knowing something about the criminal system, even at the street level, might be helpful when representing white-collar defendants. So I thought PDS might be a good destination." Tom froze his facial features, hoping she would buy this explanation.

She held his stare for a few seconds. He could tell she knew something was askew, but couldn't quite figure it out. "Very well. Katherine O'Neil gave you high marks for your work in Corporate, so we want to accommodate you." She handed him a slip of paper. "Report to the PDS administrator this afternoon."

"Thanks." He got up to leave. She pushed the Altoids across the desk.

"Take the whole tin."

***

After a lunchtime burger with Zig—"grease is the best antidote for a hangover"—Tom took a cab from the restaurant to PDS headquarters on Indiana Avenue where the courthouse, police HQ, prosecutor's office, and public defender's office were all conveniently located within a few blocks of each other.

The '60s-era building looked to be about twelve or thirteen stories. He entered and was mildly surprised to have to go through airport-style security screening. Guess by definition, PDS clients were the type of folks for whom security screening was devised. The small lobby had a vaulted ceiling, which must've been impressive when it was built fifty years earlier. He stepped into the elevator with two other men, each of whom appeared strung out on one of the many illicit substances available in the nation's capital. He nodded to them.

"How's it goin'?"

Each stared through him as if he weren't there. When the elevator reached the fourth floor, both got out. As the doors closed, Tom saw a sign reading: DC Drug Intervention Services.

He rode up one more floor and stepped into a tiny lobby decorated in mauve and cream. No doubt at one time the space had been beautiful, but wall smudges, deep nicks in the floorboards and chair rails, and tiny wallpaper tears testified to years of wear, and more important, budget priorities. He entered through a glass door where a pleasant receptionist led him to the small office of Shannelle Burk. A sign outside her door identified Ms. Burk as CJA Coordinator.

"Come in, come in. I'm Shanny—we're all on a first–name basis here, part of the foxhole mentality." They shook hands. A slim, athletic African-American woman almost as tall as he was, she appeared to be in her mid-thirties. "Have a seat." She lifted a stack of case files off the office's single chair and Tom sat down. "We don't get volunteers from firms like SHM very often, so it's refreshing to have you join us."

"Criminal law has always fascinated me." Well, not always. Actually, only after he'd recently become a criminal himself. "You mentioned a foxhole mentality."

She chuckled. "As you'll come to learn very quickly, we have an impossible job. We're required to represent the indigent, which in this town, means 95 percent of everyone who enters the system. Our budget is a sliver of the prosecutor's budget. Most all of our clients are guilty, but they watch TV and expect a million-dollar defense, and get pissed off when we can't provide it. We not only have to deal with clients who are, shall we say, unsavory, but we must also deal with their wives and girlfriends and boyfriends and kids and grannies and, in many cases, their gangs and entourages. Throughout it all, we must maintain our professionalism and our belief that everyone deserves a fair trial, or as is much more likely the case, a fair deal."

"Sorry I asked."

"No, it's good that you understand from jump what you're getting into. So how much do you know about criminal law?"

"Took several courses in law school, but it's been a while."

"We have a pretty good training program here that we jam down your throat in a day. Then it's on-the-job training."

"Not very much to defend a murderer."

She looked at him as if he'd just said the most stupid thing in the world. "Mr. Booker, Tom, you won't be defending any murderers, or handling any felonies, for that matter. That's the job of our senior staff. You and other outsiders, both those who volunteer and those who're drafted through the DC Bar, are what we call CJA attorneys, named after the Criminal Justice Act of 1964. You handle traffic cases and misdemeanors, so we have the time to represent those charged with major felonies."

Okay, maybe he did say the stupidest thing in the world. "Guess I thought I might be sitting second chair to a senior attorney in a murder case instead of the little stuff."

"Look, what you call little stuff is very important. It's ridding our communities of little stuff that improves quality of life, which then can have a cascading effect on more serious crime."

"You sound like a prosecutor."

"I was. Many of us have spent time in the US Attorneys' Office. Best training in the world." She must've read the disappointment on his face. "But don't worry. Chances are, your little stuff clients will have done some big stuff in their past. Many times the prosecutor will bring misdemeanor charges against someone who they know did the dirty but couldn't prove it. They're looking to use the charge as leverage to try to turn the perp and pull in a bigger fish."

Okay, that was sounding better. He put on his eager-beaver face. "Whatever you want me to do, I'll do it."

"Great." She stood, signaling the meeting was over. "We assign each of our CJA attorneys to a mentor. You're assigned to Eva Stoddard. She's been here three years, which makes her a veteran. You'll find her in arraignment court."

As Tom walked down the hall, he considered that maybe handling misdemeanors was a blessing. Unlike murderers, who'd be locked up and mostly inaccessible, a bad guy charged with a misdemeanor would likely be out on the street.

Where Tom could kill him.

CHAPTER 17

Thirty minutes later Tom rode the escalator down to the C level of the Moultrie Courthouse. The escalator was located in the middle of a huge, airy central lobby that reminded Tom of a shopping mall. Corridors spoking out from the center hall contained well-appointed courtrooms. Strategically located banks of TV monitors gave notice of cases being adjudicated that day—criminal, civil, domestic, and juvenile. A courthouse was a place to deal with conflict, and few of the people bustling through its corridors looked particularly happy. Most everybody was there because something bad happened.

When he reached the C level, he passed a narrow hallway over which a sign read: "To Holding Cells." Presumably prisoners were taken there from the DC Jail and held pending their court appearance. He followed the signs, turned right, and found the door to Courtroom, C-10. Two TV monitors outside the door listed the defendants scheduled to appear for arraignment or other pretrial proceedings.

As he was about to enter, the courtroom doors opened, and a mass of humanity spilled out. From snatches of conversation, Tom concluded the judge had taken a break. No one told him what Eva Stoddard looked like. A short, stocky woman whose age and the era for which her clothes were designed both appeared to be in the '50s, carried a stack of files as she exited.

"Excuse me," asked Tom, "Would you be Eva Stoddard?"

"Right church, wrong pew. I'm the AUSA"—she saw the blank look on Tom's face—"The Assistant US Attorney. That's Eva."

She pointed to a tall young woman holding an armful of manila files, leaning against the wall, talking on her cell phone. Maybe a year or two younger than Tom, she had red hair, green eyes, a slim body, and wore a don't-screw-with-me expression on her face.

He approached just as she got off the call. "Hi, my name's Tom Booker. Shanny Burk sent me over." He extended his hand.

She shook it briefly. "You CJA?"

"Guess so. Doin' a pro bono stint from Smith Hale. Shanny said you're my training officer." He offered his most charming boyish smile.

She ignored it. "Fine." She spread out the files like a deck of cards. "Pick two."

"Uh, don't think you understand. Today's my first day. Don't really know what I'm doing."

"Best way to learn to swim is to jump in the deep end. You either swim or drown. Good news here, Booker, is when you screw up, you'll survive to jump in again tomorrow."

"But what if I make a mistake? We're talking about someone's freedom."

"These are misdemeanors, and this is the District. Our jails are overcrowded, we have murders and rapes happening almost on a daily basis. Drug crime is rampant. Those are big-boy cases you won't even get close enough to sniff. It's rare for someone to serve time for a misdemeanor."

Tom's next question was key. "What if you have a felon, let's say a murderer, who maybe gets off, then gets picked up for speeding?"

"First of all, traffic matters are prosecuted by the city through the DC Attorney General's office, not the Feds. See, Booker, the District's not a state—"

Okay, acting tough was fine, but sarcasm wasn't necessary.

"—and so crimes that in a state would be prosecuted by a state's attorney are handled here by the Feds, along with federal crime. The exception is what's commonly referred to in the law as little shit. Traffic's little shit. Baby misdemeanors are little shit.

Little shit's prosecuted by the DC government. I don't do little shit. Now, if you got a perp who beat a murder rap, and he gets caught on a misdemeanor threat or simple assault, a judge can take the murder charge into account at sentencing, although they rarely do."

She checked her watch. "Gotta go back in." She handed him two files from the bottom of the pile. "Here, watch me on the first ones. Then you do the last two. The goal here is to make sure the accused understands the charges and gets out on bond. You can check out the files while I'm doing my thing. When it's time to talk about bond, always ask for PR, personal recognizance. If the AUSA wants a heavy bond, list all your client's personal connections to the community and, hopefully, Squeaky will impose a light bond."

"Squeaky?"

"The Honorable Stephen A. Mosley. Let's go."

Tom took the files and followed Eva into the deep end of the pool.

***

Two hours later, his mind was mush and his legs shook. He'd sat next to Eva as she, the prosecutor—her name was Vera Lutz—and the judge ran through one case after another. Eva appeared to be in a rhythm and, hopefully, she'd forget and handle the last two—He heard Eva say his name.

"...Thomas Booker. Mr. Booker's a CJA volunteer from Smith, Hale and Masterson, and is available for appointment to the last two cases, Your Honor." She whispered to Tom, "Stand up."

Tom rose so abruptly, his chair toppled over, eliciting laughter from everyone, including the judge.

"Welcome, Mr. Booker. I hope you will be a bit more careful with our furniture in future visits. Given our budget, that chair will need to last for another 100 years."

"Yes, Your Honor."

The judge turned to the prosecutor. "Let's keep them rolling, Ms. Lutz. Maybe we can all get out of here a little early today."

"Of course, Your Honor," Lutz responded. "Next case is Tawana White, sol pros."

The bailiff escorted a skinny black woman dressed in accordance with her profession, who looked to be in her forties, but Tom knew from reviewing her file she'd just turned nineteen.

"Afternoon, Tawana," said the judge. "I was hoping I wouldn't have seen you back here so soon."

She shrugged. "Whatcha gonna do, Judge? Girl's gotta make a livin'."

"Six convictions for soliciting," said Lutz in a monotone. "Two misdemeanor drug possessions, one felony drug possession pleaded down. Government asks for ten thousand dollars bond."

Tom jumped up, suitably indignant. "Your Honor, ten thousand for a simple solicitation is very excessive."

Tawana faced him for the first time. Her bloodshot eyes attempted to focus. "You my CJA?" Before he could respond, she turned back to the judge with an expression that could only be interpreted as, "Who's this bozo?"

Tom continued. "Sir, we believe—"

The judge held up his hand to cut him off. "What do you want to do, Tawana?"

"Could use a little break, Judge, if you don't mind. Gettin' cold out there."

"No problem. Bond's set at ten thousand dollars. You gonna plead?"

"'Course."

"Okay, I'll assign your case to Judge Hecht. How about a week?"

"Can I get two?"

"No problem. Case will be set for status two weeks from today."

"Thanks, Judge."

"You're welcome. Take care of yourself."

She smiled at the judge as she was led away. "Next case," said the judge.

"United States versus Reece Mackey," said the clerk.

The marshal escorted a tall, gaunt black man forward. Mid-thirties, stringy, dirty hair, rough beard, heavy lids over dull eyes. Dressed in street clothes, his jeans were halfway down his ass, exposing blue boxers. He wore a Washington Redskins t-shirt that may have been washed several months ago. His body odor made Tom's eyes water.

"Mr. Mackey's charged with simple assault, Your Honor," said Lutz. "Bar fight."

Tom had read the file. Mackey originally had been charged with ADW—assault with a deadly weapon—for cutting the victim with a hawk-bill knife, then punching him in the face. The AUSA in charge of intake had no-papered the felony and reduced the charge to misdemeanor assault. Both the defendant and the victim were drunk. The victim only received a superficial cut on his arm, and wasn't exactly citizen-of-the-year material.

"Defendant has a long record, Your Honor," said Lutz. "The government requests ten thousand dollars cash bond."

Squeaky turned to Tom. "Mr. Booker?"

"Mr. Mackey has a long record of arrests, Your Honor, not convictions. There's no evidence that Mr. Mackey ever failed to appear." Tom was parroting a line he'd heard Eva offer on several occasions during the afternoon. "This is a bar fight, and I'm sure the evidence will show Mr. Mackey was as much a victim as the complainant. We believe he should be released on his personal recognizance."

"One of those arrests led to Mr. Mackey being tried for first-degree murder," said Lutz. "He was acquitted when a key witness failed to appear."

Eva looked at Tom, expectantly. What did she want him to say?

Eva sprang to her feet. "Your Honor, Ms. Lutz's comments are outrageous. She's hinting that somehow Mr. Mackey was responsible for the witness' failure to appear. If that were the case, her office would've prosecuted him for witness tampering."

Right on right on, thought Tom.

"Ms. Stoddard has a point," said the judge. "Okay, Mr. Mackey, I'm releasing you on your own recognizance. You will report to

Judge Hecht's chambers three weeks from today at 9:00 a.m. for a status hearing. If you fail to appear, I'll issue a bench warrant for your arrest. Do you understand?"

"Yes, sir," said Mackey.

"Between now and then, consult with your attorney, Mr. Booker here."

Mackey pointed to Eva. "I want her."

Tom didn't blame him.

"Not your choice," said the judge. "Mr. Booker comes from one of the most prestigious firms in the city. You're in good hands. All right, think that does it, unless there's anything else, court's adjourned until tomorrow at 9:00."

All stood while the judge exited the courtroom. Tom approached Mackey and offered his hand. Mackey shook it warily.

"So, how can I get in touch with you?" asked Tom.

Mackey gestured to a big-breasted black woman wearing a pink halter top who'd been sitting near the back of the courtroom. She came forward.

"Phone," said Mackey.

She retrieved a cell phone from her purse and handed it to him. He punched a few keys and displayed the screen to Tom. The phone's number appeared. Tom quickly entered the digits into his own phone. Without another word, Mackey and his girl departed the room, arm-in-arm.

As they reached the door, the woman turned back and grinned.

For an instant his vision flickered, and it was Brit smiling at him. He blinked and she disappeared.

CHAPTER 18

Tom sat with Eva and other PDS attorneys around a long wooden table in the back of Jack's, a deli only steps from their office building. All the attorneys appeared to be under thirty-five, most under thirty. The place was packed, and the attorneys had to shout across the table to be heard. Pitchers of beer and baskets of thick, homemade pretzels covered the table.

A blond guy sitting across from them passed the pitcher over to Tom so he could fill his glass. Eva had introduced all of her colleagues as they drifted in, but Tom could only recall a few. He did remember the blond guy's name—Danny—because Danny and Eva had held each other's gaze longer than expected for two people engaged in a purely professional relationship.

"Fill 'er up, Newbie," said Danny. "You're lucky to have Eva as your mentor. She'll show you the ropes."

Danny said the last sentence in a smarmy, double entendre tone, but for the life of him, Tom couldn't see any double meaning that might be considered sexual, unless Eva was into the dominatrix thing, which he seriously doubted.

Eva responded to Danny with a glare that could cut glass. Tom couldn't believe he cared about what was happening or had happened between Eva and Danny. He had less than two weeks to plan and execute a murder and there was no time for distractions of any kind, much less romantic distractions.

Fortunately, he thought he may have found a target. Reece Mackey had murdered another human being, and therefore fell

squarely into the "bad guy" category. That he'd beaten the rap—
Tom wondered if criminal attorneys really said, "beat the rap"—
strengthened his rationalization. This vile murderer had escaped
justice, and Tom the Avenger was flying in from his secret cave to
make things right.

He turned to Eva. "So, what about Mackey? Will he plead?"

"Doesn't get him anything. The prosecutor's pissed. Mackey
beat the murder charge, probably because he did threaten a witness
like Lutz alleged. Happens all the time. So they're not going to offer him anything for a plea. The jury can't take his arrest into account when trying him on the assault charge, but the judge can at
sentencing under certain circumstances."

"Which means—?"

"Which means, even for a pissant case like this, they're gonna
do their best to make sure the vic shows up."

"Which means—?"

"Which means in four or five weeks you're going to have your
first jury trial, Booker. Welcome to the deep end."

If Tom's plan worked, Reece Mackey would not be facing a
jury of his peers in four weeks for the simple reason that he'd be
dead.

"You ought to talk to Danny," said Eva. "He defended Mackey in the murder case." She shouted over the din of the restaurant.
"Hey, Danny, Booker needs to talk to you about Reece Mackey."

"Your wish is my command," said Danny.

Tom didn't want to talk to Danny. He didn't like Danny.
And not just because he seemed to have a thing for Eva. The man
should've had "asshole" branded across his forehead to warn the
unsuspecting. Okay, maybe most of it was because of Eva. "That
would be great."

***

That night Tom drove back into Southeast. He'd decided he needed
to meet with Mackey sooner rather than later and gain his trust.
Tom figured he'd be better able to formulate a plan after spending

some time with him. But tonight he wasn't meeting Mackey. He needed another gun, one that was untraceable. His only hope was Chewy Lewis.

He'd met Chewy during his third year teaching at Jabazz. Chewy's little brother, Jerome, was a fifth grader. Jerome was very bright and had a particularly high aptitude in math and science. Tom had taken Jerome under his wing.

Chewy, not even twenty yet, was a big-time dealer. Charismatic with a high degree of intelligence. Problem was, Chewy was Jerome's only role model, and the boy made no secret of his desire to join the family business.

One evening after a parent-teacher gathering at the school, Tom had entered his car only to discover he had a passenger in the backseat. Chewy introduced himself and instructed Tom to drive to Marion Park. When they arrived, Chewy told him to get out of the car. The park lights were out. No one was in sight.

"Let's take a walk," said Chewy. "I know you're scared, but ain't gonna hurt you. Wanna talk about Jerome."

Tom's fear lessened as he followed Chewy to the eastern side of the park. "Smartest student in the class."

"Problem is, he wants to, you know, follow in my footsteps so to speak. He needs a chance, before the shit gets him. You gotta get him out."

"Out, like out of the neighborhood?"

"I hear there's this boarding school up in Northwest, offers a few scholarships to black folk so the rich, liberal assholes can feel good 'bout all their big cars and big houses and fat bank accounts. Jerome, he needs to get one of them scholarships."

"Carver Prep. Great idea, I'll do everything I can—"

"Maybe you didn't hear me. Jerome needs to get one of them scholarships."

The next day, Tom filled out the scholarship application and wrote a glowing letter of recommendation. He took Jerome shopping for a navy sport coat and rep tie. He worked with the boy, honing his responses in preparation for his interview. Jerome aced the interview, and a week after that received a letter congratulating him on his admittance to Carver Prep.

A month later, Chewy waited for him at his car after school. "Just want to let you know, I owe you, Teach. You need anything, you call me." He handed Tom a torn slip of paper with a phone number written on it. Without waiting for a response, he got into the back of a black Escalade and his driver pulled away.

***

Tom had kept that slip of paper, never believing he'd ever use it. An hour earlier, he'd dug it out from inside a rolled-up pair of socks in the back of his sock drawer. He'd walked three blocks to the CITGO, the only place left in the neighborhood with a working pay phone, and made the call. He hadn't spoken to Chewy Lewis for almost seven years. For all he knew, the man was dead or in jail. He heard the click of the call being connected.

"Hi, this is—"

Before he could finish, Chewy responded, "Same place, eleven."

So here he was, parked outside Marion Park. The lighting had been improved, although the lights on the eastern side still weren't working—no doubt shot out to create the dark ambiance one needed to properly conduct off-market pharmaceutical business.

Tom checked his watch. Ten past eleven. It occurred to him that by "same place," maybe Chewy meant the shadows of the east side. He got out of the Lexus, locked the car, then strolled into the darkness.

He walked along the deserted path, but saw nobody. He was about to return to his car when he heard, "Hey, Teach."

Tom turned and there he was. Better dressed, looking much more than seven years older.

"Hi, how's it going?" asked Tom. "How's Jerome?"

"Got a full ride to Princeton next year." Chewy didn't attempt to hide his pride. "Princeton's in the Ivy League, like Harvard."

"That's great." Actually, Tom felt a sense of pride himself due to his small part in launching a kid from an at-risk neighborhood to almost certain success.

"What you need?"

"A gun. Needs to be clean, never used in any, uh, situation."

"That's it?"

"That's it."

Chewy nodded. "Ain't much, so my debt ain't fully paid. Case you need anything else."

"Doubt it, but thanks. And tell Jerome I said congratulations."

"Take the long way around the park to get back to your car."

"Thanks. Hey, you know if Jerome becomes rich and successful, maybe you can get out of this business."

Chewy paused before he answered. "Ain't the money, Teach. Got plenty of money to meet my needs. What I got here, no price for that." He turned and disappeared into the darkness.

Tom followed Chewy's directions and, as he expected, by the time he got back to his car there was a crumpled brown paper bag resting on the front seat. His first thought was, why had he bothered locking the car?

He got into the Lexus, and for almost a full minute stared at the paper bag as if it were a foreign object. He rubbed his hand across the bag surface, feeling the outline of the weapon. He slipped his hand inside the bag and wrapped his fingers around the grip.

Unlike Gino's Ruger, this gun now belonged to him.

And time was running out for him to use it.

CHAPTER 19

The weapon rested on Tom's kitchen table as he checked out the gun on his laptop. The Glock 30 was a .45-caliber automatic. The barrel length was only four inches long, the whole gun under seven inches. The barrel bore was much bigger than the Ruger, and the .45-caliber bullet looked like it could stop a train. Tom counted thirteen rounds in the magazine, and Chewy had included a second magazine containing another thirteen rounds. Twenty-six bullets, enough to start a small war. He only needed one.

Despite its firepower and small size, the most amazing feature of the Glock was its weight. The gun frame was constructed from a plastic polymer, reducing its weight to a bit over one pound. This feature allowed it to be carried just about anywhere on one's person without discomfort and telltale sagging clothes. The only thing missing compared to the Ruger was an external safety switch.

Tom turned off the laptop and stared at the thick, stubby .45-caliber bullets protruding from the extra magazine. Would he be able to fire one of those missiles into Reece Mackey's brain? He honestly didn't know.

***

The next few days he immersed himself in his new job. He tagged along with Eva throughout the workday, accompanying her to discovery meetings with AUSAs, sitting as second chair in several cases where her client plead guilty, and in several bond reduction hearings.

At the end of the day, he visited Danny the Asshole's office to get info on Mackey. He'd learned Danny's last name was O'Brian, but liked Danny the Asshole, DTA, better.

"Come on in, Newbie. Grab a chair."

DTA's office was tiny, but as a senior member of the staff, still bigger than the workspace of most of the other PDS attorneys. DTA sat in the single, straight-back chair behind a gray metal desk that must've been issued by the government fifty years earlier. He wore his blond hair down to his shoulders, suspenders, and a constant smirk. He leaned back in his chair and put his feet up on his desk.

"So, how's it going with the Ice Queen?"

Tom pretended not to know who he was talking about. "I'm sorry?"

"The implacable Ms. Stoddard."

Implacable. Big word, impressive. "Eva's been very helpful. I'm learning a lot from her."

"Take my advice. Don't get too close or you'll get ice burns."

"Thanks. Don't think that'll be a problem. So, about Reece Mackey—"

"Lyin' dirtbag. Loves the hooch. Whatever they say he did, he did."

Music to Tom's ears. "So you think in your case there's a chance he killed the guy?"

"Not just a chance, a certainty. He admitted it to me. Hell, he bragged about it. Vic was a fellow scumbag, Mackey's partner in a string of B&Es south of the freeway. Mackey believed his partner—forget his name, may've been Jackson, Johnson, something like that—was screwin' him over. So one night the vic's walking along E street with his whore, Mackey gets out of a parked car and caps him twice in the head. Doesn't run, casually gets back in the car, and slowly drives off with nary a la-di-da."

Nary a la-di-da? Tom decided he might have to change Danny's name to Danny the Big Time Asshole. DTBTA. *Nah, too many letters.* "And Mackey scared away the witness?"

"Witness was a whore with kids—who isn't in that world?—so Mackey tells her he's gonna cap the babies unless she contracts a serious case of amnesia. She gets amnesia."

"Guess I'm going to have to meet the guy, find out what happened in the bar."

"Good luck, and Newbie, watch out for ice burns."

Ha, ha, ha, ha. Asshole.

CHAPTER 20

The good thing about working for the Public Defender Service—one of several good things, actually—was Tom could finish up at a decent hour. He'd been able to see Janie every night since he took the assignment, and now he was heading back to DC from Arlington after taking Janie and Angie to Chez Mac for burgers and fries.

He crossed into the District and headed south, caught the Southwest Freeway, which became the Southeast Freeway, and crossed the 11th Street Bridge into Anacostia, one of the highest crime areas of the city. He'd called Mackey, who had to be reminded who he was. Mackey had reluctantly agreed to meet him at Bertha's, a hole-in-the-wall dive on Alabama Avenue. Tom involuntarily patted his jacket pocket where Mr. Glock rested comfortably. He didn't intend to execute his plan—bad choice of words—that evening for the simple reason that he had no plan. Rather, his goal was to reconnoiter—another bad choice of words for the simple reason that it sounded so lame.

He found Bertha's easily enough. After parking directly under a streetlight, he crossed the street and entered the bar. Everything inside was dark; everybody inside was dark. The place was packed, and all eyes were on him.

He walked as slowly as he could to the bar. He hadn't had a drink since the morning of the orange puke, but he reasoned that if he ordered a soft drink his client wouldn't respect him and might not talk to him. Maybe he'd just order a beer, take a few sips to show his street cred.

The bartender—Bertha?—a huge black woman with tattoos covering every exposed part of her flesh, approached him warily. Her hair shot straight out from her head, as if she'd just stuck her finger into an electrical socket. Her cheeks were so fleshy, her eyes appeared as black slits in her face.

"We ain't want no trouble," she said, her voice a deep rumble.

Tom was momentarily confused, then it hit him. She thought he was a cop.

"Uh, no, I ain't a cop." *Why did he say "ain't?" He never said "ain't."* "Supposed to meet Reece Mackey."

The bartender nodded. "CJA."

"Yeah. How 'bout a beer?"

She paused for a moment, then rinsed out a glass and drew a Bud from the tap. "Twenty bucks."

Okay, he had two choices: One—tell her that was outrageous and he wasn't paying twenty bucks for a draft beer, an option that likely would result in him not escaping the establishment alive; or two—lay a twenty on the bar and thank her. After considering the matter for a nanosecond, he smiled and pulled a twenty from his wallet.

"He's over there with LaChiqua and Ball." She pointed to the darkest corner of the bar, where Tom recognized Mackey seated at a small table with his woman and a small black man with a shaved head.

Tom made his way over to Mackey's table. Half-full glasses of straight whiskey rested in front of them.

"Good to see you again, Mr. Mackey." Tom extended his hand.

Mackey ignored it.

Tom took a seat. He addressed the woman and the little man. "I'm Tom Booker, the attorney assigned to defend Mr. Mackey." Both stared at him with glassy eyes. "Uh, as you know, anything Reece tells me is confidential and can't be used against him. But, if a third party also hears Reece say something to me, then—"

"She stay." Mackey's face was devoid of expression. "She not sayin' nuthin'."

Fair enough. "No problem." Tom turned to the bald man, presumably, Ball.

Mackey caught Ball's eye and gestured with his head toward the bar. The little man frowned, then gave Tom the once over. "Make him buy me a drink. Premium."

Tom pulled another twenty from his wallet. Ball jerked it from his fingers and departed for the bar.

Before Tom could speak, Mackey drained his whiskey, then handed the empty glass to LaChiqua.

"Tell 'er I want the good stuff. CJA's buyin'." His dead eyes locked on Tom's.

"Sure. My treat." Tom opened his wallet and removed a ten.

Mackey reached over and pulled out a twenty, then gave the thirty bucks to the woman. "Tell 'er the real good stuff. And to start a tab." LaChiqua left for the bar. Mackey smiled broadly at Tom, flashing his gold tooth, but his eyes remained dead.

"Okay," said Tom, "so as I understand it, this is where the altercation occurred. Can you tell me what happened in your own words?" *Whose words would he use?* He had to stop watching cops shows on TV.

Mackey shrugged. "Tonka, he grabbed my woman's titties." Tonka was Tonka Jones, the assault victim.

"So, when Jones sexually assaulted your girlfriend, you were simply defending her."

Mackey gave Tom a quizzical look. "Didn't say sex, didn't fuck her. Well, he did fuck her, but that was last year when she was his woman. He just grabbed her titties, and when he did, he knocked over my drink. So I asks him to buy me another one, and he tell me to go fuck myself, so I cut him."

"Okay, but when we go to court, might be better if we paint this as you defending your girlfriend. Maybe your intention was simply to display the knife to deter him from further assaulting her; he pushes you and you accidentally nick him in the arm." Bending the facts this far triggered somewhere in the back of Tom's mind the concept of legal ethics, but this thought disap-

peared quickly for two reasons: first, in the great ethical continu-
um, bending the truth appeared substantially to the right of serial
murder; and second, Mackey would never lie to the jury because,
again, he'd be dead.

LaChiqua returned with a beer mug filled with whiskey and a
few cubes of ice. "Crown Preferred," she said.

Mackey grinned from ear to ear. He took the mug, raised it to
Tom in a toasting gesture, then took a long drink.

Tom couldn't insult the man so he drank half his beer. The
sight of the Canadian whiskey triggered a reflex in Tom, and he
had to struggle not to order another beverage more serious than a
tapped Bud.

He turned to the woman. "Might I get your name?"

She looked to Mackey for permission.

Tom continued. "Reece said he was defending you against
Tonka when he cut him. You could be key to his defense."

"Ain't gonna be no defense 'cause ain't gonna be no trial," said
Mackey. "Tonka ain't gonna post."

"How do you know? I must advise you that the prosecutor's
not treating this like a run-of-the-mill simple assault. They still
have it in for you for beating the murder rap, so they're going to go
all out. Which means they'll threaten Tonka if they have to, and
send a car for him to make sure he appears."

Another flash of the gold tooth. "As I said, Tonka ain't gonna
post." His tone made plain that no further comment was being solicited.

Mackey's solution posed a problem. Tom needed an excuse
to meet up with his client again in a private setting. He stood to
leave, not bothering to extend his hand.

"Great to meet you both. If I hear the prosecutor has happened upon any other evidence, I'll give you a call."

Mackey held up his mug of premium whiskey. "Thanks."

Tom drained the rest of the beer, then exited the bar. The
Lexus was still there and appeared to be untouched. As he reached
the car, he heard a voice behind him.

"Give it up."

He turned to see three black teens, one of whom was pointing a gun at his head. Interestingly, his first thought was the gun appeared to be a Glock, same as the one in his jacket pocket. He had two choices: one, grab for his gun and hope he could use the element of surprise to shoot the kid before the kid shot him; or, two, give it up.

He pulled out his wallet. "Tell you what, guys, I give you the cash, you leave my credit cards and stuff, I don't even call the cops. We look on it as a donation."

The one with the gun paused as he considered the offer, then nodded. Tom pulled out the cash, about 800 bucks, and handed it to the tallest kid.

"Think I may cap you anyways," said the kid.

"Please...no need for that..." Tom stepped back as his hand moved to his pocket, then he heard a whistle.

Tom and the teens turned to see Mackey standing across the street in front of the bar. Mackey made a cutting gesture across his neck which could either mean slice whitey's throat, or stop, don't shoot him. Fortunately it meant the latter. The three teens turned and walked away.

Tom waved his thanks to Mackey for saving his life. His client ignored him and returned to the bar.

As Tom drove away, he tried not to think of the new complication. He was planning to kill a man who'd just saved his life.

He turned his phone back on. The screen showed he'd missed a call.

He froze.

The caller ID read: *P. Castro, DCP.*

CHAPTER 21

Tom drove north on Connecticut Avenue, then turned right onto Columbia Road. Almost home. Castro hadn't left a message, so Tom reasoned the purpose of his call must not have been important. Then why was acid spraying into his stomach like a garden hose? Should he call back? Again, no message; no *please call back,* or, *you're under arrest for murder.* He checked the time of the call: 11:13 p.m. Two hours ago. Obviously, too late to return the call.

When he turned onto Biltmore, Percy Castro was sitting in an unmarked car parked in front of Tom's apartment building.

Castro got out of his car and waved to Tom. *Damn.* Tom stopped and rolled down his window. He strained to appear cheerful.

"Evening, Detective. Or, guess it's good morning." *Ha, ha, ha, you're a real comedian, Booker.*

"Out hitting the bars, Mr. Booker?" Castro was smiling, but the best Tom could tell in the limited light cast by a streetlamp half a block away, the smile was mirthless.

"No, just coming back from interviewing a CJA client down in Southeast."

Castro didn't respond, but kept the smile. Definitely *sans* mirth. Should he park? Fortunately, there were no spaces available nearby.

"Anything I can help you with?"

"Just routine follow-up on the Battaglia case."

Did he say, *"Just routine?"* Didn't he know everyone in the world who watched TV knew that whenever a cop said "Just routine" it meant the opposite?

"We found Gino's gun box on a shelf in his closet. Three sets of prints: his, those of his deceased wife, and unknown. Seeing as how you were related by marriage and were present at the time of the incident, thought maybe you might be willing to come down to the station tomorrow and get inked."

Okay, quick decision time here. "Be happy to do whatever you need, but I can tell you the third set's probably mine. When I took Angie back to get her clothes, I found her suitcase up on that shelf. Had to move the box. I admit I was curious what was inside. I shouldn't have opened it; none of my business, but I did. So I wouldn't be surprised if you found my prints on the inside as well."

Castro paused for a second. "Okay, then. That explains it." He eye-locked with Tom. Thankfully, it was dark inside Tom's car so, hopefully, Castro couldn't see the abject fear in his eyes. "Goodnight, Mr. Booker. If you wait a second, you can have my parking space."

"Thanks."

Castro took his time walking back to his car, got in, and slowly pulled away.

***

Over the following days, Tom tried to push Castro from his mind. There should be no further reason for concern. The detective had found extra prints on the gun box. He was following up, doing his job, that's all. *Just routine.* Tom had answered the detective's questions, answers that happened to be the truth. So why did Castro's image continue to lurk in his head?

Couldn't worry about it now. Tomorrow was Saturday. D-Day.

Tom needed to come up with a plan to get Mackey alone in the man's own apartment. Seeing as how Mackey intended to persuade the victim of the assault that testifying was not conducive to his health, any ruse based on discussing a plea deal would be ignored. There was no need to plead, because there'd be no case, because there'd be no victim to testify.

On Thursday night, Tom called Mackey, and was surprised when he answered after only a couple of rings.

"Mr. Mackey, Tom Booker."

Silence.

Tom continued. "So, I was interviewing one of my other clients, and he told me he heard some folks were plotting to take you out."

"Who?"

Tom lowered his voice in an attempt to sound conspiratorial. "Don't want to talk about it over the phone. And I think we should talk alone." He waited what seemed like forever for a response.

"Saturday night."

***

He'd spent Friday morning with Eva representing felony defendants in preliminary hearings—known as *"px's"* among members of the criminal bar. The ostensible purpose of the hearing was for the court to determine whether sufficient probable cause existed to bind a defendant over for trial. Defense counsel used the px as the first opportunity to cross-examine the arresting officer and gain added discovery.

They'd been sitting before Arnie Turkus, who'd once been chief deputy at PDS, and he'd been more lenient than the AUSA wanted in allowing Eva to question the arresting officers, squeezing as much information as she could before even Judge Turkus, facing a crowded docket, cut her off and bound the defendant over.

In the past, Eva had used the lunch break to return to the office, but Turkus only gave them forty-five minutes, so they both hurried downstairs to the courthouse coffee shop for a quick sandwich. Called the Firehook Bakery and Coffee House, the place served the usual crapacino array of coffee choices along with homemade soups and stacked deli sandwiches. Large travel and sports posters hung on gold-colored walls, and along with the fake mahogany tables, offered a pleasant alternative to the typical drab government-issue cafeteria.

"So, what did you think about this morning?" asked Eva.

They sat at a small, two-person table in the back corner of the loud, crowded room. She wolfed down a chicken salad sandwich while he picked at a turkey Reuben. He'd ordinarily welcome a few minutes of private social time with Eva, but his mind was focused on facing Reece Mackey the next day with a gun in his hand. Would he pull the trigger? Could he pull the trigger?

"Tom, you with me?"

"Sorry."

Before he could continue, DTA walked by, and Tom saw a flash of disappointment when Danny realized there were no extra chairs at the table.

"Room for one more?" asked Danny. He looked around for an empty chair from a nearby table.

Tom wasn't in the mood for idle conversation. "Here, take mine." He cleared his place.

"You okay?" asked Eva.

"Had a big breakfast. See you back in court." He left before she could respond.

***

The afternoon session moved more quickly. Eva had given Tom the last file of the day to handle—a murder case. Freemont James, aka Jiggy, barely eighteen with a rap sheet going back to the age of ten, was accused of shooting one Alfred Lewis, aka Spider, in the face outside a bar on 14th Street.

The prosecutor called the arresting officer to the stand. Tom was shocked to see Percy Castro approach from the back of the room and take the witness chair.

The prosecutor, a good-looking Latino who appeared as if he'd just graduated from high school, easily walked Castro through a recitation of the facts, making sure to elicit the bare elements of the crime. Took less than two minutes. The judge turned to Eva.

"Ms. Stoddard?"

"Mr. Booker will handle this one, Your Honor."

"Make it fast, Mr. Booker."

Tom stood. "Yes, Your Honor." He faced Castro, who greeted him with a bemused expression. Tom's hand shook, rattling the sheet of yellow-lined paper holding his quickly scribbled notes. Castro's eyes moved to the shaking paper. Tom dropped the paper onto the defense table.

"Uh, so, Detective, what were the lighting conditions at the scene of the alleged shooting?"

"Oh, the shooting wasn't alleged, Mr. Booker. Got a stiff with half his face blown off and two recovered 9mm slugs from his brain."

"Okay, well, what about the light?"

"The defendant popped him right under a streetlamp in front of a well-lit bar. As I said in response to the prosecutor's questions, we have three witnesses, we recovered Jiggy's Glock from his apartment, and the ballistics matched."

Eva scribbled a note on her yellow pad: statements?

Before Tom could ask the question, Castro exchanged glances with Eva. "She's probably telling you to ask me about statements. We've got signed affidavits from the three witnesses and a signed confession. The confession was videotaped, so you'll see he was fully apprised of his rights and elected to talk without a lawyer. If memory serves, his direct quote was, 'Yeah, I capped the mother 'cause he showed me disrespect by not tellin' his ho to gimme a blowjob.'"

The judge intervened. "Sit down, Mr. Booker. The defendant will be bound over. Court's adjourned." He banged his gavel.

Castro stepped down from the witness stand and offered his hand. Tom shook it.

"Good to see you, Mr. Booker. I'm sure our paths will cross again."

As he spoke, Tom imagined Castro's eyes boring into him. His knees began to shake. Could Castro see his knees shaking? *Stop it.*

A quick nod, then Castro left the courtroom.

"So, you know Castro?" asked Eva.

"Yeah, my brother-in-law killed himself, and Castro was the detective in charge."

"Sorry to hear that. Did he leave a note?"

Yeah, he left a note. One that was practically dictated to him by the guy standing in front of you. "Yes. Gino had beaten his wife to death in a jealous rage and faced life in prison. The note was asking forgiveness from his daughter."

"Now I remember reading about it. Didn't realize you were related. Sorry."

"Thanks."

"Good news for the family is you've got Percy Castro involved," said Eva. "Best detective in the city. Any loose ends, he'll find them."

Yeah, good news unless one happened to be a loose end. Tom couldn't stop his legs from shaking. His head pounded.

He had to talk to someone or he was going to burst.

CHAPTER 22

Tom patted John Carroll's ass without breaking stride. The seated bronze statue of Georgetown's founder, otherwise green with age, sported one shiny spot on its rear end. Over the years, countless superstitious students and faculty, perhaps on the way to a final exam, a tenure committee meeting, or a blind date, had rubbed John Carroll's butt in search of good fortune.

The campus was crowded as undergrads hurried to reach a 5:00 p.m. class. Tom climbed the stone steps to Healy Hall. Healy reminded him of a huge medieval castle, and today its sharp spires and cold gray stone melded perfectly with the heavily overcast late afternoon sky.

He took the elevator to the third floor, then turned down the corridor toward the faculty offices. During law school, he'd spent little time on the main campus; the law school was located on New Jersey Avenue, a stone's throw from the Capitol. But first-year law students were required to take a legal ethics class. Tom's instructor had been Father Matthew Sheran, a Jesuit who'd written extensively about ethics in general and legal ethics in particular. While not an attorney, he was highly regarded as one of the top scholars on legal ethics in the country.

Tom had called ahead for an appointment, found the office, and knocked.

"Come in." Father Sheran's deep baritone voice could easily be heard from the other side of the door.

Tom entered and closed the door behind him. The priest stood up from behind his desk and greeted him with an easy smile.

In his mid-thirties, Matthew Sheran was an inch or so taller than Tom, fit, African-American, with close-cropped hair and soft, brown eyes. He had a strong grip, and Tom was reminded of a comment he'd heard his first days at Georgetown during orientation—the Jesuits were a muscular order of the church known as God's Marines due to their founder's military background. Nobody messed with the Jezzies.

"I'm sure you don't remember me," said Tom. "As I said on the phone, I was in your legal ethics class over four years ago."

"You're right, I don't." The Jezzies also had a reputation for being direct. "Please, take a seat."

Father Sheran wore a tan corduroy sport coat over an oxford shirt, his Roman collar the only indication he was a man of the cloth. Tom recalled that the man's movie-star good looks, combined with the novelty of a black priest bearing an Irish name, convinced many females in his class it was their duty to persuade him to break his vows of celibacy. As far as Tom knew, no one had ever been successful.

The small office was cluttered with stacks of books and papers, but Tom cleared the single chair and sat down.

"On the phone you mentioned a matter of life and death. Rather melodramatic," said Father Sheran. "And if I might say, you appear rather anxious."

Rather anxious? Rather no shit. The priest's eyes bore into him.

"First, thank you for seeing me, Father. Before I go any further, I'd appreciate confirmation that anything I tell you would be covered by the priest-penitent privilege," said Tom. "By the way, you should know I'm not Catholic. In fact, I've been away from the church for some time."

"Doesn't affect the privilege, and please call me Matt."

Tom continued. "And confirmation that the privilege, unlike

the atttorney-client privilege, covers admissions of intent to commit future crimes."

The priest's expression clouded and he leaned forward. "You said you weren't a Catholic. Before you say another word, I strongly encourage you to seek counsel from a Protestant minister or rabbi or whoever represents—"

"Am I right?"

Matt held his gaze and spoke in an even tone. "Yes."

Tom paused to exhale. "Do you believe in hell? I mean really believe? Not just in man's capacity to do evil on earth, but an actual place with a head guy, and demons or dark angels or boogeymen who work for him?"

It was Matt's turn to pause. "Perhaps at this point it would be helpful if you told me a little about yourself."

Tom knew where the priest was heading, and he didn't blame him. "I'm not crazy, although when I leave here you likely will disagree." The priest held his gaze, and Tom suspected he was debating whether to continue the conversation.

"Yes, I believe in hell as a state of eternal punishment inhabited by those rejected by God."

"A state? Not a place?"

"I had a professor say once, 'Hell is as far away as the nothing beyond the farthest universe, and as close as the nose on your face.'"

"Poetic, but not helpful."

"The Bible repeatedly attributes to Jesus the description of hell as a 'fiery furnace,' and St. Peter himself pictured demons, fallen angels, lions prowling among us, searching for someone to devour. But the church has been less than definitive on these matters. I'm not sure it makes any real difference, and the truth is, irrespective of what or how strongly we believe, no one really knows for sure. For the person, the soul involved, a state of being *is* a place, a place absent of God. Now, what it's like, who staffs it, what they look like, I have no idea. Why don't you tell me why you're here?"

Tom bent forward, clasped his hands, and rested them on the edge of the priest's desk. "By midnight tomorrow night, I have to murder a man to prevent my daughter or another innocent child from dying and going to hell."

He was not surprised by Matt's stunned expression, and proceeded to tell the priest his story.

***

Tom leaned back in the chair, emotionally spent. Matt hadn't spoken a word throughout the telling.

"Tom, you can't do this. No matter what crimes Mackey might have committed, you have no right legally or morally to take his life. The events you described on the bridge were obviously delusions resulting from trauma caused by the accident."

"But there was no accident. Once I agreed to the deal, no crash occurred, so there couldn't have been head trauma."

"Okay, why you?"

"No idea. And what about the messages on my iPhone from Chad and Brit?"

"Anyone else see them?"

"No, but—"

"Do they appear on your phone's call log?"

"Showing what number? 1-800-roast-4-eternity? Look, I expected if anyone would've had a mind open enough to believe me, it would've been a priest. I should've known better." He stood and headed for the door.

"Wait." Tom turned back to see Matthew was visibly troubled. "If you're asking me whether your story is conceivably possible, to say anything other than 'yes' would betray my faith. But, I don't know you. I don't know whether you have any history of mental illness, any history of, shall we say, exaggeration. I do know that murder's a sin, Tom."

"Even in defense of an innocent child?"

"But Mackey hasn't threatened your child."

"I will protect my daughter," said Tom, his voice barely above a whisper. "I appreciate your time, Father, I really do." He opened the door.

"Tom—"

He left and closed the door behind him, harder than he'd intended.

CHAPTER 23

As he drove down Alabama Avenue the next night, Tom couldn't flush Father Sheran's words from his mind.

Murder's a sin, Tom.

Yeah, God, well, allowing the other team to take the life of an innocent child, doesn't that count as a sin? Oh, guess you can't sin against yourself, can you?

He felt his mind edging closer to...to what? *Madness?*

Concentrate on the mission. Think about Janie.

He turned right on 32nd Street, passed Naylor Gardens, then took a left on Polk. Deserted. No moon or stars; most all of the streetlamps shot out. A few dimly lit windows hinted at the location of several three-story garden apartments, which otherwise would've been camouflaged by the darkness.

When he'd asked for the street number, Mackey didn't know. He'd said he lived in apartment 201. He thought the building was either the third or fourth on the left after he turned onto Polk, and the front door was broken.

After parking across the deserted street, Tom locked the car. He suspected any attempt to protect the vehicle from theft was likely futile, and if he emerged from the building—*escaped the scene*—and his car was gone, well, he could only worry about so much at one time. Maybe the demon twins would protect the Lexus. After all, what fun would it be if the star quarterback got knocked out of the game in the first quarter?

He made his way up the steps to the third building. The

front door's lock had been ripped away, and the door offered no impediment to access.

The lobby was filthy. Trash, rolled-up dirty diapers, used condoms, and a few syringes littered the chipped tile floor. A panel of mailboxes along one wall had been partially pried from the wall, and the doors to all the individual boxes were either open or totally missing.

He climbed the steps to the second floor. Four doors, four apartments. Three of the doors displayed numbers: 202, 203, and 204. Tom knocked on the door without the number.

No answer.

He knocked harder and thought he heard the sound of movement on the other side of the door.

A muffled voice. "Yeah?"

"Looking for Reece Mackey."

"Who lookin'?"

It sounded like Mackey. "Mr. Mackey, is that you? It's Tom Booker."

"Who?"

"CJA."

No answer. Tom glanced at his watch: 11:10. He had less than an hour.

Tom was about to repeat himself when he heard the sound of a chain being unlocked. Two more clicks from other locks and his client opened the door. Mackey stepped back, allowing Tom to enter.

As he passed the man, Tom nearly choked from the overpowering stench of alcohol. He spotted a half-empty bottle of cheap gin sitting on a small Formica table that might have been white once but now was a smudgy gray. Clothes, including stained underwear, were strewn throughout the main space, including the kitchen counter and the old table. Cigarette burns peppered the frayed carpet.

Along with the gin and soiled clothing, a bag of potato chips, a tin of onion dip, and an ashtray overflowing with butts covered the table. Half of the butts were cigarettes, the rest were of the cannabis variety. An ancient TV with cables running through a ragged hole in the wall, presumably leading to a CATV connection in the adjoining apartment, sat on two stacks of magazines.

Tom glanced toward the bedroom. "So, are you alone?"

"La Chiqua comin' over later after she get off work."

"Oh, what kind of work does she do?"

Mackey gave him a curious look. "She a ho."

Okay, no problem. Just trying to make conversation here. He sat at the table without being invited. Mackey took the seat opposite him and swigged a long swallow of gin, then passed the bottle to Tom. The gracious host.

For a moment, Tom stared at the bottle lip, wondering what kind of deadly bacteria had just been deposited there. What the hell? Hopefully the gin would kill the critters. He took the bottle, nodded his thanks, and quickly sipped the gin.

The liquid tasted like rubbing alcohol. *Frank Custer's Gin* made in Akron, Ohio. *Wonder if Frank was a descendent of George?* No matter, scalping was too good for him.

At the last moment before leaving his apartment, Tom had decided to join his close friend Mr. Daniel's for a little pre-game pep rally. Just a taste to soften the edges. There'd only been a couple of shots left in the bottle, so he'd drained it and hadn't been surprised that his mind and reflexes remained unaffected. But sitting across from his soon-to-be-dead client, the previously softened edges had sharpened up again, so he took another swig of Frank Custer's Gin. Really, not so bad.

"So, what you need to tell me, Booker?"

Mackey took an even longer swig, but before he could offer his guest the bottle again, Tom retrieved a quart of 101 proof Wild Turkey bourbon from his briefcase. He'd decided at the last minute it might be a good idea to bring a peace offering for his client, a gesture that, hopefully, might lessen Mackey's natural suspicion of anybody associated with the District of Columbia criminal justice system.

"Little present for you."

Mackey's eyes lit up, and he snatched the bottle from Tom's hand. After peeling off the aluminum seal, he pulled the cork and drank as if the bottle contained spring water. Guess when one's used to Frank Custer's Gin from Akron, Ohio, everything else tasted smooth as honey.

When Mackey was finished, he stared at Tom with a curious expression. Tom realized the man couldn't remember why his lawyer was sitting across from him at his kitchen table.

Tom glanced at his watch: thirty-nine minutes. No use putting it off.

He reached for the Glock as Mackey drank some more. The bottle was almost a quarter gone. If Mackey didn't slow down he was going to drink himself to death.

Tom paused. Was that possible? Could someone drink themselves to death in thirty-nine minutes? While the man was a habitual drinker, he'd also consumed as much as a half bottle of rotgut gin. He remembered reading about a well-known singer dying of alcohol poisoning. Her death had focused attention on the subject, and while Tom recalled very few of the details, he knew time was critical—the more one consumed in a short period of time, the greater the likelihood the body couldn't metabolize the alcohol, and death would result.

Tom released his grip on the Glock and studied the man sitting across the table. Mackey's eyes were glassy and he swayed in his seat.

"Good stuff, right?" asked Tom.

Mackey responded with a lazy smile. "Real good."

"Help yourself, help yourself."

While Mackey took another swig, Tom got up from his chair and walked to the tiny kitchen. He slipped on a pair of latex gloves, then opened one cabinet drawer after another until he found what he was looking for—a 20 oz. plastic Redskins cup. "Hey, Redskins fan. Me too."

He returned to the table and filled the cup with bourbon.

"Here you go. Hail to the Redskins."

"Thank you, brutha." Mackey took the cup and drained a quarter of it in one swallow.

"Taste good? Have some more."

"Better lay off for a bit, know what I'm sayin'? Shit's got a bite."

"I hear you, man. Your TV work?"

Mackey fumbled around, looking under a clump of damp t-shirts on the table. He found the remote and handed it to Tom. Fortunately, he was too far gone to notice the plastic gloves. Or maybe that's what he thought the skin of white people looked like.

"Got to eat some grease to soak up the hooch." He jammed a handful of chips into his mouth.

Tom wasn't happy about the chips soaking up anything in Mackey's stomach, but there was nothing he could do about it. Hopefully, the salt would make him thirsty. He turned on the TV and saw the Comcast logo appear on the screen. He flipped to ESPN. They were running a tape of Maryland's win that afternoon over Penn State. In the lower right corner of the screen, Comcast showed the local time and temperature. Tom compared the Comcast time to his watch; Comcast was two minutes faster. It was 11:48. He pulled his cell phone from his pocket. Comcast was right.

"You follow the Terps?" asked Tom.

"Oh, yeah. Got a second cousin, played tight end for them while back."

Tom saw him take another long drink. Maybe the salty chips were working. Except the bag was now empty. Tom got up and found a jumbo bag of pretzels in the fridge next to a six-pack of Miller and three tins of onion dip. He quickly opened the bag and poured a pile of pretzels onto the table in front of his client.

Mackey's movements were slow and uncoordinated, and he had to squint to focus on the pretzels. Something clicked and he put one in his mouth and swallowed, then immediately took a long swig from the Redskins cup.

"Did you see that catch?" asked Tom. Mackey was having trouble seeing anything. Comcast time: 11:54. Six minutes.

This wasn't working. He'd have to use the gun. Would it be easier to pump a bullet into the brain of a man if he were drunk and would likely feel no pain?

Tom popped a pretzel into his mouth. "Damn, these pretzels are good." He put a pretzel into Mackey's hand. The man stared at it for a moment then ate it. Another long drink from the Redskins cup. Little less than two inches left in the bottom of the cup.

Tom grabbed the bottle of gin. "Touchdown! You see that?" A commercial for Bud ran on the screen, but Mackey couldn't tell. Tom clinked the bottle against the Redskins cup.

A toast. It took Mackey a long moment to understand. Then he smiled.

"Tushdown." He drained the cup.

Tom immediately poured more bourbon into the cup, but Mackey pushed it away. Tom did a quick calculation. Twenty ounces. Added on to the long swigs he'd taken from the bottle. Added on to Frank Custer's Akron gin. Was that enough?

Tom again tipped the gin bottle against the cup. "Touchdown!"

Mackey reached out for the cup, then his eyes rolled back and his head flopped onto the table. He was out cold.

Out cold, but not dead.

Tom felt his pulse. Weak, uneven beats, but still there. He glanced at the TV. Two minutes.

Tom figured it had to take some time for the alcohol to get into Mackey's bloodstream. But how much time? More than two minutes?

Mackey was making gurgling noises, like he was having trouble breathing. But he *was* still breathing. Tom watched intently, and it appeared the breathing was becoming more erratic.

He glanced at the TV. Comcast time: 11:59. He couldn't wait, couldn't take the chance.

He pulled the Glock from his pocket. Tom's own breathing

was erratic, and it wasn't from the alcohol. Comcast didn't offer the time in seconds, so he checked his watch. Forty-five seconds. His palms were wet and slippery. He needed two hands to steady the gun as he raised it to Mackey's temple.

Wait. He remembered. No blood spatter. He stood up and stepped back from the table. Both hands were shaking heavily now. What if he missed? He'd have to fire more than once and—it hit him. The sound. *He hadn't planned on dealing with the sound. Shit!* His eyes searched the room for a pillow. That's what they always used in the movies. No pillow. He could get one from the bedroom—no time.

He stepped over to the TV and turned up the volume as high as it could go. The football fans' cheering filled the room, like they were cheering for him. *Gooooo Tom! Puuuuull the trigger!* He was on the field at the one-yard line. *Time's running down, Joe. Just a few seconds on the clock. No time-outs left. Can Booker score? The fans are in a frenzy. Here he goes—*

Tom willed himself to pull the trigger.

Murder's a sin, Tom.

He told himself Mackey had killed another man.

Murder's a sin, Tom.

Mackey was a despicable human being and deserved to die. But slumped over with his face on the table, the man looked so helpless.

Murdering a defenseless, unconscious man's a sin, Tom.

Tom thought of Janie. His finger tightened. Tears poured from his eyes. He had to do it.

Pull the damn trigger!

Then Mackey vomited. Tom saw him gagging, though he remained out cold. The man couldn't breathe, he was unconscious and choking on the vomit. A thick yellow liquid dripped from his nostrils and dribbled from the sides of his mouth, but none projected out. His chest shivered in three rapid beats searching for oxygen, but his air passages were blocked.

Then his eyes flew open, looking straight at the gun in Tom's hand. Was there a glint of recognition?

More gagging, one last gasp, then his eyes glazed over.

Tom rushed back to the table and felt for a pulse. Nothing.

Reece Mackey had choked to death on his own vomit.

Tom glanced at the TV.

Comcast time: 12:00.

CHAPTER 24

Tom was almost home and still hadn't received a message from the Doublemint twins. He'd turned off the TV in Mackey's apartment, then exited quickly. Didn't want La Chiqua popping in after a long night at the office and finding him with her freshly deceased boyfriend.

He'd considered taking the bottle of Wild Turkey with him, but figured forensics would likely be able to tell the contents of Mackey's stomach contained bourbon as well as gin. Again, hide in plain sight. He'd visited his client to prepare for trial and taken him a bottle of whiskey as a gesture to encourage his client to trust him. Mackey had consumed a couple of drinks while they talked, but when Tom left, Mackey, while a little woozy, appeared okay. Of course, the likelihood of him even being interviewed was low. La Chiqua would find her man dead from alcohol poisoning. Good riddance. End of story.

Where were they? Maybe all that fire and brimstone caused interference. He needed to know Janie was saved. He needed to reconfirm the kids from hell were real, to reconfirm he hadn't just murdered a man for no reason. But did he really kill Reece Mackey? The man had drunk himself to death; all Tom did was offer the man a friendly drink. *Right.*

By the time he entered his apartment, he still hadn't received any message from the underworld. His hands shook and he needed a drink. He headed straight for the fridge and popped open a beer. Downed it in one swig, then reached for another, his last can. He hung up his jacket; no need to worry about blood.

His hands still shaking, he stripped off his clothes and, after setting his phone on the bathroom vanity, stepped into the shower. As the near-scalding water pelted his skin, his legs buckled and he slid down the tiled walls. He sat there slumped under the shower, bawling his eyes out, until the water turned cold.

***

Three hours later he lay awake, staring at the ceiling. Almost four a.m. and no word from Chad and Brit. He felt a compulsion to call Father Sheran. Good news, Matt. Didn't shoot the guy. Just shared a couple drinks. Very friendly. Watched the game. How 'bout them Terps? Poor fellow died from his own excesses, end of story.

Murder's a sin, Tom.

After another forty-five minutes, he finally fell asleep.

He awoke to a loud click. He checked his watch. Almost eleven a.m. Damn, he'd slept for seven hours.

The click came from the TV. He'd never turned it on. Immediately wide awake, he sat straight up as the images of Chad and Britney appeared on the screen. They were walking down a suburban street on a sunny day. The street looked familiar. Was it Poplar Drive? The big white house on the corner—sure looked like Poplar, two streets over from his old Arlington house.

The couple smiled and waved to Tom as they approached three girls skipping rope on the lawn of a two-story brick rambler. One of the girls twirling the rope was Janie. Emma Wong, aka Emma 2, held the other end of the rope. Angie looked on as an African-American girl—had to be Abby Jackson—easily jumped in rhythm as the rope spun under her feet.

Brit spoke to Janie.

"Hi, mind if I hop in?"

Janie shrugged. "Sure."

Brit timed the swing and jumped into the arcing rope with Abby. She chanted in sing-song in time with the twirling rope.

"TWINK-le IS my CAT, SHE'S a YEL-low TAB-by; SHE'S so HAP-py NOW be-CAUSE, TOM saved MY friend AB-by!"

Chad clapped enthusiastically. Brit jumped out of the rope swing. The two of them waved to the girls and continued walking down the sidewalk.

The picture focused on the back of their two heads. Without missing a step, both heads swiveled 180 degrees. Chad grinned at Tom. "Thanks for Reece."

Brit gave him a finger wave. "Still owe two."

The heads swiveled back and the two happy demons continued walking down Poplar Drive.

CHAPTER 25

Tom checked the obituaries in the *Post* on Sunday and again Monday morning. No mention of the untimely passing of one Reece Mackey, a good sign. Surely, if foul play had been suspected, a story would've appeared.

All day Monday, Tom was assigned to handle arraignments for the first time by himself. Fortunately, the judge was sympathetic to his rookie status, and the AUSA wasn't a jerk, so there were very few hiccups. He'd met Eva for a sandwich at a shop across the street from the courthouse. He'd thought she'd be proud of him when he told her how smoothly things had gone during the morning session, but no pat on the head. Shanny was leaving PDS, and Eva admitted being preoccupied with her application for the opening.

As they walked back to court after lunch, he received a call from Zig reminding him about the big sixtieth birthday bash for Bat Masterson that evening. Every member of the firm was expected to attend. Zig sounded excited. Not only would Bat's colleagues be there, but also the upper echelon of the city's political establishment.

As Zig was hanging up, he added, "and you can bring a date."

That he in all likelihood would be spending the rest of his life behind bars gave Tom a level of courage he otherwise would not have exhibited.

"So, that was my friend, Zig. My firm's hosting a sixtieth birthday party for the senior partner—"

'Bat Masterson."

"Right. Anyway, it's tonight and I know this is late notice, but I wondered if you'd have any interest in coming with me?"

"I'd love to."

"You would?"

She smiled. "What time?"

***

At seven p.m. he picked up Eva at her apartment in Southwest near the waterfront. When she opened the door, he struggled to hold his jaw from dropping. She looked stunning—a low-cut, emerald-green sleeveless sheath, six-inch heels, shimmering hair falling loosely to her shoulders.

"You look great."

"Thanks. Don't get a chance to polish up very often and, I'll admit, it was fun."

Unfortunately, the drive to the Four Seasons only took fifteen minutes; he would've loved nothing more than driving around the beautiful city alone with her for an hour or so. Most important, her presence temporarily diverted his mind from the clock ticking in the back of his head.

When they arrived, the doorman opened Eva's door. Tom hurried around the car so he could offer his hand to assist her exiting the vehicle. Her hand felt strong, yet soft. When she stood, she momentarily lost her balance. Tom grabbed her and she fell forward into him. She laughed as he held her.

"I'm not used to the heels."

He held her a moment longer than necessary, and she didn't seem to mind. She steadied herself, smiled up at him, then took his arm.

Once inside the lobby, they found their way to the Corcoran Ballroom by following the well-dressed couples streaming down a wide corridor. Tom recognized many of them as politicians he'd seen from time-to-time on the Sunday morning talk shows.

Unlike many other hotel ballrooms, where one had the feel-

ing he was in a wallpapered airplane hangar, the Corcoran somehow made space for 500 feel intimate. And with the firm picking
up the tab, no expense was spared to fete a man who was not only
a former governor, attorney general, and now the senior partner of
one of the most prestigious firms in the world, but also a possible
future president. An orchestra played on a makeshift stage, while
couples drank, exchanged the latest political gossip, and danced
around a spacious dance floor.

Tom felt the energy in the air, and he concluded by Eva's expression, she shared the sensation.

"How about an adult beverage?" he asked.

"Sounds good."

As they walked toward one of the many bars positioned
around the room, Tom couldn't help but notice, despite being
among many very attractive women dressed in their finest, virtually every male head swiveled to see the woman in the green dress.

The line was short, and they quickly reached the bartender,
a middle-aged man with a pencil moustache and a snooty expression. His name-tag read: Marcel. Marcel offered Eva a smarmy
smile and held up a bottle of white wine.

"May I pour the lady a glass of our Grand Cru Puligny-Mon-
trachet?"

"Thanks, but I'll take a Bud if you've got it."

At that moment, Tom wondered if anyone would notice him
dropping to a knee and proposing. Marcel's expression froze for a
moment. He responded with clenched teeth.

"I believe we have a few bottles of Heineken here, or if you
wish I can send someone—"

"A Heinie would be fine," responded Eva.

"Make that two," said Tom.

Marcel dug deep under the bar, retrieved two green bottles,
and popped the tops. "Would the lady like a glass, or would she
prefer to drink from the bottle?"

"Oh, a glass, absolutely," responded Eva. "After all, this is a
classy joint."

Marcel probably set a record for the fastest one can pour a beer into a glass, then quickly greeted the couple in line behind them.

They only made it a few steps away from the bar before the giggles came.

"Did you see his face?" asked Eva.

"Worried he might stroke out." God, he liked this girl. *God?* His expression sobered. Was there really a God who would allow innocent children to die, who would force a man to kill another human being as some sort of—? *Some sort of what? A cosmic board game? My piece can score more kills than your piece?*

"Tom, are you all right?"

Before he could respond, Zig intersected them. He had Marcie on his arm.

"There you are. And this must be Eva." Introductions all around.

"Marcie works for Senator Guthrie," Tom told Eva.

"From what I read, she has a bright future."

"Speak of the devil," said Zig, gesturing toward an attractive blond chatting with the guest of honor. Appearing to be in her mid-forties, the senator was accompanied by a tall man, a few years older, with curly brown hair streaked with silver at the temples.

"She's amazing," gushed Marcie. "She and Bill are always so gracious to even us lowly staffers."

"I've heard lots of talk about her being VP material," said Zig.

"Masterson-Guthrie would look great on a bumper sticker," Marcie added.

Tom spotted Jess across the room. She saw him and waved. Tom waved back. She appeared anxious. Maybe she was upset seeing him with another woman.

"Who's that?" asked Eva.

"Marcie's roommate. Jess also works for Senator Guthrie. We dated a couple of times." He tried to convey by his tone that it wasn't a big deal.

Marcie checked her watch. "Time to start the show." She excused herself, walked across the room, and whispered in Senator Guthrie's ear, then nodded to the orchestra leader.

The orchestra struck up "Boomer Sooner," the University of Oklahoma fight song. Tom joined in the heavy applause as Senator Guthrie, with a politician's practiced wave and smile, stepped to the microphone.

"Thank you so much for that kind welcome. Before I introduce our guest of honor, there's someone else I must recognize. Politicians' spouses often pay a heavy price, and I could not be more fortunate than to be married to such a wonderful, understanding husband and super dad to our twin boys—Bill Guthrie." Bill waved, hugged his wife, and the crowd applauded.

"But Bill and I are here tonight to honor two of our closest friends, Bat and Mary Masterson." Loud cheers. "Bat served our country honorably as a Marine officer in Desert Storm, as governor of some backwater state, forget the name"—the crowd laughed—"and until recently, as the nation's chief law enforcement officer. Since then, he's led one of the most influential law firms in the country. It's the worst-kept secret in Washington that Bat's on the short list to be the party's nominee for president in two years. Without further ado, please welcome the birthday boy, and, hopefully, the next president of the United States, Bat Masterson!"

Tom clapped politely. He glanced over at Zig who, with an adoring expression, was attempting to applaud louder than anyone else in the room. Tom had heard Zig refer to Bat as a rock star, and his friend was treating him as one. Bat bounded up on stage with his wife, Mary, two adult children, and five grandchildren trailing behind. Bat bent his wife over for a theatrical kiss, which ramped up the applause volume even higher.

As Bat began his remarks, Tom felt a tug at his coat. He turned to see Jess. She seemed highly agitated.

"I need to talk to you," said Jess.

Tom glanced at Eva, who was straining to maintain a blank, disinterested expression. "Sorry, but this isn't a good—"

"Now!" pressed Jess. "And I don't care about your fancy new girlfriend, I just need—"

"Jess," Tom spoke more sharply than he'd intended. People with disapproving looks were turning toward them, and the last thing he needed was a scene in the middle of Bat Masterson's speech.

"Jess, what's wrong?" asked Marcie. Her tone conveyed more annoyance than concern for her roommate.

"Shhhh!"

Tom turned to see Zig with his finger to his lips. "Sorry," Tom whispered.

Jess ignored Zig. "Something bad's happened, and I don't know what to do."

"What? What happened?"

She froze, her eyes focused over Tom's shoulder. He could think of no better way to describe her expression than terrified.

He followed her gaze, but everyone's back was toward them, watching and listening to Bat use his legendary oratory skills to keep all in the room enthralled. Tom thought he saw Senator Guthrie tilt her head and smile directly at Jess, but no, she was smiling at everyone.

When he turned back, Jess grabbed his lapels and pulled him close, knocking him off balance. She whispered, "Tom, I need a lawyer, and you're the only—"

Angry and embarrassed, Tom pushed her away. She tripped and fell on her back. Guests standing nearby gasped.

Mortified, Tom reached down to help her up. "Sorry, didn't mean to—"

Jess climbed to her feet and, with one last plaintive look at Tom, disappeared into the crowd.

CHAPTER 26

Tom had been in his familiar late-night position for almost two hours—lying on his back in bed, wide awake, staring at the ceiling. This time he was accompanied by a bottle of his good friend, Dr. Daniel's, to help him go to sleep. He'd briefly recalled his post-orange puke vow, but this was different. Dr. Daniel's would help him get the sleep his body needed. Medicine, that's all.

He'd had a great time with Eva at the party. After Bat's uplifting remarks, everyone had been in a good mood. He and Eva had never left the dance floor, and he believed she'd enjoyed herself as much as he had. When he held her in his arms, he felt like he was back at his high school prom, trying to ascertain whether the girl's closeness was anything more than standard dance position. Then, toward the end of the evening, he received from Eva what he'd been hoping for—that squeeze of her arm against his back, paired with a nuzzle under his neck.

He couldn't wait to drive her home. Not that he'd expected an invite to spend the night; in fact, strange as it seemed, he hoped she wouldn't extend such an offer. He didn't want to believe she was the kind to jump into the sack on the first date.

It turned out she didn't invite him in, but did give him a good-night kiss that was definitely more than perfunctory. The best thing about his time with Eva was its power to temporarily numb his mind to the horror he'd have to face in less than two weeks.

Keyword: temporary. Now the fairy dust had blown off and

he was back to reality. He glanced over to his bedside table. Mr. Glock, no doubt also wide awake, rested next to an empty cocktail glass with traces of his other pal, Dr. Daniel's. He knew he should hide the weapon, but at night he felt a sense of comfort having the gun nearby. Not that he was concerned about an intruder, or wanted easy access if he decided to blow his brains out. Rather, he viewed Mr. Glock as his partner, his sidekick, buds till the end.

"Hail to the Redskins—" His phone. He retrieved the phone from the bedside table and checked the screen. Jess. The last thing he needed was a clinger going nutso because his view of their relationship didn't match hers. But he couldn't shake the image of her face—the fear appeared genuine.

He answered. "Do you know what time it is?"

"Tom, please. I need to see you. Now. Tonight." Her voice sounded nearly frantic.

"Let me repeat. Do you know what time—?"

She responded as if she hadn't heard him. "Look, I'm sorry if I embarrassed you in front of your date. This has nothing to do with you and me."

"Then what? And why can't it wait till the morning?"

"I know something I'm not supposed to know. They want it. So I hid—"

"You hid what? What do you know? Is Marcie there?"

"She's spending the night at Zig's. I don't want to, I *can't* be drawn into it. I don't know what to do and you're the only—"

He could tell she was crying. He was awake anyway, and his curiosity had been piqued. "Okay, okay. Put on a pot of coffee."

"Thanks. And Tom, if for some reason...well, just in case someone's listening, remember doo-wop. Please hurry."

She hung up.

Doo-wop? What the hell?

***

Forty-five minutes later, he found a parking space over a block away from Jess' townhouse complex. He parked and took another swallow from Dr. Daniel's bottle—just a sip this time, as he'd been cognizant as he drove down Connecticut Avenue that he'd had a bit of trouble staying in his lane.

He walked toward Jess' place. The complex consisted of four separate, white-brick buildings, each containing three residences. Jess' place was the center unit in the farthest building from his car.

Approaching, he thought he saw movement near her building, possibly the shadow of a moving figure. He looked harder, but in the darkness it was difficult to tell. By the time he got closer, the shadow had disappeared.

As Tom passed the block of residences next to Jess' building, he vaguely sensed he was having trouble walking in a straight line, but found if he really concentrated—

A light came on in the window of the first townhouse. The door opened and an older, heavyset woman wearing curlers and a housecoat let a tiny white dog out the door to pee on the postage stamp lawn. The dog spotted him, yipped, and charged.

"Lester, you get in here this instant before you wake the whole damn neighborhood!" The dog reluctantly returned to its master. The woman scooped up Lester in one hand and closed the door.

When Tom reached Jess' building, he noticed no lights were on in her unit or the units on either side of hers. Hardly surprising, since it was almost three in the morning. With the help of a railing, he climbed the short flight of stairs to her front door. In consideration for the sleeping neighbors, he elected to ring the doorbell instead of knocking.

He heard the chimes sound inside the unit. He waited, but no one answered. He tried again. Nothing.

Heck with the neighbors. He was tired and pissed at himself for giving in to Jess. He knocked harder. Again, no response. Probably in the bathroom, he thought.

He waited about five minutes, then again rang the bell. No one opened the door. He retrieved his cell phone, scrolled to recent calls, and found her number. He was about to hit the call button when he paused.

Screw her. She'd dragged him out of bed just to play games? He was nuts to listen to the crazy bitch. Never again.

***

"...*Braves on the war path...*" He woke from a dreamless sleep with a splitting headache. Afraid his anger at Jess would've kept him awake when he returned from Foggy Bottom, just the opposite happened—he'd fallen asleep as soon as his head hit the pillow.

If it was Jess, he wouldn't answer. No, on second thought, if it was Jess, he'd unload on her, and convey as plainly as he was able that he had no intention of ever seeing her again.

But it was Zig. When he spoke, his voice sounded ragged.

"Jess is dead."

It took five full seconds for Tom to process what he thought he'd heard. "What are you talking about? I spoke to her, what, four or five hours ago?"

"She's been murdered."

CHAPTER 27

Suddenly, Tom was wide awake. "Start over."

"Marcie spent the night with me, and had to go back to their place early this morning to dress for work. She found Jess in their apartment with a bullet in her head. She called 911, then called me. I'm over here now; Marcie's kind of in shock. Hell, we're both in shock."

Tom struggled to the kitchen and on his third try, was able to insert the K-Cup into his coffee maker. "I can't believe it. We just saw her last night at the party."

"What time did she call you?" asked Zig.

"Hang on." Tom found his pants and, after fumbling through the pockets, retrieved his cell phone. "Uh, 2:49 a.m."

"What did she want at that hour?"

"Good question. She said she needed legal advice and insisted she talk to me in person. Said she needed to show me something."

"What?"

"Got me." He was about to tell Zig he'd attempted to visit Jess, but held off. No reason for anybody to know he'd been there, and it would be unfair to put Zig in a compromising position if questions were later asked.

The familiar *fizzzz* signaled his coffee was ready, and he gulped down half the cup. Tom now remembered the shadowy figure disappearing into the darkness. "How'd the murderer get in? Anybody see him?"

"They got the forensic guys over here, but no sign of forceful entry."

"I can't believe Jess would let a stranger into her house at any time, but particularly at that hour."

"I overheard a cop telling the homicide detective there may've been a witness who saw a guy who appeared intoxicated approaching Jess' house. Marcie and I are in the living room now. They don't want us moving around and disturbing anything. Looks like the place has been tossed."

Tom still had a tough time processing the news. "So they're assuming this was a burglary gone bad?"

"Marcie says Jess didn't have anything of real value. Maybe a few pieces of costume jewelry, but they're still here. She said when she found the body, Jess was fully dressed, not in her nightclothes. No outward sign of sexual assault."

"Jesus."

"Sick bastard. Hope they fry his ass and send him to hell. If there is a hell."

Oh, there's a hell, thought Tom.

Definitely a hell.

***

Tom adjusted the desk chair, lowering it to accommodate his height. One of the other PDS attorneys had to go on maternity leave, so he temporarily inherited her tiny desk in her tiny cubicle. He'd already explored the few drawers and found tissues, nail polish, lip gloss, Motrin, eyeliner, and more lip gloss. It wasn't a desk, it was a bathroom cabinet.

After three cups of coffee, dry Cheerios, and three Motrin borrowed from the new mother, Tom's brain was back in the functioning mode. He stared at the stack of arraignment files. He had to be in court in thirty minutes, and needed to go through the records to see if he could locate another Reece Mackey, some scumbag whose life he was willing to sacrifice to save his daughter. But all he could think about was Jess. She'd been killed in the forty-five minutes or so it had taken him to get dressed and drive to Foggy Bottom. His first thought had been that the murder was connected to whatever she'd wanted to discuss with him. Maybe in sacking her apartment the killer wasn't looking for valuables, but whatever it was she'd hid. Maybe—okay, he had to force Jess from his brain and concentrate.

He'd made it through four files, the most serious an unarmed B&E, when Eva popped her head over the divider.

"Got a second?" she asked.

He followed her into her office, garnering a dirty look as they passed DTA, and closed the door. Eva's good-night kiss seemed like it happened weeks ago instead of the previous night. He'd passed her in the hallway earlier, and they both had greeted each other very professionally. But now, in the privacy of her office, he wasn't sure how she'd react and so he remained standing.

As she walked past him to her desk, she briefly squeezed his hand, then took a seat. He followed suit and sat in the single uncomfortable chair facing her.

"Have a bit of news," she said.

"Me too. You go first."

"Reece Mackey's dead, so looks like you're not going to get a trial in before your pro bono term's up. Unless we find one of the other attorneys who'll agree to give you something from their docket, which is always possible."

Tom did his best to show shock. "Dead? How?"

"Mackey was a known alcoholic and he apparently drank himself to death."

"Jeez, when?"

"Over the weekend. Saturday night, Sunday morning."

Tom knew his next speech had to be Oscar-worthy. "Wow, must've been soon after I left him." He cringed inside, waiting for her to respond.

"You saw Mackey over the weekend?"

"Yeah. Wanted to go over his case and that's the only time he'd see me. Went to his place—pretty rough, by the way. He was deep into the hooch when I arrived. Gin, I think. Maybe vodka, can't remember. But he was intelligible."

In less than a second, he debated whether to mention the Wild Turkey. Hide in plain sight.

"I took him a bottle of bourbon as a gift. When I'd met him in a bar earlier, he was very wary of me, so I figured if I brought him a bottle of booze, maybe he'd trust me a little bit more. In retrospect, not very smart."

"Don't beat yourself up. How were you to know?"

"So sad. Such a waste of human life." Careful. Don't overdo it. "What was your news?"

"Even worse, I'm afraid." In this case, no acting was required. "Jess Hawkins—you remember I introduced her to you at Bat's party?"

Eva's smile never got close to her eyes. "How could I forget? Former girlfriend, right?"

"She was the roommate of my best friend's girlfriend, and we went out a couple of times as a foursome. That's it."

"Was?"

"She was killed last night."

"God, I'm sorry. What happened?"

"Apparently, a burglary gone wrong. Foggy Bottom's pretty safe, but it's still in the city."

"Any leads?"

"Possible witness. Just found out this morning from Zig, so that's all I really know."

"Again, I'm sorry."

"Thanks." He didn't know what else to say.

"So, look, I'll try to get you another trial before your time's up. In the meantime, you want to try your hand at covering px's for a few days?"

Good news. He'd have a better chance finding a potential target doing preliminary hearings where the prosecutor would be more forthcoming about the defendant's background. "You're the boss."

"On an interim basis, until they decide on a replacement for Shanny."

"They'd be crazy not to promote you." Okay, he was sucking up a little bit, but, in fact, she was the most qualified. Head and shoulders above DTA. "I had a good time last night."

"Me too."

Her phone rang. She checked the number. "Got to take this. Tell Danny I said to give you half the px files."

He left her office and found DTA hovering outside in the corridor.

"Eva said to split up the px files."

"Ooh, the newbie's getting promoted. Impressive. So, I heard you two were tearing up the dance floor at the Four Seasons last night."

"A gentleman never tells." Tom had witnessed many shit-eating grins, but had never tried one himself, so he wasn't sure how his attempt was being perceived.

Apparently, it was sufficient for his purposes, as DTA scowled and returned to his desk.

As Tom followed to collect his files, one question nagged him. Should he have told Eva about his nocturnal visit to Jess' place?

He rationalized that doing so would've only raised issues in Eva's mind about Tom's feelings toward Jess. And besides, he'd never actually seen Jess, and no one had seen—

A guy who appeared intoxicated approaching Jess' house.

Damn.

Lester.

CHAPTER 28

Tom pushed the image of the annoying white dog from his mind—
it had been dark, and it was highly unlikely the old woman would
be able to identify him.

Two hours later, he was sitting at the defense table in Willie
Cyrus Clay's courtroom. Instead of simply dividing his stack of
files in half, DTA had cherry-picked the ones involving the most
serious crimes for himself. Tom feigned disappointment and enjoyed DTA's smug look as Tom carried his stack away.

Of course, Tom didn't really want cases involving perps who
would likely remain incarcerated. He needed to follow the Reece
Mackey template—a real bad man who was charged with a minor
crime and thus out on bail.

With only a few minutes to thumb through the files, he'd
been able to identify three possibilities—Victor Ramos, Elgin
Boyd, and LaRon Walker. Each had a record of beating a murder
or manslaughter charge in the past, and was now up for a minor
misdemeanor.

Judge Clay had been around forever. Despite being long past
the mandatory retirement age of seventy, like most of his retired
colleagues, he continued to take cases on a part-time basis, both
to help chip away at the court system's expanding caseload and to
stay out of his wife's hair. Tom could tell immediately that Clay
was bored, which on balance wasn't a bad thing, since it meant he
paid little attention to the AUSA's efforts to stifle Tom's attempts
at discovery.

As he'd departed for court, Eva told him that Clay, being old school, rarely set separate bail review, and entertained motions to reduce bond at preliminary hearings, which didn't usually occur. Tom was particularly focused on Boyd and Ramos, who both remained in jail. He needed them out on the street so—so what? *So he could kill them.*

Unfortunately, Boyd had already jumped bond on two prior occasions, and Ramos was being held on an extradition warrant from Virginia, so neither of them walked out the courtroom's front door.

That left LaRon Walker. When the side door opened, Tom was shocked to see the marshal escort a black female toward his table. He quickly re-checked his file. No picture.

The bailiff announced, "US v. LaRon Walker, case No. 657452."

"My name's LaRyn, not LaRon."

Tom suspected that name mix-ups were not unheard of, as the clerk made a notation on her file with no indication the mistake was anything other than routine.

LaRyn sat next to Tom and the marshal uncuffed her. She looked like a caricature of a low-class hooker. Overweight, her butt hung out of her skintight shorts, her black hose was torn in three places, and she wore a halter top which, in its battle to restrain her heavy breasts, was hopelessly overmatched. Her eyes had the half-lidded glaze of a druggie, her hair frizzed out in a hundred directions, and her makeup resembled that of a circus clown. She was a mess.

Tom recalled from an earlier perusal of the file that she was charged with assault with a deadly weapon, blinding the victim, one LaToya Robinson, in one eye. He remembered Walker had three children, but believed his client was the father of the children. That LaRyn was the mother might make it easier to get her bail reduced.

She opened her mouth to speak, and Tom instinctively backed away. Her breath blasted an acidic mix of cheap whiskey and cigarettes. She whispered, "Where's the blond dude?"

DTA must've handled her arraignment. "He's tied up with another case, so I'm covering for him. He'll represent you at trial."

Clay nodded to Berman, the prosecutor. "Please proceed."

Berman called the arresting officer, who succinctly described a fight between LaRyn and LaToya near Logan Circle, one of the four or five spots in the city long known for scoring a quick "roadie." On the way out of town for eastbound commuters returning home to the Maryland suburbs, men would pause on the Circle; a "hostess" would hop into the passenger side of the family minivan. He'd pull into one of the dark streets spoking off from the Circle, get a quick blow job, pay the hostess twenty bucks, return to the Circle, drop her off, then hurry home to mom and the kids now completely relaxed from the stress of the day.

According to the officer, LaToya jumped in front of LaRyn when a customer stopped on the Circle. LaRyn took issue with this breach of protocol and decided to express her disappointment by removing one of her shoes and swinging its eight-inch heel as hard as she could at LaToya's face. The heel caught LaToya flush in her eye, actually partially dislodging the eye from the socket. Tom now realized if he'd read the file more carefully, he would've deduced that LaRon was of the female variety.

Tom asked a few questions, but apparently his client had admitted, indeed bragged, about her courageous stand against a violator of the sacred code of the Circle. He was much more interested in her bail. Although the thought of killing a woman gave him even deeper pause, he'd worry about that later. He had the rest of the week to find a better candidate, but the more options available on the street, the better his chances. The judge ruled that LaRyn be bound over to the grand jury. Before he could call the next case, Tom rose.

"Your Honor, I would like to address the matter of Ms. Walker's bail."

Berman interrupted him. "Your Honor, Ms. Walker has a record, including juvie, going back six years."

Tom thought, *Six years didn't sound all that bad.* He glanced at the file—she was only nineteen years old.

Berman continued. "Most are for sol pros, simple assaults. But she has one B&E, and two years ago she was charged with homicide."

"Two years ago she was a juvenile, Your Honor, and her juvenile record can't be used against her now that she's an adult," said Tom. He had no idea whether he was right, but he expressed his position with the appropriate amount of certitude.

"The original charge was murder one," said Berman. "Her case was transferred to adult court. There was a chain of custody screwup with the murder weapon, so the government agreed to return her to the juvenile system, where she pled to manslaughter. Served a year in juvie."

Tom needed some more information on the murder charge, not to assist him in making the case before Judge Clay, but in making the case to himself, if killing her was his only hope to save Janie.

"I'm sorry, Your Honor, but my file has no information on the manslaughter charge. Perhaps Mr. Berman could enlighten me." Smith gestured to Berman.

"Of course, Your Honor," said Berman. He read from his file. "At the age of seventeen, the defendant broke into the home of one Twyla Richards—"

"I ain't break in. The lock was broke an' I just opened it," said LaRyn. Clay glared at her. "I'm just sayin'." Tom put a restraining hand on her arm.

Berman continued. "Whereupon she found Ms. Richards in bed with one William Riggins, aka Acie Cat. She brutally attacked Mr. Riggins with a knife, inflicting multiple stab wounds. Mr. Riggins was transported to DC General, where he was pronounced dead."

"I ain't try to kill Acie, just wanted to cut off his dick 'cause he was fuckin' Twyla same time I'm carryin' his baby. He just wiggled around so much, ended up with a few extra slices, the cheatin' piece of shit."

Clay banged his gavel. "Ms. Walker, another outburst from you, and I'll step you back. Understand?" She nodded.

"Clearly, a crime of passion," said Tom. "Ms. Walker was a juvenile, her judgment no doubt impaired by the fact she was pregnant at the time, and obviously distressed by what she viewed as a betrayal by the child's father. I see no record of her failing to appear. She has three children who need their mother. I ask the court not to compound the tragedy that has befallen LaToya Robinson by prejudicing three innocent children."

Clay paused, then eye-locked with LaRyn. "If, against my better judgment, I let you out, you promise to stay off the Circle and show up whenever Mr. Booker here says he needs you?"

She nodded solemnly. "Yes, Your Honor."

"Defendant's released on her personal recognizance." He banged his gavel. "Adjourned for lunch."

As Tom gathered his papers, the matronly court clerk smiled at him.

"Good job, Mr. Booker."

"Thanks."

He noticed her hairpin was in the shape of a poodle. An image of the little white dog again pierced his thoughts. Arguably, he had an obligation to tell the police he saw the shadow of someone escaping from Jess' building. Conceivably, it might help with nailing down the time the crime had occurred. But he couldn't identify the individual, and it was possible all he witnessed were shadows playing tricks on him.

The last thing he needed now was getting bogged down as a potential witness in Jess' case when he was busy finding someone to murder.

CHAPTER 29

Over the rest of the week, Tom was able to take Janie and Angela out to dinner twice, something unheard of when he'd been working for the firm. Feeling his daughter's uncompromising love reinforced his resolve to do whatever was necessary to save her.

He continued handling preliminary hearings, hoping for candidates better suited than LaRyn for his purposes, his purposes being to die in a little over a week. But Judge Sylvia Hagan had taken over for Clay, and she was a real ball-buster. Wouldn't listen to any bail reduction arguments, a problem since those clients who were already on the streets had not committed any offense that, according to the Booker Code of Criminal Ethics, warranted the death penalty. He was not going to murder a young mother of three children. He would have to find someone else.

But by Friday, LaRyn remained the only candidate. At the conclusion of her bail hearing, he'd expected some form of thank you for getting her out of jail. He received nothing but dead eyes and a permanent scowl. She'd reluctantly given him her contact information, and he'd arranged to meet her at the end of the next week, hoping in the meantime he'd find a more suitable victim. LaRyn had murdered another human being and received only a slap on the wrist. Still, he didn't think there was any way he could pull the trigger. He remembered his daughter's embrace, feeling her arms around his neck. He couldn't allow the choice to come down to LaRyn or Janie.

He'd seen Eva every day, but always on a professional basis.

They'd arranged to go to dinner Friday night, and he was putting on his jacket when there was a knock at the door. Probably Zig. He'd told his friend about the date, and Zig had wormed his way in, arranging for the four of them to have a nice dinner at 1789 in Georgetown. Tom had offered resistance, selfishly wanting to have Eva to himself, but Zig reminded him that it would be the first time Marcie would have an opportunity to get out since Jess' death, and Tom acceded. He answered the door.

Percy Castro stood in the hallway, and he didn't look happy.

"Looks like you're heading out," said Castro. "Guess I should've called first."

Competing thoughts snapped through Tom's mind. Should he apologize, tell Castro he's late, and schedule a later appointment? This approach would give him time to collect his thoughts. Or should he invite him in, get a sense of what he wants, then cut the meeting short because he had to leave. He chose option two.

"I have a date, Detective, but I can give you a quick minute." He stepped aside and Castro entered. Tom purposely remained standing. He didn't want Castro to get comfortable. "What can I do for you?"

"Just following up some loose ends, Counselor, seeing as you have a connection to three recent deaths in the city." Tom purposely didn't respond. "You were with Gino Battaglia minutes before he shot himself. You were with Reece Mackey before he drank himself to death. And a check of phone records shows you were called by Jessica Hawkins an hour or so before she was shot."

Tom didn't have to fake his chagrin. "It's been an unreal several weeks. Any lead on Jess' murder?"

Castro didn't answer directly, which unnerved Tom. "I ran into Ms. Stoddard at the courthouse this morning. She asked about the Jessica Hawkins investigation and mentioned she'd met the young woman at Bat Masterson's birthday party. Said you and Jessica had a pretty intense argument."

"Wasn't really an argument," said Tom. "I had gone out with Jess several times, but it wasn't serious, at least on my part. She was at the party as an aide to Senator Guthrie, and her housemate's dating my best friend."

"All one happy family," Castro responded with a cold smile. He slowly took in Tom's apartment like a video camera panning, recording the scene.

"So, should I gather she was jealous of your dating Ms. Stoddard?"

"That's an exaggeration, Detective. She said she needed legal advice and was insistent. A nice girl, but a little flighty, if you know what I mean."

"Ms. Stoddard confirmed Ms. Hawkins' call to you later that evening. You told Ms. Stoddard that Jessica wanted you to come see her immediately, but you elected not to do so. Is that correct?"

Now what? Should he perpetuate the lie and hope it would stick or come clean? If he told the truth, Eva would learn of it and get pissed. He didn't want to do anything to upset her, not this early in what he hoped might be a long-term relationship. That is, as long-term as one could enjoy while on death row for murder.

"That's correct."

"Did she tell you what she wanted to talk about?"

"No, but she seemed scared. And she said she needed to tell me where to find something. Didn't say what it was. She was afraid her phone might be bugged. As I said, a little flighty."

Castro paused, seemingly deep in thought. "By the way, we found traces of cornstarch, magnesium oxide, and epichlorohydrin on the index finger of Gino Battaglia's right hand."

Tom's expression showed his genuine confusion.

"Powder commonly used to keep latex gloves from sticking. Interesting thing is, we found the same trace elements on a bottle of Wild Turkey resting next to Reece Mackey's body."

Tom fought to control his body, particularly his facial muscles, doing his best to force them from belying his guilt.

Castro continued. "Seeing's how you were with the two deceased shortly before they died, thought you might have an idea about the gloves."

Tom did a lousy job of feigning a thoughtful pause. "No, don't remember seeing any gloves."

"Do you keep latex gloves here?"

"Me?" *Of course, you, idiot. Who the hell else is he talking to?* "Nope, no gloves." He made a show of checking his watch.

"I've kept you too long. Might I surmise that you're seeing Ms. Stoddard?"

"Yes."

"Even though she's on the other side, I don't know a cop who doesn't respect her."

"I'll be sure to pass that on."

He reached out his hand. "Have an enjoyable evening, Mr. Booker."

Tom shook his hand. Another half smile from Castro, then he turned and left.

Tom looked down at his palms, wet with nervous perspiration.

CHAPTER 30

On any other occasion, Tom would've been having the time of his life. Eva, though dressed more casually, looked as radiant as she had at Bat's birthday party. Along with Zig and Marcie, they enjoyed a wonderful dinner at 1789, the iconic restaurant on the edge of Georgetown's main campus. The goal of cheering up Marcie had taken some time to achieve, but by the end of the evening, she laughed a few times at Zig's horrible jokes.

Maybe it had been his imagination, but Tom thought he saw Eva eyeing his third Jack. Was she counting drinks? He purposely didn't finish the third one and ordered iced tea instead.

During the table conversation, Tom appeared to hang on every word. He laughed at Zig's punchlines, though he had absolutely no idea what the joke was about. But all he could think about was Castro's expression when Tom denied having latex gloves in the house.

"...so then on the third day, the little boy comes out, and says, 'Mom, Mom!' And the Mom says, I know, you were peeing and a bullet came out. And the boy says, no, I was jerking off and shot the dog!"

Tom was angry at himself for not telling Eva—

"Tom?" Eva's expression showed she wasn't happy about his inattention.

"Where were you, man?" asked Zig. "We boring you?"

"Just your stupid jokes, which are as old as Methuselah." Tom's retort elicited another round of laughs, but he could see

Eva wasn't completely buying his deflection. During the rest of the dinner, Tom focused on participating in the conversation. He even told a joke of his own, which he knew was lame, but his three companions laughed politely anyway.

Exiting the restaurant, Zig suggested they walk along the C&O Canal and find a place for a nightcap. He wanted to locate a restaurant that served Mastika, a Greek liqueur he enjoyed on his trip to Mykonos and Santorini. Eva made the mistake of asking about his visit to the Greek isles, and for the entirety of the walk, Zig offered a frame-by-frame travelogue of his vacation. By the time they reached a small café by the water, even Eva had had enough.

"You know, I'm kind've beat."

"Makes two of us," said Tom. "Why don't we leave the two of you to enjoy your Mastika. Marcie, maybe you haven't heard about Zig's trip to Greece. I'm sure he'd love to tell you."

They all laughed. Tom and Eva said their good-byes and turned up Wisconsin Avenue toward the parking lot.

"I could tell you were preoccupied throughout the evening," said Eva. She hesitated a moment. "Were you thinking about Jess?"

"No, not at all. Again, I dated the girl a couple of times, that's it. I'm really sad she's dead, and I hope they find the killer. Maybe what you thought you saw was just my reaction to hearing Zig tell the same jokes he's told since I met him."

She held his gaze for a moment, and he could see she wasn't totally convinced. "Okay," she said. "Why don't we go back to my place for coffee."

***

As Tom followed Eva up the steps to her apartment building, he sensed a sexual tension between them. He told himself it was his imagination. To a girl like Eva, coffee meant coffee—nothing more.

But as they rode the elevator to her floor, he could not only feel, he could almost *see* the sexual energy filling the space between them. He touched her hand, and she squeezed it tight. In a moment, she was in his arms, her lips pressing hard against his. His arm around her shoulder, they were close to breaking into a jog as they hurried down the hallway to her apartment.

She giggled as she fumbled in her purse, searching for the key. In frustration she upended her purse, spilling its contents onto the corridor rug. As she quickly retrieved the key, Tom scooped the rest of the contents back into her purse. She inserted the key with one hand while wrapping her other around Tom's neck. The moment the door clicked open, they bulled through the door.

Once past the threshold, she kicked the door closed without breaking her embrace. They stumbled toward her living room while hungrily locking their mouths, refusing to let go. Her tongue explored his mouth while his hands caressed every curve of her body. Not willing to waste a second, they peeled off only the most essential garments. He easily lifted her off the ground with one arm, then gently lowered her to the plush carpet, covering her body with his.

His body temporarily assumed complete control and, for a time, mercifully forced from his mind all thought of anything other than the pleasure of making love to a beautiful woman.

CHAPTER 31

He spent the night and, as is always the case, after the first coupling the sex got slower and better. The next morning they arose and walked along the waterfront to the Odyssey Café for breakfast. Unfortunately, the light of day returned the clarity of his situation.

A thousand times he considered admitting that he'd—what was the word?—fibbed, not been as candid as he should have, slightly dissembled, misspoke? Okay, lied his ass off—about driving to Jess' place the night of her murder. But he reluctantly kept his lie to himself and hoped against hope that the fat lady with the annoying white dog couldn't identify him.

After breakfast, Tom walked Eva home, and after a warm kiss, they said their good-byes. He had to pick up Janie and Angela for a promised trip to the zoo, and Eva needed to go into the office to deal with administrative stuff that hadn't reached the top of the pile during the work week.

***

At the zoo, Janie and Angie, each munching a hot dog, watched enthralled as Tian Tian and Mei Xiang jostled over a long bamboo stalk. The giant pandas remained the most popular animals at the zoo. Before even visiting the exhibit, Tom had bought each of them a stuffed panda at the zoo store.

A roly-poly park guide, who resembled Smokey Bear in his khaki uniform, described the lives and habitats of the black-and-white bears to the two girls and a small group of other onlookers. Tom couldn't take his eyes off the girls. So young, so innocent.

One of the dark side effects of his nightmare had been the loss of his ability to enjoy the people and things he loved. But for a few hours with Eva, where carnality trumped everything, the monster at the edge of his thoughts was always there, banging the door to enter. The first few minutes when he and Janie greeted each other were always glorious, since her unreserved love was strong enough to keep the beast at bay. But, invariably, as their time together wore on, the monster would break through and his mind would return to black thoughts of death—how was he going to terminate another human life?

Tom planned on arriving at the office early Monday morning so he could look through files of defendants coming up for arraignments and preliminary hearings. Hopefully, he'd be able to find a more deserving target than LaRyn Walker.

Angie had finished all but the last bite of bun on her hot dog and tossed it through the fence toward the two pandas. Immediately, the guide reproached her.

"Young lady, do you eat bear food?"

Angie knew she'd done something wrong. "No, sorry—"

"You don't eat bear food because it would make you sick. People food is poison to bears. Do you want to poison our pandas?"

Angela was almost in tears.

"Look," said Tom. "She understands. Won't happen again. But putting the thought in a little girl's head that a bite of hot dog bun is going to poison the pandas is a stretch, don't you think?"

Before the guide could respond, Tom took each girl's hand and they moved on to the elephant exhibit.

But the guide's words had given him an idea.

***

That evening, Tom entered the Internet Café on Prince George Street in Annapolis, Maryland, to research poisons. He knew he couldn't use his own computer, and he'd driven forty-five minutes to the Maryland state capital where chances of anyone knowing him were slight. On the way, he'd stopped and bought a worn, black Orioles warm-up jacket at the Goodwill store on West Street.

While he hadn't spotted any security cameras either inside or outside the café, Tom took no chances and wore his sunglasses and Orioles gear into the establishment. He paid in cash, and when the young girl behind the counter asked for a credit card to hold, just in case he went over his allotted time, he professed to have forgotten his card and gave her a $100 bill instead. Before she could respond, he found a computer in the back corner, away from the handful of other patrons who appeared to view the venue more as a social gathering place than a research site.

After only a few clicks, Tom had before him more information than he could ever need regarding virtually every poison from the truly exotic to the most mundane. Seeing as he had neither the time nor the ability to obtain curare, sarin or monkshood, he focused on so-called household chemicals.

An hour later he settled on potassium permanganate, a common chemical used to clear iron from well water. If ingested in the proper dose, the chemical could cause death after ten to fifteen minutes.

The café had several small canisters mounted on the wall dispensing disinfectant wipes to clean keyboards after use. Tom made sure to wipe not only the keys, but the entire work station before leaving.

Heading back to DC, he pulled into a shopping center and ditched his Orioles jacket and cap into a dumpster behind a Kmart.

Driving west on Route 50 toward the city, he struggled to come up with a way to get his target to ingest the poison, but could come up with nothing. He had until Friday to develop a plan. Otherwise, he'd have to use Mr. Glock and make it look like some kind of drug-related killing.

What if he couldn't find a substitute for LaRyn? Would he point the gun at a nineteen-year-old mother and pull the trigger?

He didn't think he could do it.

CHAPTER 32

The next several days moved way too quickly. Tom became more anxious as no alternative candidate emerged who fit his criteria.

Tuesday, he'd obtained a different jacket and hat from the Goodwill store on Route 1 in Prince Georges County, donned his sunglasses, and purchased a half gallon of liquid potassium permanganate from a plumbing supply store in Waldorf, a town an hour southeast of the city.

He'd redoubled his efforts to find another victim, reviewing files on the desks of other PDS attorneys after hours. No matter what she'd done, he couldn't conceive of killing LaRyn Walker.

By Wednesday, he'd still come up with nothing.

At home, he'd smelled the chemical and found it had a strong, unpleasant odor. Worse, he touched a dab of the liquid to his tongue, and the taste was so bitter he immediately spit it out. No way he could get anyone to drink the potassium, even if mixed with booze. In Annapolis, he'd made a handwritten list of other possible household poisons, but all apparently had a strong taste.

What the hell was he going to do?

***

As was his routine, Thursday morning he awoke to *Good Morning America*, and kept the jabbering going on a low volume while he dressed. In the middle of the night he'd become resigned to the fact he'd have to proceed with LaRyn.

Brushing his teeth, he could hear the show's medical contributor discussing the need for parents to be aware of the most recent trend in teen drinking. Curious, he entered the living room and turned up the volume while finishing his brushing.

"It's called Butt Chugging, George. I guess we can use that word on morning TV. (chuckles) So as to speed up the inebriation process and avoid the smell of alcohol on their breath, both guys and girls will soak a tampon in booze. The guys insert the soaked tampon into their rectums, the girls into their vaginas. In the case of the girls, the slang term is P-Chugging."

"I know we can't say what the 'P' stands for on morning TV," said George. *(more chuckles)*

"When consumed orally," said the doctor, *"the beverage is subjected to stomach secretions, which partially neutralize the alcohol, and slow down its path to the brain through the bloodstream. But when alcohol is ingested directly into the rectum or vagina and moves immediately into the bloodstream, the chances of serious impairment, brain damage, or even death increase dramatically."*

A possibility? Maybe. All he had to do was convince LaRyn to stick a poison-laced tampon up her vagina. What could conceivably go wrong?

He decided he needed to act that evening instead of waiting until Friday. A million things could go wrong, and he wanted the extra time just in case. Also, the online data had been less than clear concerning how long it would take for death to occur. What if it wasn't instantaneous? What if it took hours, or even a day? The idea of death coming half a day later was appealing, since he would've been long gone. Hopefully, the cops would believe she was killed by a john or even her pimp. Did she have a pimp? Hadn't heard any mention of one, but even if not, she traveled in that netherworld where life was cheap, and there was a good chance her file would end up on the bottom of the pile. The problem, of course, was any delay in her succumbing would give her or someone who found her the opportunity to call 911.

He called LaRyn from the car. He had no problem if his number showed up on her phone log. Hide in plain sight. He'd wondered if he should buy a box of tampons, but concluded the chances of the young woman having tampons was very high, so why take a chance on another camera.

He was surprised when she answered on the first ring. He could hear traffic in the background and assumed she was working the streets. When he suggested they reschedule their session for later that evening, she put up no resistance.

***

It was near eleven when he drove north on 4th Street toward Howard University, passed U Street, and turned right on V Street. *V for vagina.* He found the dilapidated garden apartment halfway down the street, and after parking, entered the building. In one jacket pocket he carried a pint bottle of Grey Goose vodka. He'd emptied out all of the liquor and replaced it with the potassium permanganate. The smell was weird, but enough odor remained from the vodka to hopefully conceal it. On Florida Avenue he'd pulled into a gas station and, after wiping away any fingerprints, tossed the original bottle of potassium permanganate in a trash roll-off behind the building.

In the other pocket he carried his pal, Mr. Glock, just in case.

CHAPTER 33

LaRyn answered after one knock.

She looked bad—eyelids at half-mast, hair shooting out in all directions, makeup that appeared to have been applied in the dark. She swayed in the doorway, and had to hold onto the doorjamb to keep from falling.

"You the CJA, right?"

"Yeah. Tom Booker." He extended his hand. She stared at it as if she'd never seen someone offer to shake her hand before.

"What happened to the blond dude?"

"I'm the substitute. Remember, I represented you in court? Got you out of jail?" She squinted, clearly trying to focus her brain cells, then shrugged and stepped aside.

He imagined her apartment as a hovel, a carbon copy of Mackey's place, and was surprised to find the opposite was the case. A small, circular dining table separated a living room from a tiny kitchen. A short hallway led to three doors. One opened to a bathroom, the other two were closed. The living room furniture was old and the TV ancient. Still, the room appeared neat and clean. He saw a large milk glass half full of an amber liquid. Good chance it wasn't iced tea. The kitchen counter was clear, and Tom detected the faint smell of lemon typical of numerous household cleaning agents.

"Nice place."

For a moment, a flicker of life appeared in her dead eyes. "Thanks. My momma, she the assistant supervisor of housekeeping down the Marriott. She kick my ass hard if my place ain't clean. She always tell me, no matter how bad things get in your life, never too poor to buy soap, and there be no excuse for a dirty house."

When he got closer to her, he could smell the heavy booze on her breath. She was still wearing her work uniform—tight, shiny-blue shorts that left little to the imagination and a red halter top. He spotted a pair of red platform heels under a small coffee table.

She stepped into the kitchen and retrieved a half-filled bottle of bourbon, then moved unsteadily toward the table. She gestured toward the bourbon. "Uh, you want a drink? Also got a Coke in the fridge I think."

He knew he should take the Coke, but figured she would trust him more if he drank with her. He'd only take a small sip or two.

"I'll have what you're having. Thanks."

LaRyn nodded, pulled another milk glass from a cupboard, and filled it halfway with the bourbon. "First time my CJA come to me. Always had to go downtown."

"Door-to-door service," he said with a smile, then sat at the table.

"You ain't got no briefcase," she said.

"Photographic memory." He smiled and tapped his temple. "So, tell me about yourself. The more the jury likes you, the better chance of a favorable result."

"I ain't coppin' a plea?" She took a seat across from him and set the glass of bourbon in front of her.

"We'll always have that option, but given your record, my first goal is trying to keep you out of jail, and the best way to do that is either to persuade one juror there's a reasonable doubt of your guilt, or to persuade the AUSA there's a chance he might end up with an acquittal and he better cut a favorable deal."

She nodded and took a stiff drink. "What you want to know?"

Actually, the less I know about you, the easier it will be for me. "How did you get into your current profession?"

She shrugged and took another drink. "Got knocked up

when I was fifteen. Dropped out of school to take care of my baby. Figured once the baby was old enough, I'd get my GED."

"And the father?"

"He dead. Then needed some money for Sherril, she my little girl, and started workin' the Circle. Didn't need to be out late. White boys goin' home from work, they be gone by seven. If all's they wants is a blow job, I can make enough I come home early. They want more, cost more but take more time, so sometimes after seven I go down H Street, pick up a few extra clients. Mama, she take care of my babies while I'm workin'."

He needed to keep her talking, get her to look to him as something more than her lawyer. He took a sip of bourbon. "Your other children. Same father?"

"All different. James, he Vernon's daddy, he got himself a government job. Soon's he save enough, he says we gonna get married. In a church and everything."

"And James doesn't mind your current activities?"

She looked at him curiously. "You mean whorin'? James knows it's just business." Her glass, now, was almost empty. "You want to talk about that bitch, LaToya?"

"Yeah, sure. Mind if I use your bathroom?"

She pointed down the hall. Tom took his almost full glass of bourbon with him, making a show of sipping from it as he walked. He entered the bathroom and closed the door. He quickly opened the drawer under the sink and found what he was looking for—a half-filled box of tampons. He emptied almost all of the bourbon into the toilet, then filled the glass with the potassium permanganate from the Grey Goose bottle. The small amount of bourbon left in the glass was sufficient to tint the liquid amber, although much paler than the original bourbon. He assumed she wouldn't notice. He flushed the toilet, removed two tampons from the box, and returned to LaRyn.

She was drinking from her refilled glass, and Tom could see she had trouble holding the glass steady. Okay, it was showtime. He was about to speak when she looked up at him and smiled.

"I like you better than the blond dude."

Jesus God, what was he about to do? Kill this young woman because she'd tried to cut off her cheating boyfriend's penis and done a shitty job of it? No, of course not. It was either her or Janie, and Janie hadn't killed anybody. But at that moment LaRyn looked so young, little more than a child herself. The daughter of a woman working for hope, hope that someday her daughter will clean herself up, get a legitimate job, and be a real mother to her kids. The clean house showed there was something good inside this girl, something worth saving.

She'd poured some more bourbon into her glass. "Want some more?"

He couldn't take his eyes off the milk glass resting on the table in front of him, looking no more dangerous than a glass of weak iced tea. No. He couldn't do it. He needed to ask a few questions about her confrontation with LaToya, then get the hell out of there. He'd have forty-eight hours to come up with someone else. Maybe he'd just drive down to Southeast, find a dealer on a corner and blast away. A drive-by shooting like on TV. Like he'd originally planned weeks ago.

"No thanks. I have a couple of quick questions about LaToya—"

His cell phone vibrated in his pocket. He checked the screen: a video of Janie sleeping soundly in her bed filled the small frame.

And at the foot of her bed, Chad and Britney stood in their pj's with an index finger to their lips.

CHAPTER 34

Tom couldn't stop shaking. He was about to offer some inane explanation to LaRyn, when he saw she was so far gone that she hadn't noticed. His eyes reddened, he used his sleeve to wipe the tears from his cheek. *Why him? God, if you're really out there, you've got to stop this. NOW!*

God didn't stop it.

Now what? Just how does one introduce the subject of inserting an alcohol-soaked tampon into one's body orifice of choice? Maybe, given her profession, he should follow the commercial route. He took a full swig of bourbon. When he spoke, he didn't recognize his own voice. It was as if another invisible guest were seated at the table.

"So, I, uh, heard of this funny way to get high." *Oh it's funny all right. Yuk a minute.* He pulled the tampons from his pocket. LaRyn grinned.

"P-Chugg."

He heard the invisible person, the dude who kind've sounded like him, ask, "How much would it cost for us to maybe have a little P-Chugg party? Assuming you're up for it."

She swayed back and forth, her eyes now only slits. "Ain't nothin' I ain't up for, sugah." She peeled the wrapper from a tampon. "An' since you be my lawyer, I'm gonna give you a discount. Fifty bucks, baby."

Before Tom could pull out his wallet, she'd dipped the tampon into her glass.

"Wait." He quickly pulled out a fifty and set it on the table, then unwrapped the other tampon and soaked it in the pale iced tea. He watched as the combination of cotton and rayon absorbed the poison, like some deep-sea creature gorging itself until its size tripled. He used the cord to slowly lift the tampon, feeling its heavier weight. This time, there was no doubt it was his voice he heard.

"Want to switch?"

She shrugged and they exchanged tampons.

She pushed back from the table and unsnapped her shorts.

"You want to use the bathroom?"

She acted as if she hadn't heard him and slid her shorts completely off. He saw she wasn't wearing underwear; guess time was precious in her job. Her hand seemed to move in slow motion as it approached her legs.

No! Stop! Don't do it! The words didn't make their way from his brain to his mouth. In less than a second, her hand slipped between her heavy thighs, then pulled out without the tampon. It was inside her. She sat back down, not bothering to put on her shorts.

He was sure she was going to insist he poke the other tampon up his butt.

"Now, you want a blow job first?" Her words were even more slurred and she wasn't even looking at him. She appeared to be oblivious to the other tampon, to her surroundings, to him.

He got up, took his glass into the bathroom, and poured its contents down the toilet. He'd seen enough TV to know trace elements could be detected in drains and on porcelain surfaces. He opened a small cabinet under the sink and found what he was looking for. Toilet cleaner. Thank you, Mrs. Walker, for teaching your daughter at least one good habit.

He poured the blue cleaner into the toilet bowl and was about to use a brush from the cabinet to scrub the porcelain, when he hesitated. Could trace elements of the potassium permanganate cling to the bristles? Not wanting to take a chance, he replaced the brush, and used a towel to wipe fingerprints off the brush handle and the cleaner bottle. Which left the vodka bottle in his pocket. He'd need to dispose of that on the way home.

He heard a crash and returned to the living room to find LaRyn had fallen off her chair. Dark blood dribbled down her thighs. She vomited a putrid mixture of bourbon and blood.

Suddenly, he heard a tiny voice behind him. He turned to see a toddler, a little girl maybe one year old.

"Mommy?"

CHAPTER 35

Tom froze. God, where did she come from? Must've been in one of the bedrooms. LaRyn heard her daughter calling through the haze. She reached out to her child.

"Baby?"

The child, too far away from her mother's reach, began to cry. Suddenly LaRyn clutched her stomach with both hands and squealed out in pain. Tom was unable to move as he watched in horror while the tableau played out. He'd assumed death would come quickly and with little pain. Wasn't the booze supposed to anesthetize the victim while the poison did its work? She cried out again, this time louder.

Without thinking further, he reached between her legs and pulled out the tampon. Still holding the empty glass, he dropped the tampon into it. He had to do something—he couldn't let this woman die—and reached into his pocket for his phone. First choice, he could call 911 and remain on the scene. Hide in plain sight. His mind churned, searching for a story. A believable story. *He'd arrived late to consult with his client—she was a working girl, after all—and she appeared to be in a stupor. She suddenly got sick and he called for help.*

Second choice, he'd use her phone to call 911, disguise his voice, and get the hell out of there. As with Mackey, he could explain that he arrived, had his consult. When he left she appeared to be under the influence of something—what do you expect of a two-bit whore, right, guys?—but not necessarily ill. Any comments by her relating to Butt Chugging or P-Chugging would be laughed off, and attributed to the addled imagination of a drunk drug abuser.

The baby had crawled into her mother's arms. Sliding in and out of consciousness, LaRyn instinctively held her daughter tight to her breast as she continued to clutch her gut and moan in pain.

He liked the first choice better, but it all came down to the now contaminated glass he held in his hands. There was no way to dispose of it and remain in the apartment. He spotted her purse on the floor beside the couch. Using a kitchen towel to prevent fingerprints, he fished out her pink cell phone and dialed 911. He was about to speak in a falsetto voice when he thought of voice-prints. Were they reliable? Could they match a disguised voice?

"This is the 911 operator, please state the nature of your emergency."

He set the phone on the floor next to LaRyn's head. Hopeful-ly, the operator would hear her moaning in pain and trace the cell.

"This is the 911 operator, can you tell me your name? This is the 911 operator, I can hear you. Please keep this line open."

Tom snatched the fifty from the table, took his glass, and hur-ried out of the apartment.

As he closed the door, he saw the little girl staring at him with a curious look in her eyes.

CHAPTER 36

Fortunately, there were few cars on the road as Tom wound his way south toward the city. Because his mind raced in so many different directions, he drove purely on instinct. As had now become his habit—*his MO? Did he now have an MO?*—he tossed the Grey Goose vodka bottle and the empty glass with the bloody tampon into a dumpster behind a strip shopping center.

After leaving LaRyn's apartment, he'd parked in the shadows a block away, waiting for what seemed like hours—but was less than ten minutes—to confirm arrival of the emergency response vehicles. There was no way he could take a chance on her dying while waiting for help. He decided to revert to option *A*. He'd hide the glass and vodka bottle in his car and return to the apartment.

He reached for his phone. No use disguising his voice because his cell would be traceable. Needed a story. Okay, he'd explain he forgot his briefcase—he'd have to take his briefcase from the trunk back into the apartment—and returned to find his client lying in her own vomit. *Good story, Mr. Booker, except if she was incapacitated on the floor, who let you in? A toddler too short to reach the lock?* Okay, so how about—? Thankfully, just then he heard the sound of approaching sirens. He breathed a deep sigh of relief and drove off.

As he proceeded south, his thoughts turned to Saturday night. Less than forty-eight hours until the deadline. Two girls left, Emma 2 and Janie. The image from his cell screen continued to flash in his head. Chad and Britney in his daughter's bedroom.

In her bedroom. Were they really there? Or was the picture on the screen Photoshopped for his benefit? He assumed they had Photoshop capabilities in hell. After all, it was hell. They could do pretty much whatever they wanted, because it had become clear the big guy in the corner office on the top floor wasn't going to intervene.

He crossed Florida Avenue and turned right on R Street. At that hour the 15th Street intersection traffic light flashed red. He briefly slowed, but seeing no approaching cars from either direction on 15th, continued through the intersection without stopping.

Suddenly, out of the corner of his right eye Tom saw a small, dark-blue car with no headlights barreling south on 15th, heading straight for him. Instinctively, he cut the wheel hard left, swerving wildly, barely missing the blue car.

The Lexus spun out of control. Tom saw the streetlights swirling around him and for a moment his mind flashed back to his childhood, riding the Tilt-A-Whirl at the Maryland State Fair. Then he saw a steel-gray streetlight post flying directly toward him.

Then he saw nothing.

***

Then he saw a bright light. He squinted, and his vision gradually came into focus. An Asian guy in a white coat stepped back. Tom was in a hospital room. He could make out Zig and Eva standing behind the doctor.

"He's awake," said Eva.

"Welcome back," added Zig.

"Mr. Booker, you've suffered a concussion," said the doctor. "We've found no broken bones, probably thanks to the airbags. You'll need to remain overnight for observation, but there's a good chance you can go home tomorrow."

"Thanks." His throat felt raspy.

Tom's memory returned quickly—LaRyn, 911, the blue car. "My car?"

"Totaled," said Zig. "Saw the car. Doc's right. But for the airbags, Eva and I would be deciding the opening hymn for your memorial service. I want you to know I would've insisted on giving the eulogy."

Eva squeezed his hand. "God, Tom, what were you doing in that neighborhood that time of night?"

Tom faked wooziness, which wasn't at all that hard to do. "Memory's kind've blurry. Think I went to see a client. Only time she could see me."

"LaRyn Walker," said Eva. "Tech said you mentioned her name in the ambulance when you were fading in and out of consciousness."

Great. Wondered if the subject of a poisoned tampon also happened to emerge.

"Sorry, don't remember much now, but sure it'll come back to me."

"When you saw Walker, was she okay?" asked Eva.

"Okay for a drunken druggie whore, I guess. Why?"

"She must've overdosed or something after you left. They were bringing her in the same time as when you arrived at the emergency entrance."

"She all right?"

"She was alive when they carried her in."

A perky nurse poked her head in the door. "Excuse me, folks, but Doc says we need to let the patient get some rest."

"Just one more minute," said Eva.

Tom saw her and Zig exchange glances. Something was up.

Zig squeezed his shoulder. "See you tomorrow. And remind me to buy stock in Toyota. That Lexus saved your life." He waved, then exited, pulling the door closed behind him.

Tom could see concern on Eva's face, and he got the distinct impression it had nothing to do with his condition.

The gun.

"Tom, the police on the scene found a gun, a Glock automatic pistol on the pavement under the car. They're assuming the gun came from the car and, as you know, possession of an unregistered gun can be a felony in the District." She was too smart to ask him if it was his gun.

"A gun?" His response was pitiful, no better than a teen confronted with an empty beer can found in the family Buick. Fortunately, his circumstances permitted him to cover his response with closed eyes, rocking head, confused expression, and slurred speech. The possibility of Eva buying his performance was slim, but not impossible.

"Fortunately, since the gun wasn't found on your person or in the car itself, possession is not cut and dried. But they did use a BlueCheck on you when you were in the ambulance."

"What's a BlueCheck?"

"Portable fingerprint device. About the size of a cell phone. Most squad cars now carry them as part of their standard kit. We challenged their use when they first came out, but didn't get anywhere. So if your fingerprints were on the gun, they'll charge you. Even without fingerprints, they might still charge you."

He attempted a repeat performance. "A gun?" Worse than the first time.

She paused, trying to read him, and judging from her expression, doing a pretty good job of it. "At the risk of stating the obvious, I wouldn't discuss the matter of the gun with the cops, or anyone else for that matter. If they ask why you're not being cooperative, tell them you were acting on advice of your attorney."

He grinned. "You're my attorney?"

"For the moment." She offered half a smile. "And unless you're feeling tip-top tomorrow, stay home, take it easy."

"My lawyer and my doctor? What have I done to deserve this?"

"Not much." She bent over and kissed him lightly on the lips, then exited.

Okay, now what was he going to do? Every muscle in his body ached, but he had to get out of the hospital. And then what? Good chance his prints would be found on the gun, since he hadn't used gloves when he removed it from his bedside table drawer. Maybe a small possibility the disruption of the crash com-promised the Glock's grip, but it was a long shot at best.

Think logically. He had to kill another human being by mid-night Saturday. His weapon had been taken from him. There was a real chance the cops would be looking to arrest him and jail him over the weekend, pending bail review on Monday.

Solution? Only one, really. He had to get out of the hospi-tal, find Chewy, beg for another gun, then find a drug dealer and shoot him. First step, unhook the IV.

The door opened and the perky nurse entered. "Something to help you sleep, Mr. Booker."

"No! I don't want—"

"Doctor's orders." Before Tom could react, she had produced a syringe and squirted its contents into his IV tube. The effect was immediate.

"Please, I need—"

Sleep hit hard, no chance to dream its only blessing.

***

Five hours later, Tom awoke to find himself staring into the doleful face of Detective Percy Castro.

CHAPTER 37

Thinking he might've been dreaming, Tom closed his eyes, but Eva's voice coming from the other side of his bed quickly dashed any hope Castro was a mirage.

"Tom, don't say a word."

He figured the prints must've come back positive on the gun. A problem, but not necessarily a big problem. He'd seen in his limited time working for PDS that CPWL cases for first-time offenders carrying no prior record usually resulted in the defendant being released on his personal recognizance.

If he could get in front of a judge this morning, he'd be out by the end of the day, and have more than twenty-four hours to find Chewy, get another gun, and proceed with his crude but, he believed, fail-safe plan. He wouldn't simply fire once or twice at the target, he'd pump all of the bullets in the chamber at the dealer, leaving no doubt—wait a second. Castro was homicide. What's he doing here? LaRyn Walker must be dead. Probably fingered him before she died. But what evidence did they have? Could they have? It would be his word against—

"Good morning, Mr. Booker," said Castro. "Afraid I've got some bad news. Ballistics came back, confirmed the bullet found in Jessica Hawkins' brain came from your gun. Also, a neighbor identified you as being in the neighborhood at or near the time of the murder."

Tom heard the words, but was too stunned to process them.

"You're under arrest for the murder of Jessica Hawkins," said Castro, his voice soft, almost sad. "Please get dressed."

"That's...that's impossible."

Eva spoke sharply. "Tom, I said say nothing." She turned to Castro. "Percy, we'll waive Miranda. Can you give me a minute with my client?" Castro scowled. She pressed. "He's not going anywhere. Just a couple of minutes."

Castro paused. "Two minutes." He shuffled out of the room and closed the door behind him.

Eva interrupted Tom before he could speak. "Listen to me. I meant what I said. No comments to the cops. No comments to anybody, including, by the way, to cell mates. Most would sell their own mother for a used porn magazine."

Cell mates? Jesus. He couldn't go to jail, the clock was ticking. "What about bail?"

"Very tough in a homicide case. If the judge sets it at all, it'll be high. I'll call Zig. Maybe he can put something together by Monday—"

"Monday?" He didn't try to hide the panic in his voice. "Eva, I can't wait until Monday. I need out right away, now!"

"Sorry, but by the time they process you through intake, it'll be too late today. Bail reviews are only held for traffic and minor misdemeanors over the weekend, so Monday would be the earliest."

She must have seen the fear in his eyes. "Don't worry, it's not like in the movies, you'll be pretty safe. Just always keep your gaze straight ahead. Do not, *do not* look at any other inmate in the eye, do not agree to 'protection' from another inmate. Trust no one. Remember, inmates are notoriously good lip readers. There are no secrets. Keep to yourself, avoid even harmless chitchat. Don't try to make friends, because for each friend you acquire, you also acquire all of his enemies. The food is edible but barely enough to feed a bird. You'll need to supplement your caloric intake, so I'll make sure there's some money on your book for use in the commissary."

He could tell she'd given this speech before. How could he explain he wasn't concerned with his own safety, but had to protect his daughter?

He could feel the two minutes winding down quickly. "Where are my clothes, my wallet?"

"What do you need—?"

"In the back pocket of my pants."

She opened a closet that contained his clothing. He could see dark brown splotches on his jacket and shirt. His blood. She found the wallet and handed it to him. He quickly found the slip of paper with Chewy's number.

"Call this number. Don't wait for a greeting. Just say Tom Booker's going to DC Jail and needs protection. Then hang up. Don't wait for a response."

"Who is—?"

"Please, just do it." She nodded. "One more thing. I wasn't truthful with you. When Jess kept badgering me, I did go over to her place that night. The neighbor spotted me when she let out her dog. But I swear to you, I never went in. Knocked, rang the bell, no one answered. I left. Should've told you, but didn't want you to think I had any feelings for Jess, because I didn't. I was stupid."

He could read the disappointment on her face. "We'll worry about you and me later. For now, I'll serve as your attorney until—"

"No 'until.' I want you to represent me, Eva. No one else. I want you."

The door opened and Castro appeared with a patrolman. Castro's voice now sounded very official.

"Time's up."

CHAPTER 38

Castro watched as Tom got dressed. The nurse entered.

"Excuse me," said the nurse. "I know you guys are in a hurry, but Dr. Lin has to sign the release papers and he will be slightly delayed."

Thus, Tom, Eva, and Castro settled into an uneasy silence until Eva's phone beeped. She was needed in court and had to leave. She made a big show in front of Castro of advising Tom not to speak at all about the case. She promised to visit Tom in the afternoon "after he was settled." After he was settled? She made it sound like he was moving into a new townhouse instead of an 8 x 10 cell. For a second, he thought she might give him a peck on the cheek, but wisely she simply offered a smile and left.

Castro carefully lowered himself into the ancient visitor's chair, as if he were afraid his full weight might crush it to splinters. He nodded at the TV.

"Mind turning it to channel 47?"

Tom shrugged and tossed him the remote. Castro hit a couple keys and suddenly Oprah's face filled the screen.

"Didn't think she was on anymore."

"Reruns."

"You don't seem to me to be the Oprah type."

"My wife loved her. We both worked, so she insisted on recording her show. We'd watch it while eating dinner every night. Reminds me of Lita."

"You're wife's not—"

"Breast cancer. Two years ago this November."

"Sorry to hear that."

"Thanks."

Tom wasn't a fool. He knew the cop was trying to encourage familiarity so Tom might accidentally say something he shouldn't. The wife was probably in perfect health. But the sad, reflective expression on Castro's face appeared real.

"I just want you to know I didn't kill Jess." God, his attorney had barely left the room, and he already had violated her direction.

"Probably should listen to Eva and not talk about the case," said Castro.

"Right, sorry."

Oprah's show was more than half over, but the theme for the day must've been corruption in the church. She had two priests seated comfortably on her yellow couch.

She asked how men of God could do bad things, including abusing children.

Tom tuned out their answers and checked the clock on the wall. Less than thirty-eight hours till he'd hear from Chad and Britney. Maybe the demon twins would cut him some slack. How the hell could they expect him to offer up a new human sacrifice if he's in frigging jail? He glanced over at Castro. The detective seemed transfixed by the TV show.

"You look like a good Catholic boy, Detective. Probably go to mass every Sunday. You believe there's such a thing as hell?"

Castro didn't move, and, for a moment, Tom didn't think the cop heard him. Then he spoke quietly without taking his eyes off the screen.

"In my business you see the absolute worst of humankind. Murder, rape, child abuse. And that just includes the normal aberrant behavior. Doesn't count the true nut jobs who as a kid got their jollies pulling arms off bugs and setting cats on fire, then graduated to dismemberment, mass murder, and cannibalism."

He turned his head to lock eyes with Tom. "There is one thing of which I am absolutely certain. Satan exists, because man on his own could not conjure up the raw evil I witness every day."

Tom paused, then slightly nodded his head. He had the strange sense the man wasn't being completely candid. But why would Castro feel the need to put on an act? Weird.

They both turned their attention back to the TV as the credits rolled.

"Do not respond to what I'm about to say," said Castro. "This is not a question, I'm not questioning you. But you have me baffled. You seem like a good kid, a play-by-the rules kind of kid. Great education, great job. Great future. No trouble. Then your brother-in-law blows his brains out and you're there. Two weeks later, your client drinks himself to death and you're there. Less than two weeks later, a girl you dated takes a bullet in the brain and you were there. At about the same time, another client of yours almost dies from internal bleeding and you were there. Battaglia's trigger finger has evidence of a latex glove, and a bottle of booze on Mackey's table also has residue suggesting a latex glove. You deny you have latex gloves, but a search of your apartment reveals you were lying. You did have a box of latex gloves. Curious. Mighty curious."

"You searched my apartment?"

"When the ballistics matched, we got a warrant, executed it this morning."

"Eva told me about LaRyn. How's she doing?"

"She'll make it. Thanks to someone dialing 911 and leaving the phone near her face. Or maybe she dialed and dropped the phone. Anyway, they got there in time."

"What did she say happened?"

"Didn't say. May not come as a shock to you that LaRyn Walker has no interest in being fully forthcoming with the police. All she said was she remembered you coming over to talk with her about her case, she'd been drinking, and that's it. I'm sure some pharmaceuticals will be implicated when it's all said and done."

The door opened and Dr. Lin entered. Falsely cheerful, he nodded to Castro, then pulled a penlight from his vest pocket and shone it onto Tom's eyes.

"Sorry I was delayed. Heart attack patient had his appendix rupture right in the middle of an exam. Now, how are we doing?"

Don't know about "we," Doc, but I ain't doing too well. "Fine and dandy," said Tom. His sarcasm flew over the doctor's head.

"Good, good. I think we can let you out of here, then."

Yippee.

***

Castro escorted Tom from his hospital room to a squad car waiting outside. For no expressed reason, Castro waited until they were outside before cuffing him and helping him into the backseat. The drive from GW Hospital to the DC Jail at 1901 D Street in the farthest southeast corner of the city took close to half an hour due to typical midday traffic.

There he was turned over to jail guards, who signed a receipt that the package had been received. Just like FedEx.

Castro said, "Take care of yourself, Mr. Booker," then drove off.

A rather friendly comment from a cop who believed he'd murdered an innocent young woman in cold blood.

***

Over the next couple hours, Tom's mind was numb as he continued through processing. He was fingerprinted and strip-searched, which included a deep-cavity digital inspection. The attendant who performed the search referred to his rectum as his prison purse. Guess he needed to get used to the lingo. He received his orange prison jumpsuit, two pair of undershorts, two pair of socks, and what looked like rubber slippers. He signed an inventory of his clothing and personal belongings, then was escorted to the reception room to be questioned by a droopy-eyed, heavily jowled, African-American intake officer named Meriweather. His pallor matched the faded gray color of his uniform.

Tom looked up at the clock. Almost three p.m.

Meriweather ran down a checklist of questions. "Religion?"

Touchy subject. "Unsettled."

"Food allergies."

"Will it really make any difference in what you serve me?"

For the first time, Meriweather raised his head and offered a half smile, which communicated as clearly as if he'd spoken the words, "You gotta be kiddin'."

"Food allergies."

"None."

"Gang affiliation."

"Democrat."

No smile this time. "Gang affiliation."

"None."

Meriweather asked another page of questions, then, "We got eighteen cell blocks, each with its own dayroom and basketball court. You'll be assigned to intake Block, Northwest 3. Questions?"

"Visitors?"

"*A* to *H,* Tuesdays and Thursdays."

"Can't wait till Tuesday. How about today?"

"Tuesday. You can meet with counsel and clergy at any time. Shower twice a week, exercise twice a week for one hour. No more questions? Fine. Welcome to the District of Columbia Detention Center."

CHAPTER 39

After getting outfitted in his orange jumpsuit, Tom was cuffed, then escorted to his cell by a single guard. Guess he didn't appear to be much of a threat. To get to his new home they had to walk through the cell block dayroom, where about 100 inmates lounged, played chess, read, or watched TV. A long-term stay at the jail usually meant a year or two for a misdemeanor. But the jail also temporarily housed those awaiting trial for the most violent felonies; once convicted, they would transfer to the federal prison at Lorton, Virginia. Thus, Cellblock NW3, as the intake block, housed the most dangerous offenders in the facility.

Tom could spot only a few other white guys. Most were Latino or African-American, and most were young. He could see why Officer Meriweather asked about gang affiliation. It only took a cursory glance to see the Latinos gathered in two groups on one side of the room, while the blacks congregated in a couple groups on the opposite side.

As Tom passed through the space, his presence elicited catcalls from each of the groups:

"Hey, New, welcome to paradise!"

"Hey, New, Friday's the day you suck me, and today's Friday."

"Hey Briscoe, you bring us some Fresh? White meat, muthafuckazz, Briscoe bringin' us some fresh white meat."

The guard, a huge African-American man wearing tiny, wire-rimmed glasses, whispered, "Ignore them, keep your head down and your mouth shut, no eye contact, and you'll probably be okay."

As they passed through one of the Latino gangs, it was easy to identify the leader—a muscular, shirtless man in his early twenties with the number 14 tattooed on his chest, and a scar running from his left eyebrow to the spot where his left ear used to be. Number 14 thrust his foot out. Tom tripped and fell flat on his face.

Sprawling awkwardly on the filthy floor, his nose and mouth pressed against the grime, the events of the past weeks rushed through his brain and funneled into one searing emotion—rage.

He slowly gathered his feet under him, then sprang up with fury-fueled force. At the same time, he curled his right hand into a fist and, aided by the upward thrust of his legs, powered a crushing uppercut to the unsuspecting Latino's jaw. The man crumpled to the floor unconscious.

For a long moment, unable to believe their eyes, no one moved. Then Briscoe had his taser out and his whistle in his mouth a split second before the Latino's brethren pounced on Tom like an angry wolf pack.

"Don't!" said Briscoe through gritted teeth. "You move, you go to the hole, and the whole block loses ball and TV privileges."

Cries of "That's bullshit," came from the black groups across the room.

"Lopes tripped him," said Briscoe. "The New acted in self-defense. Case closed." Lopes regained consciousness, and his fellow gangbangers helped him to his feet.

"Don't say nothin'," Briscoe said to Lopes.

And he didn't. Instead, he locked eyes with Tom, smiled, and slowly drew his index finger across his throat.

The guard quickly escorted Tom through the day room and within a few minutes Tom was sitting on the lower bunk of cell number NW3-42.

"You made a big mistake," said Briscoe. "Lopes, he'll come for you."

"When?"

"Probably tonight. My advice—get some sleep now, because you'll need to be awake all night."

"Aren't the cell doors locked at night?"

The guard didn't answer directly. "Dinner's at six. Try to sit with the blacks. Lopes' boys won't try anything while you're with them."

Without another word, the guard departed, leaving the cell door open.

Based on all the prison movies he'd ever seen, Tom assumed at night the doors would clang shut, and he was confused by the guard's failure to confirm his understanding. The cell didn't have bars; instead, a metal door with a sliver of a window in the middle was the means of access to the space. A sink and lidless toilet were tucked into one corner across from the bunk bed. The top bunk was unmade, and Tom assumed its occupant was down in the dayroom. If his roomie was one of Lopes' boys, he was doomed. He lay back on the lower bunk and closed his eyes. His head pounded. What was he going to do? What the hell was he going to do?

CHAPTER 40

Tom awoke with a start to a loud, cracking sound. Briscoe stood before him banging his nightstick against the open metal door.

"Wake up, Sunshine."

"What time is it?"

"Little after five p.m. You got a visitor."

"Thought visiting from *A* to *H* was on Tuesdays and I'm a *B,* and *B* falls between *A* and *H*."

"A smart-ass. Here's a free tip. Smart-asses don't do too good in here. Your hot little lawyer—You want to see her or not?"

***

Eva sat alone at a table with two chairs. She smiled when she saw him.

"How's he doing, Briscoe?"

"Only been here a couple of hours and already had a run-in with Garcia Lopes."

"What kind of run-in?"

"Cold-cocked him in front of his crew."

"Jesus."

"Better talk to him, tell him what's what."

"Will do. Thanks."

"I'll be right outside if you need me." He exited.

Tom's first impulse was to take her into his arms, but a slight shake of her head held him off.

"They can see us but not hear us," she said.

Tom noticed the door had a small window for observation. "Did you make the call?"

"As soon as I said what you told me, whoever was on the other end hung up. Remember, what you tell me's privileged, Tom. Who was I calling?"

"I made a promise."

She held his gaze for a moment. "Okay, then let's talk about something more immediate. Garcia Lopes is trouble, big trouble."

"I gather that."

"He's a lieutenant in Norteños, one of the most notorious prison gangs in the country. Lopes is implicated in multiple murders. He was brought up early from Lorton for sentencing on Monday. Dan's handling it. He'll get life without parole, guaranteed."

"I know, it was stupid."

"When I leave here, I'll petition to have you moved to another cell block, but being the weekend, best case they won't hear it till Monday. So, you need to stay alive for the next couple of days."

"Good plan. What about bail?"

"I've already filed, and we have a hearing first thing Monday morning. But we're still talking about premeditated murder here, so it won't be easy."

"Eva, listen to me. I can't wait until Monday. I've been thinking. How about this? They let me out today, tomorrow at the latest. I agree to come back to jail Sunday morning. I waive Monday's bond hearing and agree to remain incarcerated for ten days without bail review."

She looked at him like he was crazy. Maybe he was.

"What's so important about Saturday night? Got a hot date? Sorry, that's not funny. What you suggest is simply impossible."

Tom dropped his head into his hands.

Her voice softened. "I know there are things you aren't telling me. I respect you and, well, I care about you. Therefore, I'll accept you have good reasons not to share with me—for the time being. So, instead, tell me about the gun."

"I didn't shoot her. Last time I saw Jess was same as you, at the party."

"How did the killer get the gun? And what were you doing with an unregistered weapon, a gun missing its serial number?"

"I live in a borderline rough area. Kept it in my bedside table drawer for protection. Obviously, the killer broke into my apartment, took the gun, used it to kill Jess, then returned it to implicate me."

"Okay, first, we never say that to anyone. They link you to the gun because they found it under your car at the accident scene. It's thin, but we at least have the argument there's nothing to connect you to the gun. It could've been tossed in the gutter by the real killer, and it was just bad luck you ran into a light pole at the same location. The fingerprint was a small partial, and I think we can attack that."

"As you said, thin."

"Their motive theory is also not particularly strong. They know you dated her—"

"A couple of times."

"—and they have the argument at the party. Their theory is you were drunk and went to her place to finish the argument. Because of your condition, things escalated and got out of hand and—"

"I wasn't drunk!" She remained silent. He worked to lower his voice. "I wasn't drunk and I didn't kill Jess."

"I believe you. Now, I'm not going to ask where you got the gun, but here are a few obvious questions. Who would want to frame you, how would they know you had a gun, and how could they get into your apartment?"

"I don't know, I don't know, and I don't know. Never checked my doorjamb. Could be signs of forced entry. So long as it wasn't too obvious, I probably wouldn't have spotted it."

"Anybody have a key to your place?"

"No. Well, I guess the maintenance guy does, but he's the only one."

She took notes on her iPad. "I'll check out the forced entry angle and run down the maintenance guy. You think about who might've wanted to frame you and how they knew you had a gun. I'll be back tomorrow. You need anything? I put $500 on your commissary book. Should be more than enough. And Tom, listen to me. Promise you'll be wary of Lopes. He's crazy and has nothing to lose."

"Hopefully, they won't try anything during the day, and at night I'll be safe behind a locked door."

"Sorry to tell you this, but many of those cell doors don't lock."

"It's a jail, how can they not lock?"

"Prisoners with a lot of time on their hands disabled them. Jail improvements are not high on the politicians' priority list. So sleep with one eye open."

"Promise." A thought occurred to him. "Actually, there is one thing. Could you call Father Matthew Sheran at Georgetown? Tell him I need to see him. It's very important." She cocked her head. "For my soul," he added. "Very important for my soul."

"Will do." Before she got up, he could feel her hand under the table, out of sight from Briscoe if he happened to be looking in the window. She found his hand and squeezed it. She held his gaze and offered a reassuring smile. For the first time her voice shed its professional tone, and she spoke to him as one lover to another.

"Don't worry. We'll get through this."

CHAPTER 41

He'd gotten through dinner without incident, electing to sit by himself. The food was edible—two dried-up fish sticks, a few damp french fries, and a spoonful of greasy collard greens—but probably consisted of no more than a few hundred calories. He'd done his best not to engage in eye contact with any of the other inmates, and most ignored him.

Tom did catch one bald, middle-aged black man hulking over his tray of food at a corner table in the far side of the prison mess staring at him. The man seemed vaguely familiar, but Tom couldn't immediately place him, although he easily could've been one of the thousands of people washing through Superior Court on a daily basis.

Tom quickly averted his eyes. Didn't need any more trouble.

Briscoe and four other guards had positioned themselves near Lopes and his boys eating at a table against the wall. For a split second, he'd been sure the face of the Latino sitting on Lopes' right morphed into a grinning Chad, but the image disappeared, and Tom chalked up the sighting to stress-induced delusion. Lopes himself completely ignored Tom and carried on as if nothing had happened. Maybe he'd forgotten the earlier incident. *Maybe pigs flew, and the 'Skins would win ten straight Super Bowls.*

Earlier, he'd checked the lock on his cell door, but couldn't tell for certain whether it worked. He'd also found his way to the block commissary located off the dayroom, and bought soap, shampoo, five packs of peanut butter crackers, five bags of potato chips, and a phone card.

He rested in his bunk while the other prisoners hung out in the dayroom, watching TV or playing board games. After consuming half his snacks, he stored the rest on a shelf built into the wall across from the bunks.

They'd confiscated his watch during intake and the only clock available hung over the TV. He'd been resting for a couple hours, so he assumed it was close to nine p.m. Exhausted, he couldn't allow himself to sleep.

"You one crazy sonofabitch."

Tom looked up to see a heavyset black man enter the cell. Appeared to be in his fifties, balding, gray hair, goatee, rimless glasses.

"You shouldn't be here, man. Lay out Lopes in front of his crew? You belong in SW2, with all the other mentals."

"I'm Tom Booker."

"Who gives a shit? Now what the fuck you doin' in my bunk?"

"Uh, sorry. Saw the top bunk had been used, so figured the lower one—"

"I use the top one to jack off. Who wants to sleep in his own jizz? Bottom one's mine." The man's glare could weld steel. "Unless you got a problem."

Oh, he had a problem. He had a you'll-never-believe-it kind of problem.

"No problem."

Tom climbed up onto the top bunk. Immediately, the smell of sweat and other bodily fluids was overpowering. He did his best to breathe through his mouth, and reflected that maybe the odor was a blessing—it might help keep him awake in case Lopes attempted a visit.

When Tom shifted the thin foam pillow in an attempt to get comfortable, he saw a photo of a smiling, heavyset black woman curled up naked on a bed. A fold mark creased through the center of the picture. He turned the photo over and saw an inscription written in what was once red ink, but now had faded to a pale pink: *Virgil, Mama's waiting for you!* Below a hand-drawn heart, the writer had inscribed, *Honey Bear.*

Tom leaned over the bunk. "Virgil, you want this photo, or you want I should keep it up here?"

Virgil exploded out of his bunk and, in a split second, grasped Tom's jumpsuit at the neck in an iron grip and yanked Tom's face so close Tom could've kissed him.

"You look at my woman?"

"No, no. Picture was turned over. Saw your name. Didn't look, man, honest. Man's woman is his own property." That didn't come out exactly right; on the other hand, he guessed the concept of women as chattel was probably not completely foreign in his current environment.

Virgil snatched the photo and smoothed it on his thick thighs, then slipped it under his pillow. He reached up and in his huge hand plucked all of Tom's remaining snacks from the shelf. "Payment for you lookin' at my woman."

"By all means. Help yourself."

A few minutes later, the doors swung closed automatically. The sound of a *click* hopefully signaled the door locking. Then the lights went out.

He rested on top of the blanket, not only to avoid Virgil's residual bodily fluids, but also to provide more flexibility if Lopes decided to stop by for a chat. Boy, a sip of Frank Custer's Akron gin would taste pretty good right about now.

With no weapon, Tom wasn't sure what he could do if Lopes opened the door. One-on-one, Lopes would likely mop the floor with him. Still, he wouldn't just be fighting to stay alive; he'd be fighting to save his daughter, and that, he supposed, was his weapon. Of course, if the lock worked, he'd be safe. He decided to violate Eva's rule and engage his cell mate.

"Hey, Virgil, you awake?" For a moment, Tom was reminded of sleeping in a bunk bed at Boy Scout camp in Pennsylvania when he was eleven or twelve. The counselors would turn out the lights, and the boys would giggle and talk about girl's body parts, and once they even snuck out and—

"Shut up, New."

Guess he wasn't in Boy Scout camp. "Just wondering about the door lock. My attorney told me—"

"Lopes comin' for you."

"So the door—?"

"All doors open 'cept the ones in the mental block."

"Any suggestions?"

"Pray."

"Got it. Don't suppose I could count on you to—?"

"He beefin' *you,* not me. I be absentee."

"When?"

No answer.

CHAPTER 42

Even if he'd been tempted to sleep, Virgil's loud snoring would've kept Tom awake. He tried counting seconds to keep track of the time, but after twenty minutes or so, he gave up. On several occasions, he climbed down and looked through the slit window on the cell door. Because of the angle, he couldn't make out the whole clock in the dayroom below, but he could see the left half. Once the little hand disappeared, he'd check periodically, and judging by the big hand's movement from the six to the twelve, he was able to approximate the time.

He'd never had any self-defense training, and his parents had always taught him to avoid confrontation. *Always better to talk yourself away from a fight, son. Not cowardice to walk from a fight. Try to put yourself in the other boy's shoes. Battle with reason and understanding rather than violence. Always ask yourself, what can I do to help defuse the situation?*

Thanks, Mom, thanks, Dad. Wonder what advice they'd offer if they saw their son in a jail cell about to be attacked by a Latino gangbanger?

Best Tom could tell it was around three a.m., when he heard a noise outside the door. Instantly alert, he hopped down from the bunk and puffed up the pillow under the blanket. His pathetic plan was based on the fact that the door opened inward. He figured his only hope was surprise. He'd hide behind the door. When it opened, Lopes would be focused on the lump in the bunk. Tom would have a split second to grab him in a choke hold from behind. 'Course, that didn't account for Lopes' posse, but one could only plan so much.

He took his place, heard a soft click, and watched as the door moved toward him. In a moment he saw a figure move into his view. It was Lopes, and he moved toward the bunks. Suddenly, Virgil's snores sputtered, then stopped. Tom could see his eyes open, take a moment to focus, then lock on to Lopes. Lopes held his finger to his lips. Virgil's gaze flicked to the right. He saw Tom behind the door.

Tom sprang and wrapped his right arm around Lopes' throat. Lopes fired his elbow back into Tom's ribs, sending pain shooting up his side. But Tom hung on, squeezing tighter. Virgil slipped out the door, not wanting to be a witness, whatever the outcome, and shut the door behind him.

Where was Lopes' posse? Maybe it was some kind of badge of honor to walk alone into the cell and take out an adversary. Some kind of *mano a mano* crap. Lopes again rammed his elbow into Tom's ribs, and this time the searing pain caused him to loosen his grip for only a split second.

Lopes instantly reached both hands behind his head and dug his thumbs into Tom's eyes. Tom attempted to twist his head away. The move again loosened his grip, giving Lopes the space he needed to snap his head back, smashing it into Tom's nose. He heard the sickening wet crunch signaling his nose had broken.

The third elbow to his ribs was enough. He doubled over. Lopes fired both hands up hard against Tom's elbows, allowing him to slip under Tom's grip.

Now freed, Lopes spun and swept his right leg against the back of Tom's knees, knocking him off his feet. Before Tom could recover, Lopes was on top of him. He pulled a knife from his pocket, pressed the tip against Tom's throat and offered a cold smile.

"Please, I don't want any trouble. I have a daughter. Her name's Janie, and she's only—"

Lopes hissed. "Shut the fuck up."

Tom closed his eyes and concentrated hard. *Chad, Brit, okay, you're getting a new soul. Me. And a day early, how about that? And it counts because I'm dying by my own hand. If I hadn't attacked Lopes, I wouldn't be about to cash out. Do with me what you will, but please save Janie. I don't want any harm to come to Emma 2 either, but Janie's my daughter. A Booker for a Booker. Please—*

Suddenly, Lopes climbed off him. Tom could see the knife better now. Six-inch blade, handle wrapped in black electrician's tape. Before Tom could speak, Lopes tossed the knife on the floor beside him.

"From Chewy, asshole."

In an instant, Lopes was out the door.

CHAPTER 43

Tom quickly pocketed the knife and climbed back up into his bunk. A few minutes later, Virgil entered.

"Surprised to see you alive, New."

"Wonders never cease."

"Don't bleed on my bunk."

Tom flipped over onto his side. He couldn't breathe through his busted nose and even the slightest movement shot pain to his ribs. He balled up the corner of the dirty sheet and pressed it hard against his nose to stem the bleeding.

He tried to rest on his back, but felt like he was bound up in an invisible straitjacket since any movement, left or right, was punished with a shot of pain across his ribs. His heavy breathing through his mouth, timed with Virgil's heavy snoring, sounded like an R & B bass line.

Despite the pain, as Tom rolled the knife back and forth in his hands he felt a glimmer of hope. He had a weapon and was surrounded by bad guys. How hard could it be to start a confrontation, escalate it, and take out a deserving felon by midnight? This was jail, right? The knife's broad blade looked to be about four-and-a-half inches long, and resembled a stubby bowie knife. Other than the tip, the blade edge wasn't particularly sharp, and there were specks of rust—blood?—near the hilt. But he had no doubt the weapon would do the trick.

If he staged it right, he'd even have a decent chance of establishing his actions were taken in self-defense. He faced one key logistical problem: the prison jumpsuit had no pockets. Probably a security measure to guard against inmates carrying around things like loose change, lucky charms, and bowie knives. He remembered the probe of his "prison purse" during his strip search, but he wasn't going to stick a four-inch bowie knife up his ass. Aside from the discomfort of have your rectum sliced through every time you sat down, the purse didn't offer quick access.

Which meant he'd have to follow the Lopes model: provoke a fight but not finish it, and hope the target would visit him later in his cell to take him out. Some of the men incarcerated in this block had been arrested on misdemeanor charges, or felonies far short of homicide. Some even for DWIs. He would have to do the best he could to cull out a killer. But if he ran out of time, he'd pick his victim based on a gut feeling to protect Janie.

He hid the knife under his mattress.

***

By morning, his ribs felt slightly better, a hopeful sign they were bruised, not broken, and his left nostril had partially cleared. He'd shuffled slowly down to breakfast, which consisted of a small scoop of powdered eggs and a floppy piece of cold white toast. He kept to himself, and Lopes and his posse completely ignored him. He'd caught the little bald black man who'd been eyeing him at dinner again giving him the evil eye, but each time Tom turned his way, the man abruptly cast his gaze down to his food tray. Tom still couldn't place him.

After breakfast, the inmates returned to the dayroom. Earlier, Tom had noticed a bulletin board mounted along one wall. A sign above the board read: *Daily Visitor Schedule.* He took a seat in a yellow plastic chair close to the board. Oddly, the hard plastic actually provided some relief to his rib pain. He'd considered asking Briscoe to take him to the infirmary, but feared he might get stuck there. What he really needed was a drink. He'd heard the compulsion to drink in the morning was a sign of alcoholism. But then, wouldn't everyone who enjoyed a Bloody Mary with their Sunday brunch be considered an alcoholic? Satisfied with his logic, Tom allowed himself the pleasure of imagining an ice-cold Stella in his hand.

Eva had promised to visit, but hadn't told him when. He absently watched the TV in front of the room until Briscoe entered and headed toward the bulletin board, where he posted the visitor list with two clear plastic pushpins. Immediately, half the inmates rose as if in church and moved to the board. Tom used his strategic position to slot himself third in a ragged line of prisoners interested in seeing who might be coming to visit on Saturday.

"Back of the line, New."

Tom recognized the deep voice as that of his bunk bud. "Virgil, I was here first and I'll be quick."

Virgil pushed him hard and Tom tripped over the yellow plastic chair, falling on his ass. He yelped out as the sharp edge of the chair hit flush across his broken nose. Pain shot up from his lower back to his ribs, but no one paid him any attention. Tom looked up to Briscoe for help.

Briscoe shrugged. "News at the end of the line."

Tom gingerly crawled to his feet and made his way to the back of the line. By the time he reached the board, the print-out had been torn in two places and was dangling by a single pushpin. The names were listed alphabetically, and Tom was surprised to see two visitors listed next to "Booker"—Zig, and his cousin, Estin. Thought he couldn't see visitors until Tuesday. Maybe the weekends were an exception. But no Eva, and no Father Matthew. He turned to Briscoe.

"My lawyer and priest were supposed to be on this list."

"Attorneys and clergy can visit anytime. When they arrive, someone will come get you."

He heard a shout from one of the inmates. "Hey, New, you got a stripe!"

Tom turned to the TV. *GMA* had switched to the local ABC affiliate at the bottom of the hour for weather, traffic, and local news headlines. A red banner decorated the top left corner of the screen like a birthday present: *Washington Intern Murder!* The crawl at the bottom of the picture read: *Washington lawyer accused of killing his jealous lover.* There wasn't much room in the middle for an actual video transmission, but a picture of Jess appeared on the left.

With its stylized image and soft lighting, the photo showed a bright, smiling girl that any parent would love to have as a daughter or daughter-in-law. The picture looked like a college yearbook photo, and made her appear not only beautiful, but innocent. Actually, she *was* innocent, and seeing her picture tugged at Tom's heart. So young, so much promise. Her life snuffed out because... because why?

Next to Jess' photo was a picture of a scowling man with hooded eyes, a purple bruise under his left eye and—holy shit! They must've used his mug shot, taken almost immediately after being transported, battered and bruised, from the hospital. To anyone watching, the face staring out from the screen could easily be a killer.

The picture changed to two women and a man standing in front of a bank of microphones. Tom recognized the woman speaking as Senator Guthrie.

"...and on behalf of their friends and neighbor Oklahomans, I want to say to Jill and Ed Hawkins, who just arrived from Norman to collect their loving daughter, Jessica, and take her back home, we grieve with you, and you have been and will be in our hearts and prayers."

Jess' mom looked just like her daughter; her father was big, rawboned with a salt-and-pepper buzz cut. Both, adhering to a Western stoicism, controlled their emotions. But anyone watching could tell from their sunken eyes and haunting expressions that each was dying inside.

The senator continued, "Jess was not only a constituent, she also worked in my office as an intern. When you spend time in Washington, it's easy to become cynical. But then, someone like Jess Hawkins enters your life. Fresh, energetic, optimistic, not a duplicitous bone in her body. And you realize she, and others like her, are the antidote to Washington fever. She reminds us what's important. Washington isn't America. Jess Hawkins is America."

Onlookers standing behind the press applauded enthusiastically, and Tom saw faint smiles on her parents' faces.

A familiar reporter from the CBS affiliate—Tom couldn't remember her name—asked, "Do you believe Tom Booker is the killer?"

Tom shuddered. His name had never been mentioned on TV before, and the thought his debut would consist of the question, *Do you believe Tom Booker is the killer?* was surreal. He was glad his parents weren't alive to see it.

"We will let the justice system work its will," said Guthrie. "But I can assure you that my office will be bird-dogging this case until justice is done. We believe in capital punishment in Oklahoma, and the monster who perpetrated this unimaginable tragedy should pay the ultimate price. Thank you."

The eyes of the inmates lingered on him for a moment. A flicker of respect? *Yeah, the white dude capped the bitch. Got hisself a stripe.*

He had to kill one of them by midnight.

CHAPTER 44

Tom remained in the dayroom until 8:00 when inmates could have access to the bank of four phones mounted along the wall next to the bulletin board. Another crowd arrived for the phone line, but this time, no one appeared to object to Tom's place at the front of the line.

Maybe his red stripe had given him a little street cred. He inserted his phone card, then quickly punched in Eva's numbers. She answered on the first ring.

"See you made it through the night."

"Yeah."

"Any problems?"

"Nothing major. When are you coming by?"

"After lunch. Going over this morning with the PDS investigator to check out the ballistics and fingerprint raw data."

"There's something else I'd like you to do." There were not even minimal partitions between the phones and he lowered his voice. "Can you find out something about my fellow campers here?"

"Who?"

"All of them. Or as many as you can. Limit it to my cell block."

"Why?"

"Some of these guys are pretty scary, and I just want to know if there are any particular nasties I need to worry about."

"Did something happen?" He could hear the fear in her voice.

"I'm fine. Zig and my cousin, Estin, are coming to visit this morning, so that'll break up the time. Did you have a chance to contact Father Matthew?"

"Said he would come. Didn't say when. But I'm curious. Why him? You're not Catholic."

"I met him at Georgetown. We bonded."

A gravelly voice behind him. "Time's up, New."

Tom looked over his shoulder and one of Lopes' posse glared at him. Guess the red stripe didn't impress him.

"One more thing," said Eva. "You may be contacted or visited by the media. At the risk of stating the obvious, keep your mouth shut and refuse to speak or meet with them. Unfortunately, your case has gained a bit of notoriety."

"I know. Got a red stripe. See you in a few hours." He was tempted to end with some sort of personal sign-off acknowledging his feelings for her, but couldn't think of anything fast enough. He hung up the phone.

***

Tom remained in the video conferencing room after Estin left, since Zig was scheduled immediately after him. Weird, talking to his cousin on a TV screen. Like big-boy Skype. Estin had tried his best to be uplifting and volunteered to testify as a character witness if called upon. Tom felt so guilty all he could do was nod. Actually, that Estin was himself a law enforcement officer wouldn't hurt if they ever got to a forum where character testimony was needed. Tom gave him Eva's number, and Estin promised to call and appear in person Monday at the bail hearing if she felt it would help.

When Zig arrived, the first thing he did was mug for the camera.

"I think maybe speed dating started out this way."

Zig's well-meaning attempt at cheerful expression came across as contrived. Tom couldn't blame him. Really, what was there to be cheerful about? Not wanting to offend, Tom offered a weak smile.

Zig's expression turned serious. "Want you to know, everyone at the firm, including Bat, is behind you 100 percent."

Tom was a bit skeptical. He doubted all the attorneys at SHM would view his red stripe with the same respect as his new camp pals.

"No one believes you could ever do such a thing," said Zig.

"Thanks, means a lot," said Tom. Actually, it did. "Eva thinks their motive theory is weak. At some point, she'll want you and Marcie to testify that the exchange between me and Jess at Bat's party was no big deal."

"No problem. Fact is, you were cool; Jess was the one who'd gone a little tilt. Besides, not like you were jealous. You had the hots for Eva."

"They say Jess couldn't let go when I dumped her for Eva. She got angry when she saw us together at the party. Later she calls me to go over to her place to, I don't know, apologize or something. We get into an argument, it escalates, and I shoot her. They find my prints in her house, and then there's the gun."

"Completely illogical. Even if the first part were true, and even if the gun was yours, why would you carry a gun into her place? And your prints were there because you'd spent the night. One night, that's it, the only time you'd been there."

"Actually, I did go over there that night. Door was locked, she didn't answer. Left without seeing or talking to her."

"They know that?"

"Some old lady saw me."

"You see anybody else?"

"Just a shadow. Looked like someone leaving, but I was too far away to be certain."

"I know there's nothing I can say to make you feel better, but just want you to know, I don't believe for a second you killed her, and I'm not going to rest until you're exonerated. I'll be in court Monday to vouch for you."

Tom was genuinely touched and was surprised to find himself choking up.

"Thanks."

***

Immediately after gulping down lunch, Tom hurried to the phone line. He had to contact Gayle and Janie. With all the publicity, good chance the media would get around to them sooner rather than later.

After four rings, she answered.

"When caller ID said DC Jail, I figured it was you since, at the moment, you're the only person I know who happens to be staying at that particular venue."

"Gayle, listen. I'm only allotted a small amount of time here. First, I swear to you on my love for Janie that I did not kill Jessica Hawkins. Second, you might've already seen a story about the case on TV and—"

"Seen it? Jesus, Tom. It's impossible to miss. Look, no matter what happened between us, I know you're not a murderer. You have your faults, but you wouldn't hurt a fly."

"I'm really sorry," he said. "Wouldn't be surprised if the media attempts to contact you, so be prepared. How's Janie doing?"

"She's okay. I think she's afraid she might get hassled at school on Monday. You know how cruel kids can be."

"Can I talk to her?"

"Just a second. And Tom, I really know you didn't do it so, you know, hang in there."

"Thanks. That means a lot."

"Hi, Daddy."

He could hear the fear in her voice. "Hi, Baby. How are you doing?"

"Fine."

"Guess you saw some stuff on TV about me, and just want you to know, honey, I didn't do anything bad to that lady."

"I know."

"And you'll probably be seeing some more stuff on TV, but no matter what you see or hear, know that I didn't do it. And also know that I love you so much it aches."

"Love you, too, Daddy."

"You listen to Mommy, okay, and I'll try to call again soon, okay?"

"Okay." Her voice sounded so small.

"One more thing. Do not talk to any strangers, no matter how nice they seem, okay? Promise?"

"Promise. Bye, Daddy."
"Bye, Baby. I love—"
But she'd already hung up.

***

Tom spent the rest of the morning sitting uncomfortably in the grimy, yellow plastic chair, observing his fellow inmates from the back of the dayroom. He'd decided to start the fight after dinner, before lights out. That way, the confrontation would be fresh and the likelihood his target would seek his retribution that night would increase. Problem was, he could think of no way to assure the visit would take place before midnight. He concluded he could probably increase his odds by targeting the biggest hothead in the group, someone who'd want to slice Tom's throat as soon as possible.

He'd listed in his mind several possibilities. His first choice was a skinny black man in his thirties, whose heavily pockmarked face sported a permanent scowl. The man already had come to blows with one of Lopes' boys over the TV remote. Briscoe and another guard broke up the fight shortly after it started, and Tom heard Briscoe call him Creek. Afterward, Tom had struck up a conversation with Briscoe, and the guard told him the man was up from Lorton for sentencing on Monday. Just as Tom was about to ask about the charge, Briscoe was called away.

At lunch, Tom purposely sat at the table in front of the table where Creek ate, so he could look directly at the man. Throughout the meal, Tom had purposely engaged Creek in a staredown. After about ten minutes, Creek flared.

"What you lookin' at, New?"

Tom held his gaze. "Not much."

Creek exploded from his seat, grabbed a plastic fork, and vaulted over his table, knocking over trays and drinks. Tom was ready for him. As Creek lunged at him like a hungry wolf, Tom swung his tray sideways, catching the black man square in the nose full force. Creek's nose split open and blood sprayed over everything and everyone within five feet. He dropped to the floor, but only for a moment.

Where the hell was the cavalry? Tom's ribs and nose screamed in pain as he stared at the bloody face and crazed eyes of a man with a single thought in his brain: ripping Tom's head off.

Tom froze. From Creek's crouched position he sprung upward, his teeth bared like a rabid dog, then suddenly flipped back when Briscoe's nightstick locked around his neck. In a second, Creek was on the ground and handcuffed.

"Goin' back to the hole, Creek," said Briscoe. "For you, be like goin' home."

Creek sputtered, his voice compressed to a croak from the nightstick pressure. "Fu—."

"No need for that," said Tom. "Just a misunderstanding. Me and Creek, we're buds, ain't that right, bro?" He locked eyes with Creek, who instantly got the message.

"Me and New, we just fuckin' around." His wide smile didn't reach his eyes, which sent Tom the message he was hoping for: I'm coming for you.

Briscoe paused, glanced at his colleagues who shrugged. He slowly loosened his grip on the nightstick. "Today's your lucky day, asshole, 'cause I happen to be in a forgiving mood."

He withdrew the nightstick, allowing Creek to stand to his full height. From a distance, Tom had seen the man as a pencil-necked beanpole, but up close, Creek was all muscle and sinew.

Briscoe pointed to the trays and food on the floor. "Both of you, clean up this shit now. Any problems?"

Creek shook his head.

"No problem," said Tom.

If things went as planned, within the next twelve hours Creek would become the solution.

CHAPTER 45

Tom shuffled into the private attorney meeting room to see Eva standing there, hands on her hips.

"Are you out of your mind?" When she got a good look at him her expression immediately switched from a punishing scowl to sympathetic concern. "Your face. Are you hurt? What did he do to you?"

"I'm okay." He offered a weak smile and sat down at the table.

She sat across from him. "I can insist you be taken to the infirmary."

"I'm okay. Really."

She shook her head. "First you get into an argument with the leader of one of the most dangerous Latino gangs on the East Coast. Then you start a fight in the prisoner mess with Joe Creek."

"What's his story?"

"Nickname's Cujo. He enjoys using his teeth to tear a chunk out of whatever body part happens to be closest. What the hell happened to 'keep your head down and your mouth shut?'"

"What's he in for?"

"Aggravated assault."

"Priors?" Tom was hoping for a homicide conviction, or at least an arrest.

"Yard long."

"Homicide?"

"No, but that doesn't mean you won't be the first."

Her answer complicated matters. If he continued with his

plan, he'd be killing a bad man, probably a crazy man, but not a murderer. Did that make a difference now?

"Aside from your recently revealed suicidal tendencies, we've got other problems," she said. "Schnabel's sitting Monday."

"I gather he's not predisposed to the defense."

"The Fuhrer? You gather correctly."

"Any chance of getting the matter transferred to another judge?"

"In a word, no. We make the best case we can. And we can file an immediate appeal when—*if*—he rules against us. Your cousin, Estin, will be there, and the fact that he's a cop will help. We'll have Zig representing the firm. I'll get someone from PDS, maybe Danny, to vouch for you."

DTA? If Danny stood up for him, Tom might be compelled to remove the TA. "But traditionally, the strongest community tie is immediate family. Unless you have an objection, I'm planning on contacting your ex-wife. I assume she'll be cooperative."

Tom didn't want Gayle and Janie dragged into his predicament, but it was in his daughter's best interest that he be freed. "I think she'll agree."

Assuming his plan worked, and he was able to take out Creek by midnight, there was a chance Emma Wong would be saved, and Janie would still be in jeopardy. What was he going to do if he couldn't get out on bail? Kill another inmate in two weeks? He answered his own question: yes. And once she was saved, he didn't care what happened to—

"Tom, are you listening to me?"

"Yes, of course."

"I need to get back to the office, work on my presentation, and make some calls. Can you please promise me you'll stay out of trouble? I mean it."

"Promise." He was hoping for an under-the-table hand squeeze, but she stood quickly. He followed her to the door, but she took a circuitous route along the wall next to the door where, for a moment, she was out of sight of anyone peering through the window. She stopped abruptly, turned, and wrapped her arms around him. Her kiss was short but deep. Without a word, she knocked on the door. Briscoe let her out, then addressed Tom.

"Don't go nowhere, New," said Briscoe. "You're Mr. Popularity today."

After a few minutes, Father Matthew Sheran entered, a somber expression on his face. Briscoe closed the door, leaving the two of them alone.

Matthew's handshake was little more than perfunctory.

"Thanks for coming," said Tom.

"You know, the prison has its own chaplain." The unsaid message was unmistakable: You're a killer, you're nuts, and you're not even Catholic. What the hell do you need with me?

Tom sat and, after a few moments, Matthew followed suit. "I need your help," said Tom.

"I took note of the untimely death of one Reece Mackey."

"Alcohol poisoning."

"And you had nothing to do with it?"

Tom couldn't hold his gaze. "He was a murderer, and his death saved the life of a seven-year-old girl named Abby Jackson."

"I remember. The demons from hell. What were their names? Brad and Buffy?"

"Chad and Britney."

Matthew bent closer. "Tom, listen to me. I'm not a shrink, but it doesn't take an advanced degree to see you need help. Don't know whether you can afford a psychiatrist, but if not, the city provides psych services to inmates. It may even assist your attorney in developing an insanity defense."

"I didn't do it."

"She was a young woman with her whole—"

"I said I didn't kill her. I swear to you on my love for my daughter, I had nothing to do with Jess' murder."

"So somebody stole your gun, shot her, and replaced the gun without you knowing it to frame you. Any idea who might've wanted to do that? Oh, I forgot, the devil's disciples."

"To my knowledge, they had nothing to do with Jess' death. That's not part of their game. You're the expert, but I would assume that if one's job title happened to be demon from hell, your skill set would include the ability to kill just about anybody you wanted. Again, they want *me* to do the killing. That's what makes the show interesting."

Tom could feel his face flush and his voice rise. "You're a goddamn priest. Why is it so hard to accept that Satan exists and does bad things? After all, he's Satan."

Matthew's expression softened. "Tom, why did you call me here?"

"In less than ten hours, if I don't take another life, either my daughter or a young girl named Emma Wong will die."

Tom expected an instant comeback, the message being some variation of the theme: you're friggin' nuts. But the priest remained silent.

"I've been thinking. Maybe if a man of God, a priest, were to be there with Janie and—"

"Sprinkle holy water over her? Perhaps brandish a silver cross and drape her with garlic?" It may have been Tom's imagination, but Matthew's sarcasm appeared forced.

"No, I want you to drive out to Arlington, and stay with her for fifteen minutes before midnight and fifteen minutes after. I'll call Gayle and make up something. If she won't let you in, sit outside the house in your car. Will you do it? Please."

This time the period of silence didn't last as long. The priest got up to leave. "All I'll promise is that I'll think about it."

"Thank you."

The priest knocked on the door, and Briscoe promptly opened it.

As the priest stepped out of the room, Tom called after him. "And a little holy water wouldn't hurt."

CHAPTER 46

Tom scrunched into the front corner of his cell, looking out the small window, attempting, without success, to read the clock in the dayroom. But he figured, best case, only about ten minutes remained until midnight. He was so frustrated he could scream.

Earlier, he'd called Gayle to tell her about Father Matthew. Prior to contacting her, he'd thought about what to say without coming across as a total nutcase. When she answered the phone, he told her some members of Jess' family were crazy for revenge and he was fearful for Janie. He'd heard from one of his fellow inmates something might be attempted that evening. His attorney had talked to the cops, but they weren't taking the threat seriously, so he'd arranged for a friend who was a former cop to watch over her. The former cop was going to dress as a priest just in case he was spotted. Tom hoped she'd let him in, maybe sleep on the couch downstairs. Otherwise, he'd probably be outside in a car.

Tom couldn't have been more surprised that she actually believed him, and said she'd call the Arlington police herself and demand a cop be stationed outside the house as a deterrent.

Now, as midnight drew closer, his stomach spasmed, and he had difficulty breathing. Where the hell was Creek? Earlier, he'd concluded he needed to take action himself and visit Creek's cell. He'd watched Virgil use a hairpin to pop the lock on the cell door, but he kept the pin attached to the band of his underwear and there was no way Tom could retrieve it and exit the cell without waking the man.

He slumped to the floor. The clock was ticking, someone would die, and there was nothing he could do about it. Should he hope—pray?—that if another little girl died, the victim would be Emma 2 instead of Janie? No, he couldn't do that. But he did. *Please, please don't take Janie. Please—*

He heard the soft sound of footsteps outside the cell.

Then the jiggling of the lock. Virgil instantly awoke and in a fluid motion reached under his mattress and retrieved a shiv. The door opened. Virgil relaxed.

"It's for you," said Virgil, and he ambled out of the cell. A black man entered and closed the door behind him. It wasn't Creek.

The short, bald black man who'd been eyeing him in the mess slipped his hairpin into his hair, then flipped a heavy pipe wrench back and forth between his two hands. Up close, Tom knew he'd seen the man before, but couldn't remember where. Whoever he was, the man looked major pissed.

"You killed my brother."

"Your brother—?" He remembered. The little guy sitting with Reece Mackey in the bar.

"Ball."

"8-Ball."

Tom could see a flicker of confusion on the man's face, probably surprised his target wasn't shaking in his boots.

"La Chiqua say when she find Reece, you just been there. Reece, he could always handle the gin, maybe nod off sometimes, but that be it. She think you had somethin' to do with him checkin' out." He slapped the wrench hard into the palm of his left hand, the sound of the crack echoing around the small enclosure.

Tom's first instinct was to deny the charge and point out the obvious—Reece was a drunk, and the hootch had finally caught up with him. But time was running out. His only thought was Janie. He felt the knife tucked into the back waistband of his underwear, the point tickling the crack of his butt. 8-Ball didn't know he was armed and he needed to provoke the man to attack him.

Immediately.

Tom backed up until he could feel the toilet bowl on the back of his leg. "Maybe I did help him along, so what?"

8-Ball took a step closer, but then paused.

Shit. Time was running out. He had to force the attack. Tom could think of only one way to do it.

"One less nigger in this world."

The black man's eyes widened, his face contorted in rage, and he sprang, swinging the heavy wrench down from above his head toward Tom's skull. Tom ducked under the arc of the wrench. The tool grazed Tom's head, stunning him, but not enough to knock him out. He reached behind his back, wrapped his grip around the knife's handle, and in one fluid motion thrust it upward toward the chest of his assailant.

But Ball easily sidestepped, locked his elbow around Tom's arm and twisted back hard, almost ripping the arm from its socket.

Tom yelped and dropped the knife.

For a moment, Ball was off balance, and Tom used the small advantage to shove the little man hard against the cell wall. Ball dropped the wrench, purposely fell to the floor, and rolled across the concrete until he found what he was searching for:

Tom's knife.

In a split second he was on his feet, nimble as a jungle cat, circling, grinning, the knife in his right hand. Tom knew any moment the man would spring. Having never been in a knife fight before, much less a knife fight where only one of the combatants happens to possess a knife, Tom was fairly certain he was about to die. He quickly scanned the small room, searching for something, anything he could use to defend himself. But all he spotted were a few empty potato chip bags.

Ball feigned left, then swung the knife upward with his right hand. Tom had played a little basketball in high school, and knew rule one when defending the man with the ball is to focus on his hips, not his arms or face. He was able to barely anticipate Ball's feint and dodged the thrust. His back now up against the bunks, he yanked a blanket off Virgil's bed and wrapped it around his arm just as Ball again attacked.

Tom blocked the thrust with his blanket-covered left arm. The sharp blade sliced easily through the worn wool, but stopped short just as the blade edge tickled Tom's arm.

With Ball's weight now forward, Tom stepped behind the man and encircled him in a bear hug, pinning both of the man's arms against his sides. The move sent waves of pain across Tom's ribs, but he held on. While smaller in stature, Ball was very strong, and Tom knew he couldn't hold the embrace much longer.

Ball bit down hard on Tom's right hand, causing Tom to let loose with a howl that had to have been heard up and down the cell row. The pain injected a new burst of adrenaline, and Tom rammed the man's head against the wall, momentarily stunning him.

Ball kept a strong hold on the knife. Knowing there was no way he could continue keeping him at bay, Tom's eyes again landed on the empty chip bags. Without thinking, he used his left arm to momentarily hold the stunned man secure, then grabbed a chip bag and rammed it down Ball's throat. Instinctively, he tried to spit it out, but Tom, sensing an advantage, shoved the second empty bag into Ball's mouth and down his throat.

Doing his best to ignore the shooting pain from Ball's teeth clamping down hard on his wrist, Tom used his left hand to brace the man's head and thrust the fingers of his right hand down the man's throat, jamming the crinkly foil deeper and deeper. Ball tried to bite down on Tom's fingers, but the jaw movement had the effect of pushing the crumpled bags deeper down his gullet.

Ball dropped the knife and clutched his throat. He couldn't breathe. His face reddened and he fell to his knees, then crumpled to the cold concrete floor gagging, clawing at his throat.

Tom hardly noticed the blood dripping down through his hair as he rushed to the door, ignoring the stabbing pain in his ribs. He had to get outside to see the clock, but the door was locked. He ran his fingers through Ball's hair, searching for the hairpin, but it must've dislodged during the struggle. He wedged himself into the front corner and tried to see the clock through the small window, but the glass had fogged from the recent activity inside.

He glanced over his shoulder. 8-Ball was lying still, but he continued to make gurgling sounds. Tom tried to rub the condensation away, but only succeeded in smearing it. Still, he thought he could see the tip of the minute hand. What time was it? *What the hell time was it?*

The rasping stopped, and he turned to see the man's eyes glaze over. Was he dead?

Tom turned to finish him off.

The door opened and Virgil entered. Tom burst past him through the doorway to the balcony where he could see the clock head on:

12:04.

He rushed back to 8-Ball, ignoring Virgil's hulk as he hovered over the man.

One more wheeze, then he was still.

"He gone," said Virgil, with the same emotion he'd exhibit commenting that he'd missed the bus. "You best get this dead piece of shit outta my room. Now."

CHAPTER 47

Tom remained frozen. Virgil found the knife, wiped down the handle on the dead man's shorts, and stuck the knife in Ball's waistband. The big man climbed back into his bunk and rolled over.

Four minutes, four lousy minutes. Maybe the clock in the dayroom was fast. Probably hadn't been checked for years. Tom extracted the crumpled chip bags from Ball's throat, rinsed them in the toilet bowl, and replaced them on the shelf. After wrapping the handle of the wrench in toilet paper, making sure not to touch the handle, he rested the tool on the body. As Virgil watched, Tom dragged the body out of the cell onto the balcony, then halfway down the cell row, where he left it in the shadows.

He removed the toilet paper, then returned to his cell and flushed the paper down the toilet. When he was finished, he closed the door and climbed up to his bunk.

He squeezed his eyes tight, but he knew there was no chance he'd be able to sleep. The image of the clock flashed in his mind—12:04—on and off, on and off. The front of the clock shifted out of focus, then reformed as a human face—8-Ball.

And he was laughing his ass off.

**

At about five a.m. Ball's body was discovered, and the block went into lockdown mode. Each cell was searched, although not very thoroughly, since there were no obvious knife wounds or blood found on the body. The discovery of the knife and pipe wrench on the victim's body was suspicious, but any further action would have to await an autopsy, and needless to say, no one saw anything. By seven a.m. the lockdown had been lifted, and the men were eating breakfast as if nothing had happened.

Tom had skipped breakfast and now waited in the day-room, his eyes locked on the damn clock: 7:55 a.m. Five minutes until he could use the phone. He'd positioned himself to be first in line.

Creek approached him and bared his teeth. "Get out of my spot, asshole."

Tom had no time for this. "Every penny on my book, it's yours."

Creek glared at him with bloodshot eyes. "How much?"

"I don't know, close to 500 bucks. Whatever it is, it's yours."

Creek paused, then nodded and stepped behind Tom.

At the stroke of eight, Tom inserted his phone card and dialed Gayle. She picked up on the first ring. And she was crying.

Tom screamed into the phone. "What? *What?* Oh, God, no."

"Tom?"

"Janie?"

"She's fine. But do you remember her little friend, Emma Wong?"

At that moment, Tom heard a familiar voice, and turned to see the *Sunday Baptist Hour* playing on the big TV. But instead of the well-known, African-American preacher with the portly frame and the booming voice, Chad stood in the pulpit wearing a black robe with a scarlet-red cross on each of its billowing sleeves. The crosses were upside down.

"Hallelujah, Thomas, hallelujah! Praise the Lord. Now, which lord would that be? Hmmmm." He stepped out from behind the pulpit and opened his robe to reveal Emma Wong in her pink Hello Kitty pajamas, her skin so pale she could've been wearing whiteface. Her neck was bent at an odd angle, tilting her head to the left. Her large brown eyes stared out at him, dead, unblinking.

"Thanks for Emma, Tom," said Chad, as he caressed Emma's

black hair. "She's as sweet as pie." He bent down and slowly ran his tongue across the top of her head. "And do you have something to tell Tom, sweetie?"

She nodded, then spoke. But her voice wasn't the gentle lilt of a seven-year-old girl. Instead, a deep whisper formed her words.

"One to go."

CHAPTER 48

Tom sat in the private, attorney interview room with his head in his hands. His ribs ached and his nose hurt. Why couldn't it all be a nightmare? Why couldn't he just wake up at home in a cold sweat and, after realizing it had all been a horrible dream, get up, eat breakfast, and later laugh about it with Zig over a beer? That poor little girl. Think what her parents were going through this morning. And it was all his fault because he couldn't kill a criminal lowlife four minutes earlier.

And two weeks from now? He vowed Janie would not die. If he had no weapon, he'd use his teeth if need be to rip open the throat of someone, anyone, before the clock struck twelve.

The easiest path, of course, was to take his own life. Since Janie was the only one left, there no longer was any chance his death would save one of the others and leave his daughter to Chad and Britney. But did suicide count? Who the hell knew?

After he'd hung up with Gayle, Briscoe had told him he had a visitor, his priest. When the door opened, Matt Sheran held his gaze as he walked purposely to the table. The priest sat down in the uncomfortable, straight-back chair before Briscoe had even fully closed the door.

The moment they both heard the click of the door locking, the priest spoke.

"How did you know?"

"You were there?"

"I almost didn't go. I told myself you were a troubled soul and my job was to bring you peace if possible. And the first step on that path was to show you how your delusions weren't real."

"Did Gayle let you in?"

"She offered. Don't know what you told her, but she was very welcoming. Still, I decided to wait in the car. Figured a little after midnight I'd take off and be in my own bed by one. Midnight came and went. I waited an extra ten minutes just in case. But nothing happened. The door didn't fly open, your ex-wife didn't come running out of the house screaming her head off. Nothing. So I left."

"And Emma?"

"I was a couple blocks away when I heard sirens. I saw flashing lights and followed the emergency vehicles back to your old neighborhood. Asked myself, could everything you've been telling me be true? But the ambulance didn't turn onto your old street. It turned one street earlier."

"To Emma Wong's house."

The priest nodded. "I stopped at the scene. I told the family I just happened to be passing by, and asked was there anything I could do."

"Died of a broken neck, right?"

Father Matt's jaw dropped. "Nothing's been in the papers, not even the neighbors knew how the accident happened. The older brother confided the information to me."

"I saw Emma with Chad this morning on TV. Her neck appeared broken. And she was wearing pink Hello Kitty pj's. What happened?"

"Emma woke up a little before midnight very thirsty. She wanted to go downstairs to get some Coke from the fridge. She tripped on the feet of her oversized pajamas and tumbled down the stairs. When she reached the first floor, her neck snapped."

"It's my fault." Tom struggled to keep the tears from his eyes.

Matt reached out and put a comforting hand on Tom's arm. Tom used his other arm to wipe his eyes. "Isn't this where you're supposed to say something like, 'There must be a reasonable explanation'?"

The priest lowered his eyes. Was he praying?

Tom continued. Suddenly he desperately needed someone to believe him. "If your faith is real, if you truly accept the concept of good and evil, of God and Satan, then you must believe me."

While a declarative sentence, Tom raised his voice at the end, positing his remark as a question. Matthew didn't respond, so Tom proceeded to describe the events of the previous night. When he was finished, Matthew leaned back and shook his head.

"You could've been killed."

"If Ball had killed me before midnight, possibly Emma would now be alive. Who the hell knows what the rules are? You're supposed to be God's agent on earth, what are the rules? Tell me what the frigging rules are?"

"I don't know."

"And in two weeks Janie will die unless I commit murder. So what's the moral thing to do, Father? Take my own life and hope my application to hell's accepted? Murder a total stranger?"

"Suicide's a sin."

"Gimme a break. Now? Today? If I knew for certain taking my own life would count and save Janie, then we wouldn't be having this conversation. I'd be hanging from my bunk bed post with my snappy orange jumpsuit tied around my neck."

Neither of them spoke for almost a full minute. Then Tom broke the silence, his voice softened.

"Sorry I raised my voice. It really has nothing to do with you personally. I guess if I've appeared hostile, it's because I'm just an average guy matched up against...against what? Demons from hell?" Even now, after all that's happened, those words sounded crazy.

Tom continued. "You have to understand, when my mom died, at first I blamed God, then quickly concluded there was no God, or this wonderful woman who believed deeply in Him would still be alive. Now, thanks to the demon twins, I do believe, but not in the God of love and goodness you and those like you

preach. A God of goodness would not have allowed that innocent child to die as if He'd just lost a few chips in a poker hand."
Tom took a deep breath. "You're the closest thing on Earth to the
cosmic good guys, and I think I've been frustrated that no one on
your side has done anything to help." He struggled to hold back
the tears. "Right now, I just need you to believe me."

Matt didn't respond; his head was bowed and it was evi-
dent he was engaged in some kind of internal struggle. Finally, he
looked up.

"When we first met, I thought you were loony tunes. But as
time passed, I began to question, not my faith but my commitment, my belief in my faith. Does that make sense?"

"Um, not really."

"I believed in God, in the power of redemption, and yes,
heaven and hell, though not so much in the fairy tale version of
those places. But I was never tested; the strength of my belief was
never tested."

Tom stood up and paced back and forth across the small space.
"I now know with absolute certainty there is an evil force roaming
this world, a force that can cause an innocent little girl to trip on her
pink pajamas and fall to her death. Please tell me I'm insane."

"If the Bible's to be believed, hell's real and demons, they're
real, too."

Tom struggled to suppress anger from his voice. "But God's
the top guy, right? The king of kings, lord of lords. Hallelujah.
You're telling me He's going to let this child, and maybe another
child, my daughter, burn in agony for all eternity?"

"There are passages in the Book of Peter which describe
Christ entering hell and releasing deserving souls. I would like to
think—" The priest looked away and lowered his voice almost to a
whisper, speaking as if only to himself. "I *have* to think, to *believe,*
He would not countenance an innocent soul suffering eternal tor-
ment. But—"

"But you don't know. Of course, no one knows. Okay, two
simple questions. Do you believe me? Will you help me?"

"Yes, I believe you. But, aside from praying for God's intercession, I'm not sure what I can do."

"I know this sounds nuts, but what about an exorcism? Somehow, these demons are connecting with me, so they must be inside me. Maybe when they stopped the car from crashing over the bridge, they, I don't know, sort've infected me. Do you guys still perform exorcisms?"

"A little over ten years ago, the church updated its ritual for exorcism, a rite which dates back at least as far as 1614. Exorcisms are conducted every year; they're not publicized in order to avoid undue attention. But there are specialists who conduct this rite."

"You're not allowed to do it?"

"Any priest is permitted to perform an exorcism, but—"

"What do we have to lose?"

That Matt was engaged in an internal conflict was obvious from his expression. "You must understand, a true exorcism is not like the movies. No green vomit or swiveling heads. It's serious business."

Tom kicked the chair, knocking it over. "Serious business? An innocent young girl's life was snuffed out and another, my daughter, her life is gravely threatened, and you don't consider that *serious business?*"

The priest didn't react to Tom's outburst, his distant gaze telegraphing his mind was elsewhere. Tom took his seat and waited what seemed like an eternity for Matthew to respond.

"It's possible," said the priest.

"Do you really believe it could work?"

"I have absolutely no idea. But there's one major problem."

"What?"

"You have to get out of jail."

CHAPTER 49

The worn shock absorbers on the old prison bus were no match for the city's potholes, and its occupants bounced around in their uncomfortable bench seats as the vehicle maneuvered through Monday morning rush-hour traffic on its way to the courthouse. The bus was full. Tom assumed Mondays were busy days in the judicial system, given the citizenry's penchant for criminal mischief on weekends.

As the bus approached the courthouse, Tom saw a midsized media gaggle, replete with satellite trucks, cameras, mic booms, light umbrellas, and perfectly coiffed news personalities gathered on the Indiana Avenue plaza.

"I wonder who they're here for?" asked Tom, to no one in particular.

"They here for you, New," said a voice from the back of the bus. "You the man with the stripe."

***

"United States versus Thomas Michael Booker."

The bailiff's booming voice carried through the door to the holding cell behind the courtroom. Tom had just finished changing into a suit and tie that Zig provided to the marshal a half hour earlier. A few other inmates had changed out of their orange jumpsuits as well, but most continued to wear the prison garb and didn't appear to care. The marshal nodded to Tom, who stepped forward while the cell door was unlocked. The marshal led him through the heavy oak door to a packed Courtroom 16. No cameras were allowed, but Tom saw reporters furiously taking notes, while at least one artist had her colored pencils poised over her sketch pad.

Eva stood behind the defense table with a welcoming smile. Zig, sitting directly behind her on the first bench, offered a thumbs up. The marshal unlocked Tom's cuffs, and he sat down next to Eva.

He saw that the AUSA was Vera Lutz, whom he remembered from the Reece Mackey hearing. He nodded a greeting, she ignored him.

"How are your injuries?" asked Eva.

"Not as bad. What about bail?"

She flicked her eyes toward the bench where the Honorable Gerhard Schnabel presided. In his brief criminal defense career, Tom had never appeared in front of Schnabel, but everyone knew his reputation. The judge leaned so far toward the prosecution that his detractors, which included virtually every other member of the criminal justice system, referred to him as the Fuhrer. With his shock of snow white hair, trimmed beard, florid face, and permanent scowl, he resembled an insane Santa Claus. His voice retained the slightest residue of his parents' native German tongue.

"The defendant will rise." Tom paused for a second, looking to Eva. Big mistake. "I said rise!"

Tom shot up as if he'd been goosed.

The Fuhrer continued. "Are you Thomas Michael Booker?"

"Yes, sir."

"Mr. Booker, you have been arrested and charged with first-degree murder, to wit: that you with premeditation and malice aforethought, did cause the death of one Jessica Marie Hawkins. The purpose of this proceeding is simply to notify you of the charges, and advise you of your right to retain counsel, and if you can't afford counsel to provide you with an attorney."

Eva stood. "Your Honor, I'll be representing Mr. Booker in this case."

The judge frowned. "It's my understanding the defendant is

an attorney in one of the largest firms in the city. Are you telling me he can't afford his own representation and is asking the hard-working taxpayers of this city to pay for his defense?"

"Your Honor, Mr. Booker is divorced, and pays substantial alimony and child support. He lives in a modest one-bedroom apartment, and drives a five-year-old car. He's assured me that he will contribute whatever he can toward his defense, which will go toward partially defraying PDS' costs of defending others who are less fortunate."

Schnabel deepened his scowl. Tom panicked. Could the judge bar Eva from representing him because she was paid by the government? After a long pause, the judge responded. "Very well. The clerk will enter Ms. Stoddard as counsel of record. Mr. Booker, you are advised you have a right not to make a statement to the police or anyone else, and that anything you say to anyone other than your attorney may be used against you. Do you understand?"

Tom was so relieved Eva was going to be able to represent him he almost smiled as he answered. "Yes, sir."

"You are entitled to a preliminary hearing to determine whether there is probable cause to bind your case over to the grand jury. You also have a right to waive the preliminary hearing and go straight to arraignment."

"Defendant does not waive his right to a preliminary hearing," said Eva.

The judge glanced down at his clerk sitting directly below him at a tiny desk.

"Monday, three weeks from now," said the silver-haired lady.

"Acceptable to you, Ms. Lutz?"

The prosecutor checked her calendar on her laptop. "Fine, Your Honor."

"Set the date."

Tom noted that the judge didn't even offer Eva the courtesy of inquiring whether the date worked on her calendar as well.

"Anything else, Ms. Lutz?"

"No, Your Honor."

"Mr. Bailiff, please call the next—"

"Excuse me, Your Honor—" Eva cut him off; he was not pleased. "Defense would like to briefly address the matter of bail."

"This is a murder case, Ms. Stoddard."

"I'm well aware of that, Your Honor. But, Mr. Booker is a respected member of the bar. He grew up in the metropolitan area. He works for one of the most reputable firms in the country, and he has been volunteering pro bono to represent the city's indigents in this court system. His daughter resides in Arlington, and he has no prior record. His former wife is here today to offer support."

Tom turned to see Gayle sitting several rows back. She offered as close to a reassuring smile as he had a right to expect. Sitting directly behind her was his cousin, Estin, who offered a thumbs up. Eva continued her pitch.

"In addition, Mr. Booker's cousin, Estin Booker, is present to vouch for defendant. Estin Booker is the sheriff of Cumberton, Maryland, and as an officer of the law, is well aware of both the seriousness of the charges and the defendant's obligations to appear when scheduled. He's ready and willing to take full responsibility for defendant's appearance. Finally, we note that the government's case is paper thin. They have the murder weapon found near his car and a partial print that likely won't survive a motion *in limine*. The trumped-up motive appears to be a very brief, minor exchange during a birthday party for his firm's senior partner. Accordingly, we request defendant be released on his own recognizance, into the custody of Sheriff Booker, or at most, be required to post modest bond."

Tom saw it as a minor victory that the Fuhrer didn't immediately crash his gavel to his desk and shout "denied." Instead, he turned to the prosecutor.

"The Government, of course, strongly opposes the defense request," said Lutz. "As Your Honor aptly observed, defendant is charged with first-degree murder, and thus will have the highest motivation to flee the jurisdiction, and even the country. We see—"

Eva interrupted. "Mr. Booker would be more than willing to surrender his passport, Your Honor. Moreover, he'd agree to limit himself to the District, Maryland, and Northern Virginia, pending his next appearance, unless specifically permitted to go beyond those boundaries by the court."

"An innocent young woman has been murdered," countered Lutz. "The government believes it has accumulated more than sufficient evidence to convict defendant of this heinous crime, in which case he'll be facing the very real prospect of spending the rest of his life behind bars. That's powerful motivation to—"

"I've heard enough," proclaimed Schnabel. "Bail will be set at three million dollars."

Eva pleaded, "Your Honor, imposing three million dollars is the same as no bail. As I said earlier, Mr. Booker is not a wealthy—" She stopped mid-sentence upon seeing the judge, bailiff, court reporter, and clerk raise their heads and look to the back of the courtroom.

She and Tom turned to observe Bat Masterson himself striding up the aisle.

CHAPTER 50

"Is this good or bad news?" Tom whispered to Eva.

"Masterson was the AG when Schnabel received his judicial appointment, so we'll see very shortly."

Masterson's voice filled the room, and every reporter scribbled furiously. "Your Honor, might I impose upon the court's largesse to very briefly interrupt these proceedings to address the court on this matter?"

Schnabel smiled, and Tom saw the two men lock eyes, as if an unspoken message was being conveyed. "The court recognizes former Attorney General Masterson."

"Your Honor, Mr. Booker has been and continues to be a very valuable associate at our firm. I can't for a moment conceive of him committing the crime of which he's charged, but that will be determined at future proceedings. With respect to the instant matter, I respectfully request the court reconsider its ruling. I will personally vouch for Mr. Booker, and assure you he'll be present for all proceedings in this court in order to fight these baseless allegations and clear his good name."

Lutz sputtered in her attempt to respond to Masterson. "Your Honor—"

Like a maestro conducting an orchestra, the Fuhrer raised one hand, and Lutz stopped her counter in mid-sentence.

After a long pause, Schnabel responded. "This court has the highest respect for Mr. Masterson, but—"

"Damn," whispered Tom.

"—releasing defendant on his own recognizance would be highly inappropriate, given the gravity of the offense. However, Mr. Masterson's support does highlight the points raised by counsel regarding defendant's community ties. Therefore, the court will modify the bail amount to one million dollars with a 10 percent bond."

"Thank you, Your Honor," said Masterson. "And we think so highly of Mr. Booker, I will present a check for one hundred thousand dollars to the clerk immediately following this proceeding to assure this innocent man not have to remain incarcerated one more minute than necessary."

The Fuhrer banged his gavel. "Next case."

**

Tom drained half the can of Bud in one swallow as he drove north on Rock Creek Parkway toward Adams Morgan. The trees in the park were now mostly bare, and though a sunny day, their stark black trunks, lined up like faceless soldiers, appeared vaguely sinister. He shivered, then finished the Bud.

It had taken till midafternoon before he'd been released. Eva had arranged to have him exit the restricted entrance in the rear of the building to avoid the media jackals gathered on the front plaza. After a quick kiss, she promised to come by after cleaning up a few things on her desk. Zig offered a ride home, but if Tom was going to save his daughter, he needed wheels. He'd insisted Zig drop him off at a Hertz office downtown, where he'd picked up a small Ford, then made a quick stop at a liquor store.

Janie was the last target. He was now free to save her. No need to worry about getting caught. One life, any life. If he knew for certain his own would qualify, at the next curve he'd veer into the nearest tree without a second thought. With one hand and a practiced thumb, he popped another beer.

He attempted to pass a big black Mercedes in front of him. As he pulled even, the driver accelerated. *Some fat-cat jerk*, thought Tom. Can't stand that a little Ford Escort or Eclipse, or whatever the hell he was driving, would pass his hotshot car. Tinted windows prevented Tom from seeing the driver's face, but he flipped the finger anyway.

The Mercedes accelerated. *One life, any life.* Why wait till the last minute? Won't have to think about an exorcism. Finish this right here, right now. Driver probably wasn't a killer, but no doubt had done some unsavory things in his life. Hell with it. *Hell with it.* Funny.

Tom saw the sharp left curve ahead. He stepped on the gas and accelerated past the Mercedes, then cut the wheel sharply to the right, attempting to force the Mercedes off the road into a huge oak hurtling toward them.

The driver slammed on his brakes. With tires squealing, the big black car spun in a full circle, out of control, heading straight for the oak. But at the last moment, the driver was able to bring it to a stop on the shoulder facing backwards.

Tom slowed and checked his rearview mirror. The driver got out. *No.* A young woman, early twenties. She opened the back door and pulled an infant from a car seat.

Oh, my God.

His shoulders heaved as the tears came and continued all he way home. He wouldn't have stopped them even if he could.

***

Tom finished the Stella. He was in his apartment, sitting across his table from Zig.

"Now that you've washed the edge off, you want to walk down to Napoleon's for some real food?" asked Zig.

"I'm starving for anything that isn't white, limp, or damp, but given my new celebrity, not sure that's a great idea." Tom got up and rummaged through his cupboard and in the back corner found a can of chicken noodle soup that had probably been there for over a year.

"Don't you dare," said Zig. He pulled out his phone and

tapped a speed-dial number. "One large, no, make that two large, with sausage, mushrooms..." He looked to Tom.

"Peppers, double peppers."

Zig finished the order, provided the address, and terminated the call.

Tom replaced the soup and returned to the table. "I know I already said this, but I can't thank you enough. And I never had a chance to thank Mr. Masterson."

"You're welcome. What are your immediate plans?"

"Good question. I don't know how I can go back to PDS. Doubt any court would approve my appointment to represent an accused. Judge would be afraid if the man were found guilty, the conviction would be overturned because of the likelihood a juror who thought I killed Jess would convict the client by association. What about the firm?"

"It's not my call, but Bat said to tell you to lie low for a few days. You know, till things cool down. And you'll continue to be paid, of course."

"Again, thank you." Tom really did appreciate the firm's help—otherwise, he'd still be living in the D Street Hilton. But although socializing with Zig felt great, he couldn't keep his mind from the exorcism to rid his body—his soul?—of the demons inside him.

If they were inside him. After the incident on the Parkway, Tom had resolved to put his faith in Father Sheran. As soon as he'd arrived at his apartment, he'd excused himself from Zig and gone into the bathroom to call the priest. Matthew explained he was working on setting up the ritual and promised to get back in touch soon. Tom resisted the strong impulse to press him further. In the meantime, he would try to act as normal as possible. Which meant engaging in discussions about his case with the people who cared about him.

Zig continued, "The free time will allow you and Eva to concentrate on your defense, and maybe even finding Jess' real killer."

Tom's response was interrupted by a knock.

"Too soon for pizza," said Zig.

Tom opened the door to greet Eva. She carried a six-pack of Bud and a bag surrounded by the seductive aroma of hot french fries. She set the beer and food on the table, then turned and embraced him.

"I never really thought you'd get out," she said.

"A lack of confidence from my own attorney is not very comforting." He smiled broadly and kissed her.

"Hey, you want I should leave?" asked Zig.

"No, no. Join us," she responded. "There's an extra burger in there."

"Already ordered pizza, but whatever's left over will keep," said Tom. He kissed her again, then opened the bag, removed a large container of fries, and ate half of them in one bite.

"A couple days in the slammer and you eat like a pig," said Eva.

Tom's voice was partially muffled by the butts of fries sprouting from his mouth. "And your point is—?"

They all laughed, and it was all Tom could do to keep from choking on the fries.

***

With Tom vacuuming in the food like a Hoover, they'd killed the burgers, the pizza, and most of the second six-pack. Tom heard Zig and Eva discussing his case, but their voices sounded like they were at the far end of a tunnel. His mind was consumed with the exorcism and the chance to rid his body, his life, of the threat to his daughter.

"Tom—Tom, are you even listening to us?" asked Eva.

"Yes, sure, of course." He tried to focus on their conversation.

"Okay, the police believe the ransacking of Jess' place was a clumsy attempt to deflect suspicion from the fact that she knew the killer," said Eva.

Zig, reclining in Tom's red chair, grabbed a beer from the lamp table next to him and tossed the two remaining cans to Tom and Eva sitting on the couch. "What do you think?" he asked.

Eva set her beer down on the coffee table unopened. "From

the discovery they've given me so far, they're probably right," she responded. "There's no evidence of sexual assault. Nothing missing from the unit—money, jewelry, were all easily findable but nothing taken. It has all the earmarks of the killer trying to throw off the cops. But don't get me wrong. At trial, we'll definitely use the spooked, robbery-gone-bad theory to try to establish reasonable doubt."

"Trial?" asked Tom.

Eva hastily stepped back. "Highly unlikely we'll get that far."

"Guys, remember why Jess wanted me to come over," said Tom. "She said she needed legal advice and was scared. You saw her at the party, she was highly agitated. Said 'they' were looking for something, which fits in with the ransacking."

"The problem is, you're the only witness to that conversation," said Eva.

"Assuming it wasn't a burglary gone bad, anyone else who'd have a motive to take her life?" Zig asked.

"No idea," replied Tom. "I mean, I hardly knew the girl. What does Marcie say? Anybody who would hate her enough to kill her? Any idea what she was hiding?"

"Clueless," Zig responded. "Although after the medics took Jess' body away, Marcie said she looked for Jess' phone so she could find contact info for her family and friends, but couldn't locate it."

'You think Jess hid her cell phone?" asked Eva.

Zig shrugged. "Who knows? Could be she had some information or pictures on the phone the intruder wanted."

"But why wouldn't Jess pass on any troubling information to Marcie? Why the cloak and dagger?" asked Tom.

"Again, no idea." responded Zig. "Marcie's still a little traumatized by the whole thing. After all, if she hadn't been with me, she could be dead. Maybe with time she'll remember something. The question is, why wouldn't Jess tell you her little secret over the phone? Or at least, where she was hiding the phone, if that's what it was?"

Now it was Tom's turn to shrug. Suddenly, he remembered

Jess' last words. "She did say, just before she hung up, she said if something happened to her, remember doo-wop."

Eva appeared perplexed. "Doo-wop?"

"What the hell's that supposed to mean?" asked Zig.

"Got me. I assume it's some kind of code."

"Maybe a location to whatever 'they' were looking for," said Zig. "If you find what she was hiding, it could lead cops to the real killer."

"Why didn't she just tell me? Why the code?"

"It could be she was worried your phone was bugged. Or maybe she thought you were with somebody. Who knows?"

Tom shook his head. "Doo-wop's music from the late '50s, early '60s. I don't see a connection to anything."

Eva turned to Zig. "I need to get into some attorney-client stuff here with Tom, so why don't you excuse us for a little bit, and then if he wants to see you later, he can call?"

Zig smiled. "If he calls to spend time with me instead of you, then he no longer has to worry about conviction, 'cause he'll have a slam-dunk insanity defense no jury could deny."

Eva chuckled as Zig got up and moved to the door. "I think there's a compliment in there somewhere."

"Hey—" Tom rose from the couch and embraced his friend. "Thank you."

Zig slapped him on the back. "You'd do the same for me." As he closed the door, he paused for a moment and turned back.

"And think about the doo-wop remark. Could be key."

CHAPTER 51

With Eva's help, Tom cleared the empty beer cans and food trash from the table.

"You're lucky to have a good friend like Zig," she said.

"I know. I'm sure he's the one who pitched my case to Masterson. Still can't believe the firm posted a hundred grand for me."

"To them, it's a rounding error. And not to diminish his good deed, but the firm had two choices—throw you under the bus, or indignantly proclaim your innocence and the gross injustice of your arrest. Luckily, and maybe it was Zig who tipped the balance, they opted for door number two."

When he cleared the last unopened beer from the coffee table, he reached for the pop-top.

"Tom—" Eva eyed the beer. An uncomfortable silence. "Look, it's not my place to—" she purposely didn't finish the sentence.

Tom momentarily froze with embarrassment. His voice sounded weak. "Uh, you're right. Probably had enough."

"I'm sorry, I have no right—"

"No, you're absolutely correct. I have to be careful." He placed the unopened beer can in the fridge. He knew on occasion he probably drank too much, but he felt he was always under control. Fact was, he had no idea how long it would take for the priest to get back to him, but if it happened soon he'd need to have his wits about him. He doubted an exorcism would work if he'd been drinking. "I need to have a clear head to assist in my defense."

In two steps she was in his arms. She kissed his neck and whispered, "I really care about you and don't want anything to happen to you."

Her warm body pressed tight against him felt wonderful. Despite his attempts to stop it, her embrace loosened the last remaining bricks in the wall—the tears trickled at first, then flowed unabated. She squeezed him tighter as his body heaved; the emotions from the last two months spilled out and there was nothing he could do to stop them.

After a while he pulled back, grabbed a paper towel off the roll on the kitchen counter, and wiped his eyes. "Sorry about that."

She kissed him. "Don't be. You okay?"

"For the moment. Just, you know, the whole thing, everything, seems surreal."

He blew his nose into the paper towel with a honk loud enough to call a gaggle of geese. They both laughed much harder than the honking deserved.

Eva put on hot water for tea. "Look, on the drinking, my brother was a functioning alcoholic, and it ruined his life. As I said, I have no right to nag you, but maybe at some point if you decide you might need some help, I have a bunch of contacts."

"Thank you. I mean it when I say I'll keep that in mind. But for now, what's the attorney-client stuff you mentioned?"

She readied two cups with a chamomile tea bag and a squirt of honey from the bear-shaped squeeze bottle. "We need to talk about the gun."

"It was mine."

"I assumed that. Why did you get it and who did you get it from?"

Tom paused as he struggled with how to respond. He didn't want to draw Chewy into this case. Also, how was he supposed to answer the "why" question? Tell the truth? That he needed the weapon to kill random citizens so his daughter would remain safe from two preppy demons from hell? The last thing he wanted to do was lie to Eva. He'd already done that once. Maybe his only path was to tell the truth about not being able to tell the truth.

"I promised you I would never lie to you, so I'm very sorry, but I can't answer either of those questions. I know what I tell you is protected, but my reasons go beyond my case, and I'm sure you're curious, and maybe a bit angry I'm not telling you everything, but please trust me that I have no choice."

She held his gaze for a moment, then poured the boiling water into the cups.

He took hold of her arms and turned her around. "I will also repeat what I hope you already know—I had absolutely nothing to do with Jess' death."

"I know, and I hate that you're keeping things from me, things that may help me keep your butt out of jail. I appreciate you not telling me something that isn't true, but—"

"Eva, I need, I really *really* need you to trust me." He held her gaze and neither spoke for several moments.

"Okay," she whispered. "But you have to promise you'll tell me all you can the moment you're able to."

"Promise."

He kissed her and his heart soared when she kissed him back. She pulled back, took a cup of tea, and returned to the table. Tom followed suit.

"I met with Percy Castro before I came over. He gave me full discovery and didn't seem displeased you were out of jail. My guess is, he knows the government's case against you is not overwhelming, and he's hoping you'll do something stupid to strengthen it. So be careful of everything you say. I doubt if your phone's tapped, but it's possible. And that, of course, also means your cell. When you and I talk on the phone, you must keep your comments very vague. The only time we can have a substantive discussion is when we're alone together like this."

"Guess that means we'll have to be spending more time alone together." He attempted a smile.

She didn't reciprocate. "I'm serious, and you need to take this seriously, unless you really took a liking to prison food."

"Anything interesting come out of your meeting with Castro?"

"Yeah, noise. Or more precisely, the lack of it. All neighbors were interviewed and no one heard a shot. Given the sound made by that model of Glock, one, if not both, of Jess' neighbors should've heard the shot."

"So?"

"So maybe the shooter used a silencer, and lucky for you, no silencer was found at the scene of your crash or in the search of your apartment."

"Are the cops buying this silencer theory?"

"Castro was noncommittal. Key question. Was your gun threaded, you know, so a suppressor could be screwed onto the barrel?"

Tom thought for a moment. "I know I sound like an idiot, but I don't remember. Can't you make the cops show you the weapon?"

"Yeah, just trying to save time."

"Is there a way for ballistics to tell if a silencer was used?"

"Depends. The new ones don't leave a trace, but older versions, going back to the Vietnam War, used baffles or wipes, inner chambers made of plastic, rubber, or foam to suppress the sound from the exploding gases as the bullet passed through. These wipes would often leave a mark on the bullet. And to answer your next question, yes, I have an appointment set up with the ballistic lab tech assigned to the case to see if there was any evidence of a wipe stain on the bullet that killed Jess."

"Even if all this pans out, the cops'll just say I ditched the silencer."

"Probably. But if you ditched the silencer, why not the gun? Remember, all we have to do is instill reasonable doubt in a single juror."

He barely heard her words. He was consumed with a gun, but it wasn't the one in police custody. He needed a new weapon to take one more life, and he needed it now.

"Don't look so down," said Eva. "You're out of jail, and while it's an uphill battle, we have the time to plan a defense that'll keep it—are you with me here?"

"Sorry." He looked at her across the table, so beautiful, so trusting, and he realized he needed his mind to blank out for a while. No more thoughts of demons and death, of jail and juries. He stood, walked around the table, bent down and kissed her.

She smiled. "We really need—"

He kissed her again, this time lingering longer. She stood, and they embraced, then she reached for the buttons of his shirt.

CHAPTER 52

By noon the next day, Tom had called Father Matthew twice to check on the status, reminding the priest of the approaching deadline—emphasis on *dead*—just over four days away. After the second call, the priest told him to stop calling, he was moving as fast as he could.

The time seemed to drag on forever. Tom felt imprisoned in his own apartment. He couldn't go to work for either PDS or the firm. Because of his notoriety, he was reluctant to go out in public. Tuesday and Wednesday afternoons he arranged for Gayle to bring Janie over to see him for a couple of hours while she and Angie went shopping. He felt a need to spend every moment hugging his daughter, but he didn't want to creep her out. He helped her with her homework, and they watched TV and snacked on popcorn. Those few hours were some of the happiest in his life, and his heart cracked each time he heard Gayle knocking on the door to take Janie back to Arlington.

Eva and Zig came over with takeout Tuesday and Wednesday nights. For a couple of hours, Tom did his best to forget about his troubles. Wednesday, Zig brought Marcie, and the four of them watched a movie. But the monster—not the murder charge, but the *big* monster—always lurked in the back of Tom's mind.

After the movie, at Eva's prodding, the four of them discussed the case, which mostly consisted of Eva gently questioning Marcie about anything she may have forgotten about Jess, her missing phone, her mood changes, her associates, and any secrets Jess may have confided that could've slipped Marcie's mind.

Marcie genuinely tried to help, but it became clear after a few sessions that she really knew nothing that would contribute. During these discussions, Tom struggled to appear interested—after all, he was charged with first-degree murder, and his friends were trying their best to assist him. But his mind was on one thing only—his exorcism to save Janie.

Several times, Eva caught Tom checking his phone and asked him about it. He couldn't tell her he was waiting for word from a priest on scheduling his exorcism, so he did what he promised her he would never do and lied, telling her he was expecting a call from his cousin Estin.

Wednesday night, Eva stayed over, although she complained that his nightmares—she reported in the middle of the night he'd shout out angrily to some guy named Chad—kept her from a good night's sleep.

Thursday morning he received a bit of good news. A city councilman had been discovered having secret affairs with young teenage girls. The politician got a big red stripe of his own and, Tom fervently hoped, the fickle public would forget about the Intern Killer.

Thursday night, he and Zig decided to test his hoped-for fall from celebrity, and went out to Napoleon's for a burger and beer. To Tom's delight, although a couple of patrons stared for a few seconds, nobody bothered him. When Zig brought up the case and the doo-wop reference, Tom cut him off.

"Let's not talk about the case for one night."

"You're absolutely right. So let's talk about our favorite subject."

"Sports?"

"Women. You and Eva look like maybe you might have something going there."

"Don't know about her, but I really—"

Tom's phone vibrated in his pocket. He looked at the screen to see a text from Father Matthew: *Be at your apt in 1 hr.*

***

After making a feeble, bullshit excuse—he had a headache, he had a stomachache, he couldn't recall which—he'd left Zig at the bar and jogged home, making it in under ten minutes. Having pushed for this time to come, he now felt hesitant, maybe a little scared. Maybe a lot scared.

His only understanding of the exorcism rite came from an old movie. The previous night, when Zig asked him if he had any flick requests, he'd mentioned *The Exorcist* as casually as he could.

Though he'd seen the movie a number of times, it still scared the crap out of him. The sight of Linda Blair's head swiveling 360 degrees, spewing green vomit, the vile profanity coming from her young character's mouth, the rising bed, the screams.

Matthew had said a true exorcism was nothing like the depiction in the movie, but Tom was skeptical. The goal of the rite was to force Satan or his demons from their warm nesting place inside a human body. If Chad and Brit were indeed camping out in his soul, then evicting them would be no walk in the park.

Tom sat at his small table and watched the clock on the kitchen wall. Forty more minutes. His eyes fell on his bed. Would he be lying down? Standing? Sitting at the kitchen table chatting with the priest? He realized his bed was in its usual state of unmadeness, which probably wasn't a word. He knew very few men who made their beds unless their wives or girlfriends told them to do it, or if mixed company were expected. Why make a bed when you're just going to mess it up again in sixteen hours? But a priest was not like a regular guy, so he probably ought to make the bed.

He took his time, carefully folding each corner of each sheet and each blanket. He fluffed up the pillows, then concluded it was probably time to change the pillow cases, actually, long past time. When he was finished, he figured he'd probably set a record for the amount of time a heterosexual male took to make a bed. Then he wondered if there was a bed-making category in the *Guinness Book of Records*. Then he wondered if the Guinness book guy was the same as the Guinness beer guy? If so, there probably was a bed-making category, male division. Then he wondered if he were going mad.

Then there was a knock on the door.

Tom jumped to answer it. The priest entered along with a woman. Like the priest, she was dressed in black.

"We're early," said Matthew. Tom immediately saw that he was carrying a large black satchel.

"No problem," responded Tom. "Actually glad. I've been getting a little stir crazy waiting around."

"This is Sister Irene," said Matthew.

Probably only a few years older than Tom, Irene would've been generally considered attractive with even a modicum of makeup. As it was, she came across as a warm, wholesome woman, with clear eyes and a disarming smile. Her garb consisted of a long black skirt and a plain white blouse. No white apron and nothing on her head.

"Pleased to meet you, Mr. Booker." She smiled, no doubt reading his thoughts. "I teach at Georgetown, where more contemporary clothing is permitted."

"The rite requires two participants other than the afflicted," said Matthew.

Tom remembered the last scenes of the movie, where Father Karras assisted the exorcist, Father Merrin, when he performed the rite on Linda Blair.

"Sister Irene is fully aware of the nature of your affliction," added the priest.

"Sure, great, good to meet you. The more the merrier." Should he offer them a beverage? Probably not. They weren't here to—

"You by any chance have a Coke?" asked the nun. "My throat's a little dry."

"Yeah, sure."

"Make that two," said Matthew.

Tom performed his host duties while Matthew talked.

"First, as I told you, I've never done this before. But I checked with the diocese, and, while I will concede they weren't overly thrilled, they advised me to proceed. Sister Irene and I have been going over the liturgy, rehearsing if you will, and I think we're ready."

"As ready as we'll ever be," said the sister.

Tom handed each of them a glass of Coke on ice. "So, do I lie down on the bed for this, like in the movie?"

Matthew hesitated only for a moment. "If you wish." He glanced at Sister Irene. "There's another less comfortable alternative, maybe a bit more radical, but possibly more effective."

"I'll do whatever it takes to increase the chances of success."

"The idea would be to place you in the same position as Christ when he died for our sins."

Tom stood against the wall with his arms outstretched. "No problem."

"Your arms will tire, and no one really knows what to expect. Chances are, absolutely nothing will happen. But if something does occur, you might decide it safer for yourself and us if passive restraints were employed."

"Passive restraints? Sounds so...passive." Tom figured if the demons were indeed inside him, they might become royally pissed if they were evicted. "Sure, why not?"

Matthew surveyed the room until his eyes fell on the double casement windows behind the kitchen table. With Irene's help, he moved the table aside. The casements were only half windows—the sill looked to be about shoulder height. At the base of each window, a brass handle used to crank the window open protruded out from the sill. Matthew opened his satchel and removed two red silk scarves. He wrapped one of them around a crank handle and pulled hard, testing the handle's strength. The handle appeared solid.

"Do you need to use the restroom first?" asked Sister Irene. "I'm afraid once we start, there won't be an opportunity."

"I'm good."

Tom stood in front of the double windows, spread his arms, and allowed Irene to tie his wrists to the crank handles. She moved quickly, like an experienced nurse preparing a patient for surgery. He tugged against the silk, testing it. "You learn how to tie those knots in Girl Scouts?"

"As a matter of fact, yes." She must have noticed his quizzical expression. "Nuns don't descend from Mars, Mr. Booker. We all have had lives prior to entering our chosen work, lives that for the most part were pretty normal."

Tom wondered if "pretty normal" meant she wasn't a virgin.

Her eyes twinkled. "And the answer to the question that's popped into your head is 'yes.'"

She stepped back and removed a white surplice from the satchel, then helped the priest don the tunic. Matthew withdrew a purple stole and draped the scarf around his neck. He pulled a black case about the size of a large coffee mug from the satchel, unzipped it, and removed a silver flask.

"Holy water?" asked Tom.

The priest barely nodded. Irene closed the blinds on the windows and turned out all the lights except a single reading lamp next to the couch. Matthew withdrew two black prayer books from the satchel and handed one to Irene. Bookmarks allowed each of them to find the appropriate page. They positioned themselves ten feet away from Tom.

Matthew took a deep breath and glanced at Irene, who responded with a reassuring smile. They closed their eyes in silent prayer, and the only sound Tom could hear was his own breathing.

Hail to the Redskins, Hail Victory—

"Jesus Christ," exclaimed Tom and Matthew, almost in unison.

Braves on the war path—

It was his damn cell phone. Irene reached into his jeans pocket.

Fight for old DC—
"Other pocket!"
Run or pass and score—
Sister Irene yanked out the phone and turned it off, then set it on the table.

"Uh, sorry."

The priest didn't look amused. He and the nun reopened their prayer books.

CHAPTER 53

The priest had barely begun, and Tom felt the sweat dampening his clothing. He wondered if he should keep his eyes closed, like praying in church. He kept them open.

The priest intoned, "Our Father, Who art in heaven, Hallowed be Thy Name..."

The nun, reading, responded, *"Deliver us from evil..."*

"Thy kingdom come, Thy will be done, on earth as it is in heaven..."

"Deliver us from evil..."

"Forgive us our trespasses, as we forgive those who trespass against us..."

"Deliver us from evil..."

"All holy saints of God..."

"Intercede for us..."

"Save your servant..."

As the priest and nun continued the rite, Tom tried hard to feel something, but so far, nothing stirred inside him.

The priest continued, "I command you, unclean spirit, whoever you are, along with all your minions now attacking this servant of God, by the mysteries of the incarnation, passion, resurrection, and ascension of our Lord Jesus Christ, by the descent of the Holy Spirit..."

As Matthew read from the holy book, he made the sign of the cross on his own chest, then stepped forward and repeated it on Tom's brow, lips, and breast.

The nun opened the silver flask and handed it to the priest. He stepped back and sprinkled water from the flask the length of his body.

"God and Father of our Lord Jesus Christ, I appeal to your holy name, humbly begging your kindness, that you graciously grant me help against this and every unclean spirit now tormenting this creature of yours, through Christ our Lord."

Tom couldn't feel a thing. The priest stepped forward again, made the sign of the cross over himself and Tom, then draped one end of the purple stole around Tom's neck. He rested his right hand on Tom's head.

The priest raised his voice. "I cast you out, unclean spirit, along with every Satanic power of the enemy, every spectre from hell, and all your fell companions, in the name of our Lord Jesus Christ. Begone and stay far from this creature of God. For it is He who commands you, He who—"

Tom didn't know whether he was supposed to say anything, but he interrupted anyway. "Uh, Father, not really feeling anything." Both the priest and nun acted as though they hadn't heard him.

"I adjure you, ancient serpent, by the judge of the living and the dead, by your Creator, by the Creator of the whole universe, by Him who has the power to consign you to hell, to depart forthwith in fear, along with your savage minions, from this servant of God—"

"Father? Matt?"

The priest returned to his position across the room from Tom. "Tremble before that mighty arm that broke asunder the dark prison walls and led souls forth to light—"

Tom figured the priest was so deep into the ritual that he didn't hear him. Tom raised his voice. "Matt—" His lips felt dry, and he extended his tongue to moisten them.

Except his tongue didn't extend. And his lips didn't move. He shouted, but he knew his mouth remained closed. They couldn't hear him.

"Depart, then, transgressor—"

Suddenly, Tom heard clapping.

He turned his head to see Chad and Brit, dressed as Redskins cheerleaders, sitting at his kitchen table watching the exorcism. Each ate from a bag of popcorn.

"It's them! They're right here!"

Neither the priest not the nun could hear him.

Matthew continued the ritual. "Give place, abominable creature, give way, you monster, give way to Christ—"

Tom struggled with the bindings, twisting back and forth. He lifted his feet off the ground, sagging against the restraints with his full weight. The restraints held. Tom noticed Matthew's eyes widen, and the priest exchange glances with Sister Irene. *They think it's working, that I'm possessed.*

"Depart, seducer, full of lies and cunning, foe of virtue, persecutor of the innocent—"

Tom hears a high-pitched screech, and, for a moment, the demons' images faded to near nothing—little more than a shadow. Was it working? *Oh, God, thank—*

The images returned.

"Almost had us there," said Chad. "Great show. Don't you agree, Brit?"

She applauded. "Excellent. Three stars."

"Only three?"

"Love the writing, but I wonder if the performance wouldn't benefit from a few special effects."

Chad said, "Why don't we give them what they're expecting? After all, Matt and Irene have gone to a great deal of trouble on Tom's behalf."

The priest continued, "Therefore, I adjure you, profligate dragon, in the name of the spotless Lamb, who has trodden down the asp and the basilisk, and overcome the lion and the dragon—"

Tom felt his stomach wrench. He gagged, his mouth opened wide, and green vomit dribbled out onto his shirt. The only time he could remember anything smelling so vile was when he and his dad had found a dead cat under the front porch that had been there for weeks.

"Love it," said Chad, clapping like a child.

Matthew and Irene froze, unable to take their eyes from the vomit.

"More, more!" exclaimed Chad.

Brit giggled, gargled a popcorn kernel in her mouth, then spit it toward Tom, hitting him in the gut. Suddenly, Tom felt the surge from his stomach. When the viscous liquid rose, it scorched his throat. He opened his mouth to scream and rid his body of the vile invader; the contents shot out like a fire hose, spraying green slime across the priest's vestments.

Matthew stood his ground, and Tom could see the fear on his face, on both of their faces. The priest's words increased in their urgency. "Tremble and flee, as we call on the name of the Lord, before whom the denizens of hell cower, to whom the heavenly Virtues and Powers and Dominations are subject, whom the Cherubim and Seraphim praise with unending cries—"

Chad clapped even louder. "Yes, yes!" He turned to Brit. "I'm getting very excited." He extended his tongue; it split at the end and each prong encircled toward Tom's face. Tom tried to scream, but no one could hear him. The tongue prongs tightened around his neck.

"Please, I can't breathe." No one heard him. He struggled violently against the restraints, using all of his weight and power in an attempt to rip loose the crank handles, but to no avail.

The prongs constricted tighter. Tom could feel his air cutting off and his face turning red. Couldn't the priest see he was being strangled?

The tongue snapped back to Chad's mouth. He extended it again and wrapped it around Brit's head, each prong caressing her hair.

Brit's breathing became heavier. "I need you, baby," she said.

Chad glanced at Tom. "Here? Now? What about Tom? You know how embarrassed I get."

"Tom's family," she responded. "Aren't you, Tom? You wouldn't mind if we got it on, would you?"

Matthew, his eyes closed in prayer, continued the rite. "Therefore, I adjure you every unclean spirit, every spectre from hell, every satanic power—"

Chad took Brit's hand and gently led her to Tom. She reached around Tom and grasped the window sill on each side of him. Her face was inches from his. She raised her hips and rubbed them back and forth against Chad's crotch.

The priest made the sign of the cross on his own head, then traced the sign onto Tom's brow, his hand moving freely through Brit's image as it would through dust mites.

"Depart from me, you accursed, into the everlasting fire that has been prepared for the devil and his angels—"

"Now comes the good part, Tom," whispered Brit. She ran her black tongue across her lips.

Chad unzipped his fly, and pulled out a glass tube. He smiled, and tugged on it so Tom could see it was the neck of an empty Wild Turkey bottle. He winked at Tom, and lifted Brit's burgundy skirt.

"Oooo, baby." Brit's eyes closed as Chad entered her. But Tom could still see the black orbs as if the lids were made of cellophane.

The priest's voice moved toward crescendo. "An unquenchable fire stands ready for you and for your minions, you prince of accursed murderers, father of lechery, instigator of sacrileges, model of vileness, promoter of heresies, inventor of every obscenity—!"

"Stop," shouted Tom. "Everybody, just please stop!" Chad laughed and continued to pound into Brit.

Tom could feel her putrid breath exhaling onto his face. He looked into her eyes and saw nothing but black emptiness.

Behind her, Chad sang: *"Hail to the Redskins—"*

Brit joined in. *"Hail Victory—"*

The priest shouted, "Depart, then, impious one, depart, ac-cursed one, depart with all your deceits, for God has willed that man should be His temple—!"

"Braves on the war path—"

The priest and the copulating demons moved to climax.

"Begone, now! Begone, seducer! Leave this soul and return to—"

Chad and Brit howled as they reached orgasm.

"FIGHT FOR OLD DC! Aaeeeoooohhhh!"

"—the FIRE!" Matthew trembled and had to steady him-self against a wall to keep from collapsing. Irene helped him to a chair, then quickly filled a glass with water and offered it to him.

Chad withdrew and they both rearranged their clothing. "That was amazing," he said. He pulled a handkerchief from his pocket and mopped his brow. Except Tom saw it wasn't a hand-kerchief.

"Where did you get that?"

Brit dangled it in front of Tom's eyes. It was white with pink and yellow elephants decorating the edges. Gayle had kept it in a small trunk in the bedroom closet along with other keep-sakes.

It was Janie's baby bib.

CHAPTER 54

Tom bucked his body up and down, back and forth. "Don't you touch that! Leave her alone!"

From their surprised expressions, it was clear that Matthew and Irene had heard him. He was back on the air.

"Tom, are you okay?" asked the priest.

"Leave who alone?" asked the nun.

"Take these damn things off!"

***

An hour later, Tom and Matthew sat across from each other at Tom's kitchen table, Matthew on his second beer and Tom into his second Jack on the rocks. He'd thought briefly of his exchange with Eva about his drinking, but he assumed she would understand surviving an exorcism starring copulating demons qualified as special circumstances.

Sister Irene had appeared shaken by the experience. Tom supposed she hadn't witnessed the whole green vomit thing before. As soon as they'd untied him, after a quick blessing for Tom, she'd asked Matthew to be excused and he readily agreed.

When Tom described what had occurred, Matthew was nearly inconsolable.

"We should've located someone who'd done an exorcism before. I'm very sorry."

"Forget it," said Tom. "Something tells me the outcome would've been the same if the Pope himself had performed the rite. So, I need to take another life in nine days or my daughter dies."

"You know I can't—"

"What? Condone murder?" Tom struggled to keep his voice on an even keel. "So what would you do if you were me? You don't have any kids, but what about a sister or brother? A loving mother or father? Would you willingly let them not only die, but sentence their souls to burn in hell for eternity? Or would you attempt to find a bad guy and take his life?"

After a pause, the priest whispered, "I don't know."

"And by the way, where's the frigging cavalry?" Tom took a deep breath. He knew he was close to losing it. "Sorry, Matt. I just feel abandoned. Where are God and Jesus and the angels, the whole merry band?"

"Sorry."

"Okay, I get it. We're on our own here. Look, I assume God wouldn't have a problem with self-defense. I know there's the whole 'turn the other cheek' thing, but we're not talking about a slap in the face. Does God condemn a man who shoots an intruder about to kill his kids and rape his wife? Or is He okay with letting the good guys die to protect the sanctity of the bad guy's life?"

"We're not talking about self-defense here. Your targets to date did not threaten you."

"But they'd killed before."

"So now you've moved beyond self-defense to vigilante justice as your justification. Big leap."

"Still haven't answered what you'd do."

Matthew pushed himself away from the table and headed for the door. "I'm so sorry, Tom." The priest paused, his eyes indecipherable, then left without another word.

The click of the door closing acted as a remote and the TV turned on.

The screen filled with a replay of the exorcism, including the copulating demons. Without breaking his rhythm, Chad's face turned to him.

"We had such a wonderful time and we know you did too, so we thought we'd give you a chance to enjoy the replay."

Brit smiled at him. "Just one little matter we wanted to pass on. The fact you tried the exorcism, no matter how much we enjoyed it,"—she lowered her voice to a conspiratorial whisper—"well, it caught the boss' attention, and for some reason he was in a cranky mood."

"Very cranky," added Chad.

"So, I'm afraid we have a rules modification. Not a big thing, really."

Chad added, "Not big at all."

"Your deadline's been moved up a week."

Tom shouted at the screen. "No! You can't!"

Chad and Brit spoke in unison. "Two days."

The screen went black.

CHAPTER 55

After a long, mercifully dreamless sleep, Tom woke Friday morning and immediately grabbed his phone from the bedside table. He knew Janie had the day off for teacher in-service training, and called Gayle to see if he could take Janie and Angie to lunch. She readily agreed. Something about David also having the day off and the two of them going antiquing.

Tom remembered tagging along with her for antiquing excursions when they were married. They usually occurred on Sundays and every few minutes he'd check his watch, concerned he wouldn't be back home in time for the Redskins kickoff. He'd been an ass and wished he could rewind those years. He really wished he could rewind to that morning on Memorial Bridge, but no rewinds in life, unless you'd cut a deal with the devil.

He thought about asking Gayle to check the keepsake trunk to see if the baby bib was missing, but when she found it gone, as he knew she would, how would he explain himself? He arranged to pick up the girls at eleven thirty.

After dressing in jeans and a sweater, he found a poppy seed bagel in the fridge. As soon as he picked it up, almost all of the poppy seeds fell off, signaling the bagel was beyond stale. No problem. Anything to soak up the acid he felt in his stomach. The bottle of cheap vodka lurking behind the milk carton caught his eye. A step above Frank Custer's Akron gin, but a small step. A little sip to calm his nerves wouldn't hurt. He hesitated; Eva's image filled his brain. He replaced the bottle and closed the fridge door, then exited the apartment before he changed his mind.

It was all he could do to keep from running full speed to the Shell station. As Tom approached, he spotted an old woman standing in front of the pay phone with a stack of quarters resting on the tiny, scuffed-metal shelf. Judging by her clothing and the supermarket cart parked nearby, stacked high with clothing and other paraphernalia, Tom assumed she was homeless.

"Hey—"

She turned, eyeing him suspiciously. "I'll give you twenty bucks to let me make my call first." She didn't respond, and he quickly dug a twenty from his pocket and handed it to her. She snatched the twenty, grabbed her quarters, and stepped aside, standing guard next to her cart. She never took her eyes off him.

Tom ignored her and dialed Chewy's number. He could hear breathing as the connection was made.

"Chew, uh, I mean whoever's listening, I need a gun."

He was surprised to hear Chewy's voice.

"Sorry, Teach. We're even. Stay free."

"No, wait. I've got less than two days and—!"

The click terminating the call resonated inside Tom's head. He immediately called back, but this time no one answered.

"Phone broken?"

He turned around to see Percy Castro standing behind him.

Tom tried to conceal his shock. "What, you're following me? You have nothing better to do on a Friday morning?"

The detective didn't answer him directly. Instead, he looked up to a camera mounted under the eave of the roof overhanging the station's service bay.

"Nowadays, everything's on camera. Don't know about you, but kind've gives me the creeps. Somebody's always watching."

Tom hadn't noticed the camera before, and he had a bad feeling.

"Of course, as an investigative tool, it's very helpful. Take your case, for example. We routinely check all the cameras in the neighborhood to see if a target's engaged in any suspicious behavior. To tell you the truth, the Big Brother thing makes me uncomfortable as hell, but the greater good and all that."

"I'm trying to think why I care, but nothing immediately springs to mind," said Tom, with a bravado he certainly didn't feel.

Castro continued as if Tom hadn't spoken. "Then, when we do see our guy—you, in this case—using a public pay phone, we got to ask, why, in this age when every five-year-old has his own cell phone, would you be needing to make a call from a gas station pay phone? Could it be you didn't want the call to be traceable?"

"You know you're not allowed to talk to me without my attorney present."

"So, we check the logs from the phone company—Ma Bell. Remember when we used to call the phone company Ma Bell? Good old days, right?—and trace your call to an unlisted cell phone, which switches the call to another unlisted phone in Poland. *Poland.* Then from there to some country I never heard of and can't pronounce. Very sophisticated, like you'd read in cold-war spy novels."

"And?"

"And we don't know who you were talking to, but we suspect it might've been a local drug kingpin named Chewy Lewis."

"First, that's ridiculous, and second, I said I can't talk to you, so unless there's something else, I'm going to go pick up my daughter."

Castro stepped aside. "By all means. But there is one thing you may want to pass on to Ms. Stoddard. Something she'll be pleased to hear. The gun that killed Jessica Hawkins had a threaded barrel."

"And ballistics?"

"Evidence of a wipe smudge. So it appears a noise suppressor, an older model silencer, was used."

"I'll be sure to tell her."

Tom hurried past him and jogged back to his apartment. They're monitoring him, maybe even following him. The likelihood of obtaining a gun had evaporated. There was always a knife, but that meant he couldn't follow his plan of spraying a street corner full of drug dealers in a hail of bullets from a passing car. He'd have to get up close and personal.

But those were thoughts for a few hours later. Now, he had an aching need to see his daughter.

CHAPTER 56

By its usual standards, the noise and chaos in the restaurant compared favorably to Tom's earlier visits with Janie—only three birthday parties filled with screaming kids. A quiet Friday afternoon at Chuck E. Cheese's. Janie and Angie sat across from Eva and him in the multicolored plastic booth, finishing up their burgers.

"Uncle Tom?"

"Yes, Angie."

"Do you think my mommy and daddy are in heaven?"

Janie spoke before he could answer. "Everybody goes to heaven. Isn't that right, Daddy? When I die, I'll go to heaven?"

He froze. Blood drained from his face. *Afraid she's burnt to a crisp.*

Eva looked at him curiously. "Tom?"

One to go.

Eva jumped in. "Yes, honey, you and Angie and everybody will go to heaven when they die, but that won't be for a long, long time." She covered Tom's hand with hers. "You okay?"

"Yeah, sorry." He had to get control of himself.

Janie whispered into her cousin's ear, and Angie's face appeared to soften. She whispered back.

"Whispering in front of someone's impolite," said Tom, struggling to make his voice appear normal.

"Angie wants to know if Eva's your girlfriend," said Janie.

Tom glanced at Eva, not sure how to answer.

"I'd like to be your daddy's girlfriend, if that would be okay with you."

By her solemn expression, it was clear Janie took her responsibility seriously. She whispered in Angie's ear again, then both girls covered their mouths to suppress the giggles. Angie's blues had at least temporarily faded.

Janie rendered her verdict. "It's okay."

"So now you got to kiss," said Angie.

"Do I have to?" said Tom. The girls nodded in unison. Tom turned and kissed Eva, holding it longer than was probably appropriate for Chuck E. Cheese's on a Friday afternoon. He passed a handful of tokens across the table. "Why don't you girls go try your hand at Skee Ball?" Janie divided the tokens evenly with her cousin, and they took off for the bowling game set up on the far wall.

"She's delightful," said Eva. "So full of life."

Tom struggled to keep his eyes dry. Yeah, full of life, unlike Emma 2, whose body was about to be locked inside a small white casket underground, the decomposition already begun. And whose soul was—

Stop. He'd promised Gayle not to talk about Emma 2 unless the girls brought it up, and so far they hadn't. But watching Janie run toward the games, laughing with her cousin, so innocent, he knew he didn't need a gun. He would strangle a man, any man, with his bare hands to protect her.

"Tell me about your run-in with Castro," said Eva. "You were rather cryptic on the phone."

"That was just a tactic to persuade you to join me for lunch."

At that moment, a tableful of seven-year-olds wearing party hats screamed as the birthday boy opened a present revealing the latest video game.

"Why would you need a ruse to invite me for a quiet, romantic lunch?"

They both laughed easily, then Tom recounted Castro's information about the silencer.

"It's good news," said Eva.

"Only good?"

"Remember, anything that can raise a reasonable doubt in the mind of a single juror is good. We add that to the very weak motive, the fact that the gun was not technically in our possession, the fact that they only found a partial print and it gives us a fighting chance."

"But?"

She held his gaze, now the attorney, not the lunch date. "I'd rather have their case than ours. Her place was tossed, yet nothing valuable was taken. Clearly evidence of a fight, maybe a fight that got out of control. The proximity of the gun to your car is strong circumstantial evidence. We both saw there was no evidence of anyone breaking into your place. So unless you can explain how your gun magically flew out of your apartment, killed Jessica Hawkins, then flew back, we have a tough sell."

Truthfully, Tom didn't care. He knew he didn't kill Jess. He also knew he had less than two days to identify a bad guy and take his life. After that, after Janie was safe, he could deal with whatever happened. A thought occurred to him. If somehow he could persuade Eva to get him a list—

"Both you and Zig said the best way to clear me was to find out who really did it."

"You've remembered the clue, the doo-wop thing?"

"Not yet. Look, in all likelihood, whoever killed Jess was no amateur. He's probably killed before. Can you get a list of defendants who are either out on bail for a murder charge, or beat a murder rap?"

"In this city that won't be a short list."

"Limit the list to those who've murdered in the last, say, five years."

"And then what?"

"PDS has an investigator. He can run down where they were on the night she was killed, any previous connections to her, you know, like—"

"Like on TV. Only it doesn't work that way in real life. Depending on how long the list is, you're talking about a major undertaking, which, I've got to be honest, smells like a wild goose chase."

"Sometimes, the wild goose gets caught." He offered his most charming smile.

She sighed. "Okay. It'll probably take several weeks to—"

"No." Realizing he'd spoken too sharply, he quickly continued. "To save time, as you get names, why don't you pass them on to me, and I'll see if maybe they're familiar. Maybe even this afternoon? You know, just a few clicks of the computer." He again tried his grade-*A* charming smile, with even less success.

"Today? Friday afternoon? Do you realize you're talking about the federal government here? Are you nuts?"

"I don't know, maybe I heard Jess mention their name or something."

"No promises, but I'll see what I can do. My guess is, Jess would never have known the men who'll end up on your list. They're going to be really bad people."

Good.

CHAPTER 57

Later Friday afternoon, Zig called.

"Good news, Booker. Starting Monday morning, you're back to work."

The powers that be at SHM had decided that since they were paying him, they might as well get some billable hours in return. Zig explained his name wouldn't be attached to any particular project, for fear the client might not take kindly to representation from the only suspect in the formerly red-striped Intern Murder.

After Tom thanked him for his concern, Zig asked, "So, how's your nose? To tell you the truth, it improves your look. People pay a lot of money to get a nose job, and you got yours for free."

"Screw you." Tom had to smile. He knew Zig was ragging him to help bring him back to normal, and he appreciated it. Normal. Funny.

"What's new with your case?" asked Zig. Tom explained the revelation about a silencer being used. "I didn't know they could do that."

"I'm not sure what it means. Eva says I need to try to decipher Jess' doo-wop clue."

"Come up with anything?"

"I haven't spent a lot of time thinking about it."

"Are you crazy? What's more important than keeping your ass out of jail? What the hell have you been thinking about that's more important?"

Well, did I mention I'm waiting for a list of candidates from which to select the lucky man whose life I intend to take in less than thirty-two hours? "I don't know, nothing, everything." Very wimpy answer.

"Just to help you along, I e-mailed you the link to a list of the most popular doo-wop groups of the '50s and '60s. Promise me you'll look it over."

"Promise."

"Got to get back to the salt mines. Study the list and call me if anything strikes a *chord*."

Tom responded with the exaggerated groan he knew Zig was expecting, then hung up, music the last thing on his mind.

**

At three on Saturday morning, Tom sat in the Ford, dressed in black, watching the dilapidated row house in East Baltimore. The city was dead, but as he'd moved deeper into the poorest neighborhoods, he'd seen more activity. Every twenty minutes or so, he'd observe three or four youths, most wearing the ubiquitous hoodie, sauntering down the street, seemingly without a destination. So far, apparently no one had noticed him in the dark shadows, but he locked the car just in case.

He laughed to himself. Here he was about to kill one of the local residents, and he was worried about being accosted.

A little after six, Eva had called and told him she'd found only one name so far—Sean Williams—a white male dirtbag who fit the criteria, but she expected a much larger list by Wednesday. Sorry, four days too late, so Sean was the lucky winner. He'd been charged with first-degree murder for a drive-by. Key witness caught the amnesia bug on the second day of trial. Because the trial had begun and jeopardy attached, the case not only had to be dismissed for lack of evidence, but Williams couldn't be re-tried. Tom insisted on Eva revealing Williams' address—he'd moved to Baltimore—and e-mailing his mug shot.

Tom wished he'd had a gun. Not just because of the increased chances of success, but because a gun was impersonal. He could've stayed in his car and pulled the trigger. He rolled the wooden handle of the eight-inch serrated kitchen knife in his hand. The knife would require him to be up close and personal.

He didn't care—*one to go*—he'd be killing a cold-blooded murderer to save his daughter—*one to go*—the man deserved to die, his daughter was an innocent seven-year-old—*one to go*.

Tom saw the row house door open; his grip tightened on the knife. But it was a young black woman with an infant in her arms. He relaxed. What was she doing out at this hour? Could that be Williams' wife? Girlfriend? Maybe the kid was his, and Tom would be ensuring the kid grew up without a father. Tom shoved those thoughts from his mind. He had to focus.

The woman appeared angry. She walked down the three, stained marble steps to the cracked sidewalk, where she greeted a group of young men and women passing by and joined them, moving away from the house. When do these people sleep?

After another hour, there was still no sign of Williams. Maybe he was sleeping. Maybe he wasn't there. Maybe he'd never been there, and Eva had given him—

The cracked wooden door to the row house opened again, and Williams emerged.

Tom's stomach tightened and he breathed harder. His target appeared short, maybe 5'7", and he couldn't have weighed more than 150, 160 pounds at most. *Good.*

Williams looked up and down the street. Probably searching for the young woman. In his bare feet, wearing only a black t-shirt and what looked like pajama bottoms, Williams gave the clear impression he'd been sleeping. He shivered from the night chill, crossed the stoop, and walked down to the sidewalk. Tom also checked the street and saw no activity. The man was alone and vulnerable, his reflexes still dulled from sleep. Tom had to act now.

Tom slid the knife's blade up into his coat sleeve, maintaining a grip on the handle, then exited the car. The sound of the car door opening and closing drew Williams' attention. Though Williams was white, Tom assumed anybody, including Williams, who saw a white guy in this neighborhood at three a.m. would conclude he was a cop. At least that's what he hoped. Otherwise, there was an excellent chance Williams would run into his house and come back shooting.

He saw the man tense up. Tom tried to act authoritative, but each of his four limbs shook inside his clothing.

"You Sean Williams?" asked Tom.

"What you want?" asked Williams. "I ain't done nothin'."

"Got some ID?" asked Tom, deepening his voice to sound official.

"You know who I am or you wouldn't be here."

"Hold your hands out wide so I can see them." Williams complied, just as Tom had hoped. Tom moved closer toward the man. Could he do this? Could he plunge a knife into another human being?

One to go.

Tom's eyes widened. He couldn't breathe. He pulled the knife from his sleeve and stepped inside Williams' open arms. He was close enough to kiss the man. He saw Williams' eyes widen in surprise, then glance down at the knife; surprise turned to fear. *Now!*

Tom hesitated for a fraction of a second. Williams instinctively stepped back, tripping on the step. He fell backwards and hit his head on the sharp marble, momentarily stunning him.

Tom stood over the semi-conscious man. One quick plunge of the knife into his heart. Or, even easier, a deft slice of his exposed throat. Still no one around.

One to go one to go one to go.

Tom crouched down and positioned the serrated blade under Williams' ear. The man regained consciousness and stared up at him, terror in his eyes. He had sunken cheeks, heavy acne scars pocked his pale skin, and greasy brown hair hung straight down into his face.

"Sorry," whispered Tom. Tom didn't know why but he felt compelled to explain. "See, if I don't do this, my daughter, she'll be killed and—"

Williams tried to get up, but Tom exerted more pressure on the knife, and the young man stopped his resistance.

"Why me? I don't know you. I ain't done nothin' to you."

"You killed a man and got away with it."

Williams became animated. "B. Chop? You talkin' 'bout B. Chop? Man, that was self-defense. He pissed I took his woman, and he say he gonna double tap her and my son to teach me a lesson. So I seen him comin' down the street toward my house. He sees me and reaches inside his jacket. I drew first and he went down. That's it, man, I swear."

Tom figured the man was probably lying, but it made no difference, right? *Right?* He felt his eyes well up. "Sorry." He pressed the blade against the man's throat, drawing blood. One quick slice. That's all he had to do.

Now, *DO IT NOW!*

"Shiiiiitt!"

He tossed the knife into a nearby shrub and shuffled back to his car.

"You better run, motherfucker!" shouted Williams. "You cut me? You cut *me?*" The man crawled to his feet and ran into the house. Tom reached the Ford, jumped in, and drove off, just as Williams emerged with a gun in his hand. He fired wildly at Tom's car as it sped away.

A part of Tom wished the bullet had found its mark.

CHAPTER 58

There was no way Tom could sleep. He had less than twenty-four hours to save his daughter. He knew he couldn't kill again, and he hated himself for it. His own—cowardice?—wouldn't allow him to take the life of an unarmed, nonthreatening man, no matter what heinous crimes the scumbag may have committed. He knew now, even if he had a gun and could distance himself from the act, he couldn't do it.

Which left—what? He rolled out of bed and stumbled into the kitchen. He had to get some sleep.

After carrying a highball glass to the fridge and filling it with ice, he added three fingers of whiskey. He took a healthy sip, then hesitated. What would Eva think? Wouldn't she want him to get his rest? *Shit.* He dumped the rest of the whiskey into the sink.

He found the remote, slumped into the kitchen chair, and channel surfed. At that hour, the pickings were slim. After a few minutes, he turned off the TV.

Looking at the double casement windows, he still found it nearly impossible to believe that days earlier he'd been tied to the brass handles and subjected to an exorcism. It was crazy. *Crazy.* Maybe he was the one going nuts. He could still see Matt and Sister Irene chanting their verses while the demon twins were screwing right in front of them. *Holy water my ass.*

The priest. Tom paused while a thought tried to form in his mind. *The priest.*

He'd assumed Chad and Brit had kept Janie until last to

motivate him. But there could be another explanation. The priest. What if Janie had been marked a week ago? What if she'd been the one at risk instead of Emma 2? Maybe she wasn't selected because the priest was outside watching over her. Sort of like Passover. The angel of death passed over those families whose homes were marked with goats' blood. Could the priest have acted in the same capacity? Could the demons have passed over Janie because she was protected by the presence of a man of God?

He got up and fumbled through his pants pocket for his phone. After six rings, he was about to hang up, when he heard Matthew's slurred voice.

"Hello?"

"It's Tom."

"You have any idea what time—?"

"You're my last hope."

***

"I win!" Janie shouted. She looked over the back of the couch to Tom sitting anxiously at his kitchen table. "I beat Uncle Ziggy!"

"She got lucky," Zig said, sitting next to her. They'd been playing Madden NFL '15, the iconic NFL video game, for a couple of hours. Tom had imbued his daughter with a love of football, and she'd become a devoted 'Skins fan. He'd taught her how to play Madden, and she'd become so adept that Gayle had complained their daughter was spending too much time in front of the TV instead of playing outside.

Tom had arranged for Janie to spend Saturday night at his apartment, and Gayle offered no objections. The temporary absence would allow her and David to spend some quality time with Angie, who'd begun to exhibit manifestations of depression, the impact from the loss of her parents now slowly kicking in. When Zig popped in unexpectedly, Tom's original thought was to tell him this wasn't a good time, but she'd responded so enthusiastically to the sight of her Uncle Ziggy, he decided his good friend could provide a diversion for his daughter until the priest arrived.

If he arrived. When Tom had conveyed his theory on the phone, Matthew had sounded skeptical and responded coolly to Tom's entreaty that he spend the midnight hour with them. When Tom explained the alternative was roaming the streets searching for a random innocent to kill, the priest reluctantly agreed. But Tom worried that Matthew, with the benefit of a clear head unclouded by sleep deprivation, might change his mind and not post.

At almost ten p.m., everything seemed so normal. No threatening clouds, no howling winds, or ominous music, or wisps of smoke rising from the floor. Just a normal fall night in the nation's capital. Weird.

"Can I play again, Daddy? Please? Please?"

"You don't want to make your Uncle Ziggy feel even worse, do you? Now go brush your teeth and get in bed, and I'll come in to tuck you in."

"Just one more game?"

"Better listen to your daddy," said Zig. "If we play again, you'll win and that'll make me sad. You don't want to make me cry, do you? Give me a hug and scoot off to bed."

She wrapped her arms around Zig, gave him a quick hug, and scurried into the bathroom wearing her Redskins pajamas. Tom's mind flashed to the image of Emma 2 in her pink pajamas, the blood drained from her skin.

A minute later, the bathroom door opened, and Tom followed Janie into his bedroom. In their familiar ritual, she stood against the wall, Tom yelled "Hike!" and she ran toward the bed. In a single leap, she was on top of the bed, scrambling to get under the covers.

"Touchdown!" they shouted in unison.

He hugged his daughter so tight he heard her grunt. "Sorry."

"Daddy, why are you crying?"

"I'm not crying, sweetie. Just allergies."

She reached up and gingerly touched his nose. "Your nose doesn't look as fat as before. Does it hurt?"

"When you touch it, all of the pain goes away. Listen, a good friend of Daddy's, a priest named Father Matt, might come over to talk to me tonight, so if you happen to wake up and see him, don't be scared, okay?"

"Okay. Love you, Daddy."

"Love you, too, Baby."

He kissed her again, then exited the bedroom, closing the door behind him, then stopped in the bathroom to pop three ibuprofen. The medicine had done a good job in reducing the pain in his ribs.

When he entered the living room, he heard his cell phone ring. Matthew? Telling him he wasn't coming? If that happened, Tom had a contingency plan. He'd take Janie to a church and keep her there until midnight passed. Would the demons pass over a church? Who the hell knew?

"You going to answer your phone?" asked Zig.

Tom saw from the screen that it was Eva.

"Hi."

"A bit of news, Tom. My cousin works for PD labs, and that partial on the gun? I'm afraid it's no longer a partial. They were able to lift the rest of the print. Faint, but identifiable. It's yours."

Of course it's his print. It was his gun he was planning to use to kill a young mother. "Thanks. Let's talk about it tomorrow."

"Uh, all right. Are you okay?"

"Janie's here, and Zig. Didn't mean to be short." Tom realized he needed to try to sound normal. "What are you up to tonight?"

"Just sipping a glass of wine here alone at home. Listening to Ravel's *Bolero,* enjoying the city skyline. Look, I'll let you go. And Tom, don't worry about the print. We'll still mount a strong—"

He interrupted her. "Hold on." It hit him. "Skyline." He stepped over to the computer, logged on, and quickly found Zig's doo-wop list.

"What's up?" asked Zig.

"When Eva said 'skyline,' it reminded me. The Skyliners. In the car with Jess, I remember the DJ mentioning the Skyliners." He ran his finger down the list of groups and their hit songs.

"Tom, what's going on?" asked Eva into his ear. He put the phone on speaker mode.

"Here. Let's see. *'Since I Don't Have You,' 'This I Swear,' 'Pennies from Heaven,' 'When I Fall,'*"—He looked up from the list. *"Pennies from Heaven."*

"I know where Jess hid the phone."

CHAPTER 59

"Where?" asked both Zig and Eva in near unison.

"'*Pennies from Heaven*.' What's on the back of the penny?"

This time Zig beat Eva to it. "The Lincoln Memorial."

"The phone's behind the statue, in the fold of Lincoln's robe."

"Not sure I want to know how you know that, but I'm on my way," said Eva. "Have Zig stay with Janie and meet me there."

At that moment, Tom couldn't care less about the phone. "It's been there all this time, it'll be there tomorrow."

"I'll go get it," said Zig, reaching for his overcoat.

"I'm closer," said Eva.

"Just bring it by tomorrow morning," said Tom.

"I'm not waiting." She hung up before Tom could respond.

Tom checked his watch. Where was the priest? He probably ought to ask Zig to leave. Who knew when Matt—?

"Get your coat."

Tom turned to see Zig standing by the door in his overcoat. In his quivering hand, he held an automatic pistol with a silencer.

And it was pointed at Tom's head.

CHAPTER 60

The gun shook so violently that Zig had to steady his grip with both hands.

"I'm really sorry." His voice trembled, beads of sweat formed on his brow.

Tom felt surprisingly calm as he tried to wrap his brain around the image of his best friend pointing a gun at his face. A gun with a silencer.

His mind flashed back to waiting in the holding cell, prior to entering the Fuhrer's courtroom. Zig had brought him a business suit to wear. *A suit from his closet.* Which meant he had a key to the apartment. He'd forgotten. When he'd moved in, he'd given Zig a key in case of an emergency. "You? Jess?"

"Man, I'm so sorry."

"Stop telling me you're sorry." Tom checked his watch: 10:37. "Look, Zig, I'm sure you got a story, and I'd love to hear it but—"

"We need to go to the memorial and get the phone."

"I don't care about the phone. You go. Get the phone. You heard me tell Eva where it is. What you do with it, I don't care. Burn it, throw it in the Potomac. Just leave me alone with Janie for a couple of hours."

"Eva will likely get there before we do, so I need you to call her and tell her to wait for us before she does anything."

"Zig, please, I know you, and I know whatever you did, you had good reason. Please, I'm begging you—"

He was interrupted by a knock at the door.

"Who's that?" asked Zig, not attempting to hide the alarm in his voice. Tom noticed his gun hand had gotten even shakier.

"A friend, a priest."

"A priest? You're not even Catholic. Get rid of him."

Tom paused for a moment; he had an idea. "Okay, here's how it's going to work. I'm going to let the priest in. He's going to take Janie and leave. I will not give any indication that you are armed."

"No, just open the door and tell him—"

"And if you don't play along, I will not accompany you. You can shoot me, but I won't call off Eva, and she will get her hands on the phone and be miles away before you even arrive."

Another knock, this one louder.

Zig paused only a second before nodding his assent. He stuck the gun into the deep overcoat pocket. Tom had no doubt the barrel was pointed at him.

Tom opened the door and motioned Matthew to enter. He introduced Zig as his best friend, and couldn't help a sideward glance to see Zig's reaction. Zig purposely avoided Tom's eyes.

When the priest extended his hand, Zig had to pull his right hand from his pocket. For a brief instant, Tom considered tackling Zig to the ground, but the handshake was perfunctory, and the right hand returned to the pocket before Tom could react.

"Good news, Father. We think we've uncovered evidence that will clear me. We're heading off to retrieve it now. Be back shortly. Janie's asleep, so make yourself at home. Beer and soda's in the fridge, leftover chicken—"

"You're leaving?" Matthew's eyes locked on Tom, the unspoken message clear: You're leaving, when in less than two hours, there's a good chance an otherworldly force will attempt to kill your daughter?

"Just down to the Lincoln Memorial and back. Be home long before midnight."

"We better get moving," said Zig, stepping into the doorway. "You coming?"

Tom's eyes fixed on Zig's pocket. He could see by the shape of the bulge that Zig was pointing the gun at the priest.

"You bet." As he passed Matthew, he whispered, "Do whatever you have to do. Save her, please."

He followed Zig out into the hall and closed the door before Matthew could respond.

***

The Ford was parked a half block away. Zig was visibly nervous, not an ideal condition for someone with a finger on a trigger.

"I'm really sorry," said Zig. "It wasn't supposed to turn out this way."

"I honestly don't care right now. I can call Eva, tell her I was wrong about the clue. Call her off. You go get the phone, do what you want with it. Just let me go back to Janie."

They'd reached the car. Tom stopped and looked at his former friend in the eyes. "Zig, I swear to you on Janie's life, I will not call the cops. I'll forget the last ten minutes ever occurred. Whatever your reasons, I'm sure you felt they were justified at the time, but—"

"Do you take me for an idiot? You don't know what's on that phone, but you have a pretty good idea it could exonerate you. And you'd be right. So you'd have me believe you'd never tell anybody? That you'd go to jail, maybe for life, if I let you go?"

Tom thought he saw a flicker of hesitation in Zig's face. Maybe he was trying to find a way out.

"Get in the car," ordered Zig. Away from the streetlight, it now was dark enough for him to remove the gun and point it directly at Tom as he unlocked the car and got behind the wheel. Zig quickly slid into the passenger seat and Tom pulled out. "Drive the speed limit—no traffic stops."

Tom's mind was spinning. He had to come up with a possible out for Zig, a way for the man to rewind the last ten minutes. *Tom Booker—life rewind master.* "Look, we're not yet beyond the point of no return here. I call off Eva. You let me go. You get the phone and destroy it. Later, I'm sure there's something you could provide me, some piece of evidence that would keep you in the clear but allow Eva to raise a reasonable doubt."

Zig paused. Tom saw the man at least wasn't rejecting his proposal out of hand.

Zig shook his head. "Never work. Now call Eva and back her off. Otherwise, if she's there, I may have no choice but to use this on both of you."

"You'd kill Eva in cold blood?"

"Just make the call!"

"Okay, okay." As he dug out his phone from his pocket and punched in her speed-dial number, Tom wondered what he was going to say. He needed to get her away from the memorial; the last thing he wanted was to put Eva in harm's way.

She answered immediately. "Tom? I'm almost there. Where are you?"

"I was only half right. The penny thing? Lincoln? Jess wasn't referring to the memorial, but to her car. Her grandfather had an old Lincoln Continental. I remember her telling me that when he died, she got the car. A real boat, but it reminded her of her grandpa so she kept it. She must've hid the phone in her car."

"Where's the car?"

"We assume it's still parked in front of her townhouse. Zig's trying to track down Marcie. We figure she has access to the keys. We're heading over there now, so meet us there."

"Are you sure? The memorial sounded right."

Zig poked him in the ribs with the gun, then nodded to the speedometer. Tom was already going almost 50 in a 30 mph zone. He eased off the accelerator and tried to come up with an answer for Eva.

"She knew I understood how much that car meant to her. Let's try that first. If we don't find the phone, we can all go over to the memorial."

"Okay, I'll turn around. Should be there in about twenty minutes." She ended the call.

"Very good," said Zig. "She really had a Lincoln?"

"No idea."

"You've turned into an accomplished liar, which undercuts your rewind proposal." Zig immediately cut off Tom's protest. "No more talking."

The Ford wasn't a big car, and it seemed even smaller with Zig's gun pointed only inches from his body. Tom considered slamming on the brakes and grabbing the gun as Zig's body was thrown against the seat belt. He'd seen the maneuver in countless movies and TV shows. But there was always a chance the force would cause Zig to reflexively pull the trigger. He couldn't risk it.

They rode the rest of the way in silence. While Tom was beyond curious about Zig's involvement in Jess' murder, he remained focused on getting back to Janie before midnight. Besides, he assumed the less he knew at this point, the better. His most immediate task was persuading Zig not to put a bullet in his head.

When they reached the memorial, Tom pulled over. "Go get the phone," he said. "You can take a cab back and pick up your car."

"Find a parking place."

Before he pulled away, he decided to confront the issue. "Are you going to kill me?"

"There's a space. Park the car."

"Because if you do, it's a whole new ball game. Besides, I thought of another way, a win-win."

"I said, park the car."

Tom quickly pulled into the open space. They got out and made their way along 23rd Street toward the memorial.

Zig said, "No one was supposed to get hurt."

Tom decided empathy was the best approach. "I'm sure you got yourself into a jam and made some choices you'd like to take back. News flash, that makes you human. I'm not going to judge you. In fact, I want to help you. Jess is dead. Heartbreaking, but nothing anyone says or does will bring her back. I really think we can rewind this, but you've got to let me go."

He reached into his pocket and retrieved his car keys. "Here. You go get the phone, then take my car. I'll catch a cab. Tomorrow, we'll meet for brunch and sort out any loose ends."

"First, let's get the phone. If it's not there—"

Zig didn't need to finish his sentence, and for the first time Tom wondered if maybe his deduction from Jess' clue might've been in error. If so, things were going to get ugly. He felt his phone vibrate in his pocket and pulled it from his jeans.

"No calls," said Zig.

"It's the priest." Tom read the text message to himself.

Tom, decided to increase our chances, should be in a church at midnight. Closest is Nat'l Cath. Been there for ecumenical service. Come through Bishop's Garden, south side. Small maintenance entrance near Herb Cottage always open. God protect us.

He closed the phone.

When they reached the memorial, fortunately, it appeared deserted. The two men jogged up the marble steps. Zig followed Tom to the back of the statue. Tom reached up to the fold. Nothing. Maybe he wasn't reaching deep enough. He jumped up and plunged his hand as far down into the robe's fold as it could go. No phone—empty.

Zig's eye's hardened, and he pulled the automatic from his coat. "You knew—"

"I swear. This had to be what she meant."

"I will shoot you. They'll find your body back here with a bullet to the brain. You know I'm smart enough to remain in the clear. So tell me, where's the goddamn—"

"Looking for something?"

CHAPTER 61

Both men turned to see Eva step out from behind a pillar, holding a black cell phone in her hand.

With Zig's attention momentarily diverted, Tom stepped to the side and, using both hands, grabbed Zig's gun. Zig resisted, but while he was bigger and stronger than Tom, Tom's two arms and hands were stronger than Zig's single-hand grip. Tom attempted to rip the gun away, but Zig held on. With both of his hands wrapped around the gun, Tom couldn't block Zig's left fist. He twisted to Zig's right side and was able to divert the punch to a glancing blow off the side of his head. Tom wrenched the barrel down toward Zig's leg. He pulled the trigger. Nothing—Zig hadn't disengaged the safety. Holding Zig's gun arm down toward the floor, Tom ignored the stabbing pain to his ribs, and twisted his back so his hip served as a fulcrum against Zig's elbow. Using all his strength, Tom rammed the arm backwards. Zig screamed in agony, and a second later Tom had the gun.

He jammed the barrel into Zig's face.

"Don't know whether you can see from there, but I'm switching off the safety, and if you so much as twitch, I'm pulling the trigger."

"Okay, okay, don't shoot!" Zig looked angrily at Eva. "Why'd you have to show up? We could've fixed this. Ask Tom, we were going to rewind."

"I called Marcie. She said Jess drove a Camry. Didn't have a chance to see what's on the phone, but got a feeling it's going to be mighty interesting."

Tom checked his watch: 11:00 p.m. He did his best to keep the panic from his voice. "Eva, I've got to go."

She had her own cell phone in her hand. "Go? What are you talking about? I'm calling the cops, they'll put this piece of shit under arrest, confiscate the phone as evidence, and interview us. First thing Monday morning, I go see the AUSA and get all charges dropped."

"Fine, no problem. But I need to postpone seeing the cops for at least an hour. Call them, give them the phone. Tell them I'll meet them at Second District HQ in two hours." He offered her the gun. "Here."

"Are you out of your mind? You're going to leave me here with him? Wherever you're going, I'm going. Where are you going?"

"To church."

CHAPTER 62

The Ford headed north on Massachusetts Avenue, past the Naval Observatory where the vice president resided, and Embassy Row. Zig drove, with Eva in the front passenger seat. Tom sat in back so he could more easily train the gun on Zig's head.

"I know you would never pull the trigger," said Zig.

"My daughter's life is at stake. I'd shoot anybody to save her, especially a piece of shit who killed an innocent young woman and allowed his best friend to take the blame."

"I told you before, no one was supposed to get hurt."

"Okay," said Eva, "Tom, I'd like an explanation about the threat to your daughter because, frankly, you've been more than mysterious about the subject. But first—"

She pulled Jess' phone from her pocket, found the video app, and hit play. She held the phone up so both she and Tom could easily see it.

Jess' face filled the small screen. From the angle, it was clear she was filming herself. Seeing her alive and hearing her voice was unnerving.

"Hi, guys. Forgot my briefcase—no comment on my supposed habitual absentmindedness needed, Dad—so thought since no one's around I'll give you both the nickel tour."

The jumpy camera panned a long, brightly lit hallway with a high ceiling and cream-colored walls. Rich mahogany doors lined the corridor. Every fifth door was marked with an American flag on one side, and a state flag on the other. Jess continued, "This is the third floor of the Russell Senate Office building." They could hear her steps as she approached one of the mahogany doors. "And here we are at the offices of the junior senator from Oklahoma." Tom could make out the iconic state flag—an Indian war shield on a sky-blue field.

The camera pointed at Jess' purse, then the floor. "Got to find my keys; here they are." Tom heard the sound of the key in the lock, and the polished corridor floor surface gave way to the darkened interior. They heard the door close, then the soft flick of a light switch revealing the royal-blue carpet. Jess refocused the camera and panned the reception area. "This is Bonnie's desk; she's the receptionist. Ancient. Been with Liz Guthrie since the senator first started practicing law in Norman. Really nice. You'd love her, Mom."

The camera showed four doors leading from the reception area. As the camera lingered on each door, Jess continued her narration. "That's Mark Anderson's office. He's the LA, which means legislative assistant. This next door is the AA's office. Harvey's the administrative assistant. Between us, he's a bit of a stick in the mud."

The camera moved toward a third single door. "This is what we call the bullpen, where your hotshot daughter works. Oh, before we go there, I'll give you a peek at the senator's office." The camera approached double mahogany doors. She opened the door and the camera jumped as she flicked on the light.

A scream.

"Oh, my God, sorry!"

The cell phone screen clearly depicted the junior senator from the great state of Oklahoma with her back on her desk. She was naked from the waist down.

And her legs were wrapped around the naked loins of former Texas governor, former attorney general of the United States, and leading candidate for president, Bat Masterson.

The camera caught the flashing expressions of Guthrie and Masterson—surprise, anger, fear. Then greater anger.

"What the fuck are you doing?" shouted Guthrie, as she slid down the other side of the desk to the floor and straightened her skirt.

"I didn't know—"

"Get out!" Guthrie screamed.

"Jesus, is that a cell phone?" asked Masterson. "Is she filming this?"

The camera went dark as Jess apparently shoved it into a pocket, but the sound of Masterson's voice still came through.

"Give me that phone! Now!"

Tom heard Jess panting as she apparently ran from the office. He heard the outer door close and the click of her shoes on the hard corridor surface.

Then silence.

CHAPTER 63

"My God," said Eva. "You killed her and set up your best friend to prevent your mentor from being ensnared in a sex scandal?"

Zig didn't speak for a moment, focusing his eyes on the traffic ahead. Then his voice was almost too low to hear.

"He promised me chief of staff. I would run the White House. Really run the whole damn government."

"You're disgusting," she replied.

She handed the phone back to Tom, who glanced at it dismissively and put it in his pocket. A part of Tom was curious how he had been dragged into Masterson's little conspiracy, but that could wait for another day. "Speed up," he ordered.

"Don't want to get a ticket," Zig responded.

"Speed up," Tom repeated, and Zig goosed his speed up by 10 mph.

Eva asked Zig the obvious questions. "Why Tom? Why his gun?"

"Bat told me about the phone video, said I needed to retrieve it and, if necessary, use lethal force. I didn't own a gun. I remembered glimpsing Tom's gun in that paper bag at Napoleon's, and I had a key. I figured I would use the gun to scare Jess, retrieve the phone, then return the gun to Tom's apartment with no one being the wiser."

"Masterson says 'jump' and, like a toy poodle, you jump," said Eva.

"This country's going to hell, and I believed the only person to right the ship was Bat Masterson. So it was in my view for the greater good. Like collateral damage in war—sad, unfortunate, but necessary for a noble goal. Besides, no one was supposed to get hurt. I felt energized that he was trusting me to handle this very delicate problem. I believed he was testing me. If I could make the Jess Hawkins problem go away, he could trust me with much more sensitive matters threatening the country when he was elected."

"You're sick," said Eva.

Tom, only half listening, pointed to the spires of the cathedral in the distance, lit up against the dark sky. "There it is."

Eva ignored Tom and pressed Zig. "Obviously, something went wrong."

"When I knocked, she was dressed. She said she thought I was Tom. I hadn't counted on him being on his way to her place, and I had no idea how soon he'd arrive. Bat had asked me to check to see if the barrel was threaded. It was. He provided me with a silencer left over from his military service days, just in case. I kept the gun in my coat. I was counting on convincing her it was not only in her best interest, but in the country's best interest, to turn over the phone to me. I was authorized to offer her money, a job, whatever it took. I would only pull the gun as a last resort to scare her. That's it. Scare her. Worst case, fire a suppressed bullet into the floor."

They had to stop for the light at the intersection of Massachusetts Avenue and Wisconsin Avenue. Tom checked his watch: 11:19 p.m. *Damn.*

"The second the light changes, turn right on Wisconsin," he said.

"What's the hurry?" asked Eva. "You won't tell me what we're doing at the cathedral. You asked me to trust you. Fine. But aren't you curious about how Jess really died?"

"Yeah, sure. Lay it on us, Zig. Explain how you decided to take the life of an innocent young woman."

"She was very nervous. Kept saying she didn't want to get in trouble, didn't know what to do. Said she'd seen enough Washington scandals on TV to know it usually was the little guy who got thrown under the bus. I tried to assure her, but she insisted on waiting for Tom. If Tom advised her to turn it over, she'd tell me where it was."

"But you couldn't do that," said Eva.

"No. I believed with more time I could've convinced her, but I had no time. Tom could be popping in at any moment. I panicked and pulled the gun. Just to scare her, that's it, I swear. She went berserk and threw a lamp at me. I ducked and fired reflexively, not at her but at the lamp. When I looked up, she was sliding to the floor with a bullet hole in her forehead. An accident, Tom. A horrible, horrible accident. My turn to panic. I did a quick search of her apartment, couldn't find the phone, then got the hell out of there."

The light changed. "Go, go!" ordered Tom. Zig turned right on Wisconsin. Tom saw the sign for Pilgrim Road. "Turn right here."

"And so you framed your friend," said Eva.

"I returned the gun. We had no idea that Tom would be arrested. Bat and I couldn't do anything over the weekend, but he arranged to get you out on Monday. He had some contacts—people I don't know and don't want to know—who he arranged to swear they were driving by and saw a black man running out of her house right before you arrived. Everything would be smoothed over."

"Except the phone was still out there," responded Eva.

"Park there," said Tom, pointing to an empty lot on the south side of the cathedral.

Zig did as he was told. When the car stopped, he turned back to face Tom. "I swear to you, I would never have let you take the fall."

"What about being king of the world?" asked Eva.

Tom spoke before Zig could respond. "Okay, Eva, I want

you to wait here with Zig." He gave her the gun and checked his watch. "At midnight, call the cops. I'll meet you back here."

Zig's voice quivered. "Tom, you've got to believe—"

Tom ignored him, jumped out of the car, and disappeared into the shadows.

CHAPTER 64

He made his way as quickly as his bruised ribs would allow up the steep, grassy hill. He was familiar with the Cathedral Close, the grounds of the cathedral, having visited the site on several occasions during his early days as a college architecture major.

He passed the Bishop's Garden and the Herb Cottage on his right, followed the narrow path to the south side of the structure, then carefully wound his way around chunks of carved stone—pieces which had fallen off the cathedral during the earthquake back in August 2011.

Tom looked up. This close to the cathedral, the central tower seemed to rise all the way to the sky. A full moon slipped away from a dark cloud and cast the rich Indiana sandstone in a pale glow.

There was an unnerving stillness—he could no longer hear the sound of traffic from Wisconsin and Massachusetts Avenues. He felt a sense of foreboding. Imagined? Or justly caused by the presence of evil?

He checked his watch again: 11:41 p.m. He followed the south wall until he came to a small door, half hidden behind heavy shrubbery. The knob turned easily and he entered.

The narrow, dimly lit hallway led to a staircase, at the top of which he spotted another door. What if it was locked? But then, the priest wouldn't have been able to gain access, and presumably would've called. *Presumably.* Tom climbed the staircase two steps at a time and tried the knob. The door opened.

He found himself in the southwest corner of the narthex and moved quickly into the nave. Like its twelfth century Gothic predecessors, the Cathedral was laid out like a Christian cross. The nave made up the long piece of the cross and represented the largest segment of the floor plan. Cavernous—50' wide and 150' high. The walls of the nave featured three rows of stained-glass windows, each of which illustrated famous stories from the Bible or, in some cases, images of Americana.

The moonlight, filtered by the multicolored glass on the south wall, illuminated the space in eerie shades of pale blues and reds.

The vaulted spires met in the center of the ceiling, creating a spine down the middle. In the shadows, Tom could barely make out the bosses—flat, circular keystones that separated the opposing arches and kept them from collapsing in on themselves. The bosses appeared as a row of huge, decorative buttons running down the length of the center spine, some measuring almost five feet in diameter.

He heard something from far down the aisle toward the transept, the crosspiece that intersected with the nave.

"Janie? Matt?"

"Daddy?" Her voice was faint.

Tom hurried down the aisle to the south transept, the baptistery, breathing heavily to reduce the dull stabs of pain every time he moved. Janie, still in her pajamas, sat next to the priest on a wide bench under a three-paneled stained-glass window. She scooted down from her seat and jumped into his arms.

"Baby, you okay?"

She stretched back so she could see him and nodded. "Father Matt, he said we were going to meet you in a church and it would be fun, and afterwards, you'd let me stay up for ice cream."

"Father Matt was right, honey." He squeezed her again. He turned to the priest. "Anything?"

Matthew checked his watch. "Nothing so far."

Tom sensed there was more. "But?"

"But I feel, I don't know—the presence of an intruder."

"What's an intruder, Daddy?" asked Janie.

"Uh, it's like a headache. Father Matt has a little headache, but I'm sure it will go away soon." He looked toward the apse, the high point on the cross floor plan where the altar was located. "Why here?" he asked Matt.

The priest pointed up to the third lancet of the stained-glass window. The bottom panel showed Jesus standing over a cowering Satan. "Renounce the devil. That's what the panel depicts. Of all the glass in the church, this is the only one where Satan is shown defeated. Seemed an appropriate place to wait it out."

"Wait what out, Daddy?"

"Wait until the midnight ice cream store opens, sweetie. Why don't you tell Father Matt your favorite—"

The sound of footsteps. He hugged Janie close and turned to see Eva and Zig approaching. They stopped in the center of the nave. Tom now saw there was a third person with them.

Bat Masterson's calm baritone echoed inside the cavernous space.

"Tom, this has to end, this *will* end—now."

CHAPTER 65

Tom couldn't leave Janie, but if Masterson was there, good chance he somehow had taken possession of the gun.

He set his daughter down. "Baby, you go keep Father Matt company for a minute while I talk to these folks."

"Uncle Ziggy!" She waved, and Zig, with a sickly smile, waved back.

Tom checked his watch. Ten minutes. He left Janie and the priest, and hurried up the aisle to the trio.

As he reached them he saw that his suspicion had been correct. Masterson, with Zig at his side, held the gun on Eva.

"I need the phone, Tom," said Masterson, his voice calm, authoritative.

"I'm sorry," said Eva. "He must've been tracking Zig's—"

"I don't care. Here." He pulled the phone from his jacket and tossed it to Masterson. Tom pivoted to return to Janie.

"Hold on," ordered Masterson.

"What are you going to do, Bat? Shoot me? And Eva, and a priest, and my daughter? Go destroy the evidence. I couldn't give a shit about your political career. On Monday, you figure a way to get me off, and we'll pretend nothing happened. Without the tape, no one would believe Eva and me anyway. I've got to go. Give us ten minutes, then we'll talk. Have a seat. Maybe the both of you should take advantage of your surroundings and pray for forgiveness."

Tom took Eva's hand and pulled her toward the baptistery, hoping Masterson wouldn't shoot him in the back.

"What's going on?" asked Eva, not attempting to hide the fear in her voice.

"If I had the time to tell you, not only wouldn't you believe me, but you'd think I was bonkers. And right now, I don't have the time. Hopefully, nothing will happen."

"You're scaring me."

They reached the priest and Janie.

"Can I go see Uncle Ziggy?" asked Janie.

"Maybe later," said Tom. "Now let's do what Father Matt says."

Matthew bent down to Janie's eye level. "Honey, do you know any prayers?"

Janie looked up at her dad.

Other than as an architecture student, Tom hadn't been inside a church since his mother's funeral. When Janie was younger, Gayle had raised the question of their daughter's religious upbringing. Tom had made it clear that Gayle could take her to Sunday school if she wished, and Gayle had done so.

"What about the prayer you say with Mommy right before you go to sleep?" asked Tom. She nodded.

"That's a good prayer," said Matthew.

Tom thought sure he smelled something. He looked around, but nothing seemed out of place. He noticed both Masterson and Zig had indeed taken a seat. Zig held his head in his hands. Maybe he was praying.

Tom sniffed.

"Sulfur," said Matthew. "The smell of hell."

Eva raised her voice. "Damn it, will somebody please tell me what's going on?"

Tom tried to calm her. "Eva, if you can just give us—"

"What are you doing with your daughter and a Catholic priest inside an Episcopal church at midnight?"

Matthew and Tom simultaneously checked their watches. Five minutes.

"I'm sorry," Tom responded. "I know this looks weird, but

you're just going to have to trust me. Stay close and keep your eyes open."

"For what? Keep my eyes open for what, Tom?"

Before Tom could respond, Matthew and Janie were reciting the familiar children's prayer, each with their eyes closed:

"Now I lay me down to sleep..."

CHAPTER 66

Tom thought he felt a slight vibration, then it stopped. Probably his imagina—

This time there was no doubt. The shaking increased to a low rumble.

Eva's frightened face looked up to him. "Tom?"

The floor trembled below their feet.

Janie stopped praying. "Daddy?"

Tom heard the scraping sound of stone against stone. In moments, each of the columns in the nave shook.

Eva screamed and turned to run from the building. Tom grabbed her and held her tight.

"If you try to escape, you'll die!"

He didn't understand how he knew that to be the case, but he was as sure as anything in his life.

Janie ran to him and leaped into his arms. With one arm around Eva and the other holding his daughter to his breast, he encouraged her. "Let's keep praying, sweetie." He joined Matt. *"Now I lay me down to sleep..."*

After a few moments, first Eva, then Janie joined in. *"...I pray the Lord my soul to keep."*

The rumble deepened. Heavy dust and bits of stone descended down upon them from the vaulted ceiling.

Masterson and Zig leaped from their seats and rushed toward the baptistery.

Tom heard a loud boom. He looked up to see the spine of the

nave crack apart from one end to the other like a time-lapsed bolt of lightning.

Now the entire cathedral shook with the sound of an onrushing freight train.

An even louder ripping sound filled the church. Tom saw a huge boss being pulled from the ceiling spine, like a button torn from a coat by an invisible hand.

The 2,000-pound stone dropped toward the cathedral floor.

"Run!" Eva shouted to Zig and Masterson.

Zig tripped, then scrambled to his feet, looked up, and froze. Tom saw the stark terror on his face, and followed his eyes.

"Zig!"

The massive stone crushed his head against the floor, splitting it like a ripe cantaloupe.

Eva screamed. Tom pressed Janie's head tight against his chest to keep her from witnessing the fate of Uncle Ziggy. He pulled them under the wide bench seat.

Matthew stood defiantly in the center of the baptistery. His arms outstretched, he tilted his face heavenward, his eyes closed, his expression serene. He shouted the next line of the prayer. *"If I should die before I wake—"*

"Jesus!" shouted Masterson. "What the hell's—?"

Eva pointed to the carved stone wall behind the high altar. In the center of the wall, surrounded by angels and archangels, a seated Christ held a globe. Suddenly, the Jesus figure appeared to come to life. It stood and jumped down to the floor.

"I pray the Lord my soul to—" The priest saw the animated figure walking toward them and froze. The Christ figure shimmied, then spun twice full circle.

And there was Britney, dressed in Christ's limestone-colored robe, grinning from ear to ear.

CHAPTER 67

The shaking ceased.

Suddenly, the cathedral was still—the rising dust from fallen stone was the only sign of movement inside the cavernous space.

Then Tom heard a sound, and turned to see that Bat had fainted, falling to the floor.

Britney broke the silence. "Hi, guys." She smiled and offered a finger wave.

The priest stepped in front of her and raised a Bible in front of her face. The book burst into flames. The flames caught on Matthew's clothing, and he screamed as the fire enveloped him. No one could speak.

Then the flames extinguished as suddenly as they'd appeared. Matthew seemed to be unharmed and his clothing untouched. He raised his head, faced Tom and grinned.

Only, it wasn't Matthew. "Hi, guys," said Chad.

Tom was staring at Matthew's face, but the eyes and voice were that of Chad. "What did you do with him?"

"Who? Matty? Let's see, he's around here someplace." The thing's eyes rolled back for a moment, then returned. Must've gone out for some fresh air. He was getting rather hot in here."

Both Chad and Britney giggled like ten-year-olds.

"Daddy, what's happening?" whispered Janie, the fear apparent in her voice. "Is this your surprise?"

"Yes, honey," said Chad, "this is Daddy's surprise. Do you like it so far? Looks real, huh?"

Janie curled tighter into Tom.

Brit approached the bench. "Aren't you guys all scrunched up under there?" she asked. "Come on out."

Eva tugged on Tom's sleeve. She tried to speak but couldn't get the words out. He kissed her, then placed Janie in her arms and crawled out from under the bench.

"Daddy!" Eva hugged Janie close.

Tom spotted Matthew's ornate flask filled with holy water on the bench. He grabbed it and shook the contents at Chad and Brit, sprinkling droplets on each. He stepped back, apprehensive.

Brit licked her lips. "Holy water? Mmmm, my favorite."

"Ditto," said Chad. "Especially good to rid one's throat of all of this dust."

Brit stepped over to the heavy marble baptismal font, ripped the bowl from the pedestal, then lifted the bowl and drank. When finished, she let loose a tiny burp. "Oops, sorry," she grinned. "Not very ladylike."

Chad bent over so he was eye level with Janie as she cowered in Eva's arms under the bench. "Come on out, honey. Uncle Chad wants to show you something."

"Daddy, help me!"

Tom stepped in front of the bench. "Take me. Please, leave her alone."

Chad made a show of looking at his wrist. He blew stone dust from Matthew's watch. "Oh, sorry. Midnight's passed. Rules are rules. Am I right, Brit?"

She nodded solemnly. "Rules are rules." She took a step toward the bench.

Tom pushed her, but his hands passed through her robe into what felt like fire. He screamed, then yanked out his hands—they were red and swollen with first-degree burns. Without thinking, he buried them into what remained of the holy water in the marble bowl. Smoke rose from the bowl as if he'd just dipped a lighted torch into the water.

"Daddy, take me home, I want to go home!"

"Don't worry, Janie," said Brit. "You'll be going home soon. To a new home actually. Won't need a coat."

Chad chuckled.

The blood had drained from Eva's face as she witnessed the confrontation. Her eyes widened in terror, but she nevertheless rolled out from under the bench and positioned herself in front of Janie.

"I don't know who you are or what you're up to, but you're not taking this little girl anywhere."

"So brave," said the Chad-Matt thing. He spread his arms theatrically, as if reciting a Shakespearean soliloquy to a crowded theater, and lifted his face skyward. *"Yea, though I walk through the valley of the shadow of death..."*

Eva's body slowly levitated from the floor. Her piercing scream echoed inside the giant cathedral vault.

"...I shall fear no evil..."

Tom leaped for her, wrapping his arms around her waist, the rush of adrenaline momentarily masking the pain from his burnt hands. Immediately, he felt a powerful electric shock and released his grip. "Eva!"

"...Thy rod and Thy staff, they comfort me..."

She rose upward—ten feet, twenty-five feet, fifty feet. "Tom, help me!"

Tom pivoted, anxiously searching for something, anything, he could use as a weapon. He ran to the high altar and grabbed the cross. Ignoring the stabbing pain in his ribs, he wielded the cross like a sword, swinging with all of his might at the Chad-Matt thing's head.

The cross sliced through its neck, severing the head. The head rolled off the thing's shoulder, then dropped to the floor. But the face kept talking as if the head had remained attached.

"...surely goodness and mercy shall follow me all the days of my life..."

Eva had now risen to the highest point of the vaulted ceiling—nearly 150 feet. Were she to fall from that height, she would surely die.

"...And I will dwell in the house of the lord forever."

"Please, don't hurt her!" Tom pleaded.

"Sorry, Tom, but you failed to live up to your end of the bargain," said Brit.

"As an attorney, you know there must be penalties for breach of contract," Chad added.

"If there were no consequences, everyone would feel free to break agreements, large and small," said Brit. "Lawlessness and anarchy would prevail."

"A civilized society is built on a man's word being his bond. You have to agree with that, Tom," added Chad. The head floated up through the air and reset itself on top of Matthew's body. He again checked his watch. "Love to stay and chat, but duty calls."

He looked up at Eva and winked.

She shrieked, and her body dropped toward the cathedral floor 150 feet below.

CHAPTER 68

"No!"

Tom froze, not believing his eyes. He rushed down the aisle, his eyes glued to Eva, and tripped over Bat's crumpled body. He yelped out in pain as his healing nose smashed hard against the cold stone floor. He scrambled to his feet, blood pouring down his face, and stumbled forward as Eva's body tumbled down toward him.

Then she stopped in midair. Then she was pulled upward again, yanked like a dancing marionette. She shrieked as her body performed involuntary backflips, turns, and twists over the length of the nave—a trapeze artist without a trapeze.

Her gymnastic maneuvers sent her back toward the high altar. Tom ran toward her, but knew any rescue attempts would be fruitless.

The circus act had concluded. She shot upward to the height of the ceiling again, her terrifying shriek piercing Tom's brain.

And now she was falling. In a split second she would crash to her death.

Tom dove forward, his arms outstretched, but he couldn't reach her in time.

"*Evaaaaah!*"

But when her flailing body reached five feet above the floor, she suddenly stopped, hovering there for a moment. Tom leaped to his feet and rushed under her.

Eva softly floated into his arms.

Janie ran to him, and he held both tightly to his body. Janie and Eva were shaking. Or was that him?

He turned to Chad and Brit, anticipating their wrath, knowing he was helpless to stop it.

But something was wrong. By their expressions, Tom could instantly see the save had not been the work of the twin demons. He followed their eyes to the western entrance.

The door was open. A figure—at once both familiar and unfamiliar—ambled down the aisle toward them. The figure's face was obscured by the low light and the dust still filling the air. The figure paused when he reached Zig's body, looked down, and shook his head. He continued toward them and glanced at Masterson's body lying unconscious on the floor.

Oh my God, thought Tom.

Detective Percy Castro.

CHAPTER 69

The moonlight coming through the stained glass reflected off the residual dust in the air, creating a blue glow around the man as he moved steadily toward them.

Tom whispered to Eva, "You shouldn't have called—"

"I didn't."

Castro looked left and right, up and down, taking everything in as he walked down the aisle. For the first time, Tom noticed his eyes. Or more accurately, his lack of eyes. White orbs stared out from his eye sockets, reminding Tom of a character from cheap horror movies back before CGI existed.

Then the eyes flared for an instant, lighting up the cathedral as if 100 klieg lights flashed simultaneously. Tom squeezed his eyes shut and used his hand to cover Janie's face.

After another few seconds, the light had subsided.

Tom's voice cracked as he spoke. "Detective?"

The cop ignored him, his focus on Chad and Brit. When he spoke, his voice sounded normal. Almost normal.

"Enough."

Chad snarled, "Never enough."

Suddenly, Tom felt Janie ripped from his embrace.

Her body fired through the air to Brit. The demon wrapped its arm around the girl. Janie's panicked scream echoed throughout the cathedral.

Don't worry, sweetie," said Brit, "you'll be fine so long as you can—*fly!*"

"Daddyyyyyy!"

In an instant, Chad and Brit levitated from the floor with the girl, then crashed through the baptistery's stained-glass window, shattering the glass, leaving one remaining panel—the depiction of Satan. The head of the satanic figure looked down on Tom and grinned.

Tom turned to Castro, beseeching—"Do something!"

"Come," said Castro, his voice eerily calm.

"Who are you? Where are we going?" asked Eva.

"They've taken her to the tower."

Tom remembered a number of years earlier his class took the Saturday Tower Tour offered by the cathedral—300 steps up a winding staircase to the central tower, soaring over 300 feet above grade.

Tom studied Castro's face. Nothing unusual. Had the whole blinding light from the eyes thing been a hallucination?

He ran toward the door that he knew led to the stairs. He wasn't sure Castro was fit enough to handle the climb, but he couldn't wait. "Let's go!"

Eva followed him, but Castro moved steadily in the opposite direction. "Where are you going?"

"Elevator."

The ascent took less than a minute. Castro had led them through a door marked "Staff Only" to a single service elevator. The pain from Tom's hands was nearly unbearable, and he noticed blisters had already formed on both palms. He willed the pain from his mind.

During the ride up, both Tom and Eva stared at the detective. A cop chasing the bad guys. Doing his job, that's all. The elevator rose to a secondary level, where they took another elevator to the top interior space of the central tower—the bell level, named for the fifty-three huge, bronze carillon bells hanging from a steel superstructure, and the ten smaller peal bells hanging above them.

Tom raced from the elevator and quickly circled the space. "Where are they?"

Suddenly, he was nearly knocked off his feet by the deep clang of the largest carillon bell, measuring over eight feet in diameter and weighing several tons. Unlike the peal bells, the carillon bell itself didn't move: carillon bells remain stationary while the metal clapper inside strikes the casting.

The vibration from the sound shook him to the bone. He saw Eva holding her hands to her ears. Castro appeared unfazed, his attention drawn to a small cubicle in the center of the space where the carillonneur would play the bells using a keyboard.

Tom saw the keys on the board moving, like a player piano. Immediately, the space shook with the sound of fifty bells chiming. The sound was not melodic; Tom was reminded of a two-year-old sitting at a piano, haphazardly pounding the keys.

"Where are they?" he shouted, but he knew that Eva and Castro couldn't hear him. Then he saw, more than heard Eva scream, pointing at the cubicle.

Chad sat at the keyboard, pounding the keys, harder, harder. Still using the priest's body, he was dressed as a '50s rocker—Jerry Lee Lewis bangin' the ivory with his fingers, fists, elbows, ass, and feet—a toothy grin spread across his face. The carillons clanged louder each time he'd pound the keyboard, the sound rattling even the steel structures from which the massive bells hung.

Tom and Eva squeezed their ears tighter, but to no avail. Each strike of a bell felt like a hammer crashing the inside of Tom's skull. Chad began to sing, the tune bearing no resemblance to the discordant sound of the bells.

"Goodness gracious—"

Tom charged him, his blistering hands covering his ears. "Where's my—?"

"Great balls of fire!"

"Tom!"

Somehow, this time he heard Eva's warning. He looked up to see the peal bells swinging angrily back and forth from the ceiling. With each swing, a small fireball shot out of the ten bells, one after the other, like a Gatling gun stitching instant death across the floor.

Tom ran back toward the shelter of the elevator, dodging the fiery projectiles. One burst at his feet; he tried to dodge the waist-high flames, but his pants caught on fire. He screamed in pain, then in an instant he was on the floor. Eva had tackled him hard, rolling his body back and forth to extinguish the flames.

With her help he scrambled to his feet, and together they headed toward the elevator, but the door was closed. They pounded the call button. Tom yanked Eva back as a fireball crashed against the polished steel elevator door. *Castro! Where was Castro?*

There. Strolling toward them from the other side of the floor, seemingly without a care in the world. He veered toward the cubicle. When Chad saw Castro, he pulled his hands from the keys. The fire stopped; the bells stopped. He grinned at Castro, waved, then in two giant steps leaped through the narrow window.

For a long moment, no one spoke. Then Tom screamed in frustration.

"Where is she?"

Castro gestured upward.

"They have her on the tower roof."

CHAPTER 70

They followed Castro to a door in the far corner of the space behind the largest carillon. The door led to a narrow stairway.

Tom climbed the stairs three at a time, then burst through the heavy metal door to the tower roof, where the icy November wind hit him hard in the face. Heavy fog now shrouded the tower, but, best Tom could tell, the roof was flat, maybe forty-five feet square. Tall, pointed pinnacles, stone spires, rose over thirty feet from each corner. Stone carvings of angels surrounded the middle of each spire, while small gargoyles ran up to the sharp point of the spires like festering sores.

"Daddy!"

Tom didn't wait for Eva and Castro. He rushed through the fog to the other side of the roof.

"Daddy! Help me!"

Her voice came from above. He looked up. Brit stood on the tip of the northwest spire, holding Janie loosely around the shoulders with one arm. The little girl's body dangled in midair. Tom glanced down; the fog cleared enough for him to see the concrete plaza over 300 feet far below. To his right, standing tall on the corner of the apse roof some 200 feet beneath them, a slim bronze cross rose heavenward.

"Hi, Tom," said Brit. "Lovely daughter. She'll be great to have around the house, so to speak."

"Let her go!"

"If you wish." Brit loosened her grip and Janie screamed as she slipped through the demon's arms.

"No!" Tom shouted.

In the last instant, Brit grabbed Janie's wrist. The girl shrieked in pain as her body jerked to a stop.

"You bitch!" Tom shouted.

"Great catch, Brit." Tom heard Chad's voice behind him.

He glanced over his shoulder and saw Chad balancing on the point of the northeast spire. He waved. Then Chad's attention moved away. Tom followed his gaze to see Castro standing nearby.

"Afriel, you do not belong here," said Chad.

"You already have taken the life of one innocent child, Moloch, there will not be a second."

"Rules are rules," echoed Brit.

"Xelbeth, release her."

For a long moment Castro and the demon twins froze, as if someone had pushed the pause button.

"Tom?" Eva's voice was barely audible.

Tom felt both cold and hot at the same time. A bead of sweat trickled down his spine. Unable to wrap his mind around what he was witnessing, he closed his eyes like a child who believes if he can't see bad things, they don't exist. When he opened them, nothing had changed.

Castro raised his gaze skyward.

The detective's eyes rolled back, now showing nothing but white orbs, their glow casting a light glaze over Castro's jowly face.

Suddenly, Tom heard a loud hiss. Blinding light beamed out from his eye sockets, cutting through the fog.

Tom vaguely heard Eva scream.

My God, thought Tom. *My God!*

Brit shook her body, shedding her human trappings. At first Tom thought she'd disappeared, and Janie was somehow suspended in space. But with the help of Castro's illumination, he could barely make out a shimmering form. Nearly transparent, little more than a black film. Changing edges. No edges.

Janie's eyes widened and the terror stole her voice. Mercifully, she fainted.

"You heard what he said," said Chad. Tom saw that he'd also transformed; Matthew's body had disappeared, and, like Brit, Chad's voice emanated from an oily shadow. "Release her."

"No!" screamed Tom. He turned to Castro. "Help her!"

Suddenly, his daughter's limp body dropped from the seemingly invisible hook that had held her suspended.

Castro turned and focused his eyes on the center of the northwest spire. The light shattered the spire, sending chunks and shards of stone into the air.

"Look!" said Eva.

Tom saw that four of those stone chunks, the carved angels, weren't falling. They were flying. He looked down and watched the four tiny angels swoop under Janie, catching her, then softly setting her down on the lawn.

Castro turned to the two greasy shadows, flitting around the tower like filmy bats.

Brit's voice, coming from the closest one, was barely recognizable. "You have broken the rules, Afriel. There will be consequences."

"Go home," Castro whispered.

The beam of light from Castro's eyes bore through the shadow, breaking it apart into tiny pieces of soot. The soot scattered and disappeared into the darkness.

Then Castro trained his eyes on the Chad shadow, knocking it backwards out of the air like a laser anti-aircraft gun. The shadow flipped and twirled, then dropped. Tom heard a shriek—he thought he recognized traces of Chad's voice. He looked down. Hard to make out, but it appeared the shadow had impaled itself on the bronze cross, mounted on the crest of the apse roof. It squirmed and shifted like a fish on a pike, screeching, howling.

Then a flash like a struck match.

A split second later the flame dissolved into the black night.

CHAPTER 71

Tom sat on the cold grass, cradling his sleeping daughter in his arms. He looked up at Castro.

"What will she remember?"

"Very little. Take her home. When she wakes in the morning, she'll remember she went to sleep in your bed."

"And Eva?" She was inside the cathedral checking on Matthew.

"She'll remember walking into the church with you. That's it. She'll assume she was knocked unconscious by falling debris."

"And me?"

"You will remember everything."

Tom nodded. That was how it needed to be.

"Tom?" Tom turned to see Matthew being led from the western entrance by Eva. "Is she alright?"

"Fine, just sleeping."

"We were waiting for you, then the earthquake hit, and I must've been struck by debris. Lucky to be alive. Guess you know your friend didn't make it."

"Yeah."

"There's another guy in there dressed in a suit. Still breathing, but we need to call—"

"On their way," said Castro.

"This is Detective Castro," said Tom. The priest nodded to the cop, then sat down on the lawn.

"When I woke up and didn't see Janie, I was fearful that

she—" He glanced at Castro, then locked eyes with Tom. "Uh, might've wandered off."

"She's safe," said Tom.

Matthew smiled broadly. "It worked. Thank God."

Tom struggled to keep from looking at Castro. "Yeah, thank God." He turned to Eva. "How are you doing?"

"Okay, I think. Things are a little fuzzy."

They heard the sounds of approaching sirens. Tom climbed to his feet, clutching his sleeping daughter to his shoulder. "What do you say we go home?"

Eva froze, looking back toward the western entrance. Tom turned to see Masterson, covered in dust, emerging from the cathedral. When he saw Castro, he got confused.

"Bat, have you met Detective Castro?"

Momentarily startled, Masterson quickly regained his composure and his imperious demeanor. He strode over to Castro and offered his hand.

"Detective, I'm glad you're here. My associate, Mr. Zigler, had informed me that Mr. Booker was heading to the cathedral to take his own life. Apparently, the weight of his crime against Ms. Hawkins, something I'd been previously unable to accept, became too much for him to bear."

Tom had to hand it to the man—he was inventive. Castro remained passive as Masterson continued.

"Tragically, Mr. Zigler was killed by falling debris." He paused, as if trying to read Castro. "As an officer of the court, I must report I heard Mr. Booker confess to the killing in a prayer, just before the earthquake. I will be pleased to provide a statement first thing in the morning. And Tom, I'm afraid I'm going to have to redeem the bond. I'm sorry." He waved to Castro. "Heading home, Detective. The chief has my personal number."

"You're not going anywhere." Castro strode toward him. "You're under arrest for conspiracy to murder Jessica Hawkins."

"That's preposterous," Masterson sputtered.

Castro spun him around and handcuffed him.

"You get Chief Ranier on the phone this instant. Kate is a dear friend, so, if I were you, I'd start looking for another line of work."

"We told Castro everything," said Eva.

"Told him what? You have no proof of anything. My word against yours. You have nothing."

Tom pulled a black phone from his pocket and punched the keys. A second later, sound emanated from Masterson's pants pocket.

"*Hail to the Redskins, Hail Victory, Braves on the war path, fight for old DC!*"

"I gave you my phone," said Tom. He waved the phone in his hand. "*This* is Jess' phone." He tossed it to Castro.

Masterson knew enough to shut up as Castro read him his rights. The sirens were close now. Tom caught the detective's eye. Castro nodded for Tom to go, which was what he was hoping for.

With one arm around his daughter, and the other around his girl, Tom walked toward the parking lot.

Somewhere, he had to find some ice cream.

EPILOGUE

From his table next to the half wall separating the bar from the dining area, Tom checked out his former reserved bar stool in the back of Napoleon's bar. When he arrived, he'd tried sitting there, but it was just too weird without Zig at his side.

His new vantage point allowed him to watch the TV mounted behind the bar, currently tuned to a cable news station. Footage of the interior of the cathedral appeared on the screen. The bar was almost empty so he was able to make out the familiar voice-over from the blond cable babe.

"...and preliminary reports show no structural damage to the cathedral. Experts say most of the damage constituted surface cracks. Some decorative stonework will need to be replaced, along with one stained-glass window. The surprise earthquake measured only 3.2 on the Richter scale, but was enough to cause the damage. Crews on site to repair damage from the 2011 quake will undertake the new work, and it is estimated the cathedral will be open for visitors again in less than four months."

It had been a week since the "quake," the shorthand name that he, Eva, and Matthew had assigned to the night at the cathedral. Of course, unlike Eva and Matt, he remembered everything.

The previous Monday, the AUSA had dismissed all charges against him. That afternoon, he'd submitted his resignation to the firm. Because of Bat's arrest, a number of the firm's largest clients were pulling out. A group of young partners and associates announced their intention to form a new firm, and there was every indication that many of the departing SHM clients would follow them. The new group had extended an offer to Tom, and he was tempted to accept.

Through Eva's intercession, he'd also been offered a full-time position at PDS. Much lower pay, much lower prestige. Now he was meeting Eva to discuss his options.

Tom waved for the waitress, then turned his attention back to the front of the restaurant, expecting Eva. Instead, Castro's bulky form filled the doorway.

He approached Tom and sat, not waiting for an invite. Tom shivered, and instinctively leaned back.

"How's it going?" asked Castro.

"Fine."

"Janie?"

"Fine."

"Eva?"

"Fine."

Castro smiled. Then turned to the TV. Tom followed his lead. The image of the cathedral had been supplanted by footage showing Masterson, in handcuffs, being led into the second district police station by two uniformed officers. Tom noticed the red ribbon cutting across the upper left-hand corner of the screen screaming the words: *DC Sex Murder Political Scandal!* Sex, murder, politics, and scandal. The cable Nirvana.

Bat Masterson got his stripe.

"How's the case going?" asked Tom.

"He's fighting it. Admits to the affair, says Zigler was an overzealous subordinate who committed the murder in an attempt to please the boss. Says he had no knowledge of it."

"Will it fly?"

"We linked the silencer to Masterson. Guthrie's singing like a bird. Pillow talk. Apparently, Bat confided in her what happened after the fact. That, combined with your and Eva's testimony, will sink him."

Tom nodded, but couldn't help feeling his conversation was

beyond surreal. He was sitting here talking to a cop who'd made an arrest that would clear Tom of a serious crime. No problem, except for the teeny-weeny fact that the cop was some kind of frigging avenging angel.

"Uh, the name the Chad thing called you? Afriel? Googled it. Afriel's the name of the angel of light whose mission is to safeguard young life."

Castro didn't respond.

Tom thought, in for a dime, in for a dollar. "So, is that you?"

No response.

"In fact, you can get a fiber-stone replica of the angel, Afriel, for your backyard pond for only $99.95. The picture doesn't exactly look like you. Young, cherubic, and a lot thinner."

The last comment elicited a small smile.

"I suppose the reference to a dead wife, that was all bullshit."

Castro didn't respond, but there was something in his eyes that suggested there might've been some distant truth to the story. Did angels lie?

"Do you wonder, Tom, why I erased the memories of Janie, Eva, and Matthew, but not yours?"

Tom didn't know how to answer, so he remained silent.

"You were directly or indirectly involved in the deaths of four people. Your revelation to Rosie that you knew of her lesbian relationship led to her death and, with your active assistance, the death of her husband. You goaded Reece Mackey to poison himself with alcohol. True, you killed his brother, Willis, in self-defense, but you'd set up Creek for the fall, and that Willis was the first to walk through your cell door was merely a matter of bad timing."

Tom couldn't help himself. "And what was I to do? Let my daughter die? Allow her innocent soul to burn in hell for all eternity just so the Mackey boys could continue their lowlife criminal enterprises? You're telling me that's what your boss wanted?"

"Gino wasn't a lowlife."

Tom's voice softened. "I know. Look, if I'd thought taking my own life would've—"

"Your memory wasn't erased because you need to know—not just suspect, not just think there may be a possibility, but truly *know*—there will be consequences for your actions, both good and bad. Probably not in this life, but thereafter."

Tom gulped, his throat too dry to respond.

"But the good news is, you're young and have the time, if you so choose, to atone."

"How? What do you want me to do?"

"Do good."

"Like what?"

He got up from the table without responding.

"One question," Tom said. "Can I ask one question?"

"You can ask."

"Emma Wong, Gino, Rosie. Have they been rescued from—?"

Castro smiled. Was that a slight nod? He turned toward the door just as Eva entered. He exchanged a brief greeting, then exited the restaurant.

She approached quickly, gave Tom a fast kiss, and sat down. "What did Castro want?"

"Just letting me know Bat's going to fight the charges, and we'd probably need to be witnesses."

"Poor Jess."

"Yeah. Also, can't help but feel bad for Zig. I believed him when he said he didn't intend to shoot her. Blind ambition got him killed."

"It's Washington." She picked up the menu.

The waitress appeared.

"I'll have an iced tea," said Eva.

Tom held Eva's gaze. "Make that two." Her smile of approval was empowering. "I've decided."

Eva studied the menu. "Good, what are you having?"

"No, I've decided on the job."

She put down the menu. "And?"

The decision had been very easy. He believed for commerce to function, lawyers were a necessary evil, and some of the finest,

most ethical men and women he'd ever met had been corporate attorneys. Yet, he also knew he'd never been happier than when he'd
been working with young kids. And young kids needed an advo-
cate.

"One request. I'd like to be assigned to the juvenile division.
Maybe if we can get these kids when they're young—"

"Request granted."

"And, uh, those contacts, you know, from your brother's
drinking situation?"

She squeezed his hand. "Second request granted."

Tom couldn't stop grinning, and he couldn't take his eyes off
her. She looked beautiful—her eyes, her face—a glow seemed to
radiate from the air around her. *Like an angel.* He smiled at the
thought.

"Why are you smiling?"

"Nothing. Everything."

The waitress came with the tea. As she walked away, he said,
"Probably should ask, what's PDS' policy on sleeping with the
boss?"

Now it was her turn to grin. "We encourage it."

***

Four thousand miles east, the *macchinista* engineer drove the train
toward the tunnel as he'd done for what seemed like a thousand
times before. The run from Monterosso to Vernazza along the rug-
ged Italian coast was just the first leg for tourists connecting to the
five Cinque Terre villages that sprouted like multicolored flowers
from the rocky cliffs overlooking the Mediterranean. One car was
filled with children, including his own son, on the morning run
from the villages to school in La Spezia, a large city at the end of the
line.

The engineer entered the short tunnel; when he emerged,
he would only have to make one switch to the western track,
and then five more minutes into Vernazza. His phone vibrated,
he pulled it from his pocket, and checked the screen. He'd quar-

reled with his wife when he'd left for work, and he saw the message was from her. The train emerged from the tunnel. His eyes on the phone, he reached up to the control panel above his head and turned the knob as he'd done many times before.

Suddenly, he heard a horn blaring. He looked up to see the northbound train on the same track heading right for him. *Dio mio! He'd flipped the wrong switch!* He slammed on the brakes—*too late.* The sound of screams and colliding steel crescendoed in his brain—then blackness.

***

The engineer awoke nearly upside down. He glanced out the window to see two of the train cars, including the one carrying the school children, hanging precariously over the cliff, 300 feet above the roiling sea below. He crawled out of his seat and stumbled back to the first passenger car. It still remained upright, though off the tracks.

He moved as fast as he could past the rows of seats on his way to the children's car. He shouted to the passengers, "Quick, you must get off the train!" He paused. Something was wrong. None of them moved. Not because they were unconscious or dead; they appeared frozen in time. He checked outside the window. The whole world had stopped. *Was he dead? What about Mario? Dio mio. He had to get to him before the car tipped over the cliff—*

He heard a noise and turned.

A young tourist couple, cameras swinging from straps around their necks, walked down the aisle toward him.

They smiled and waved.

ACKNOWLEDGMENTS

First, I'd like to thank my amazing agent, John Rudolph, and the folks at Dystel & Goderich. *Cheers*, John.

Using the word "family" to describe a business organization is greatly overused, but in the case of Oceanview Publishing, it's true. Many thanks to Bob and Pat Gussin, Frank Troncale, and the rest of the team for their wonderful support, and for welcoming me into the family.

Thanks also to Adam Rodriguez for his insightful early editing.

Given the story of *One to Go*, I would be remiss if I didn't mention the thousands of people across the United States who work in our criminal justice system. Prosecutors, public defenders, judges, bailiffs, court reporters, marshals, sheriffs, clerks, prison guards, and secretaries, just to name a few. Virtually none of the cases they handle make Court TV. And while a casual observer might conclude the daily processing of criminal charges through the system more resembles a heartless assembly line than the administration of justice, nothing could be further from the truth. All participants play their parts, toiling day in and day out to ensure that both the rights of the accused and the rights of the community are well protected. While far from perfect, their tireless efforts continue to ensure that the American justice system remains the best in the history of the world.

M. P.
West River, Maryland
2014